The Saviours

Author Biography

Originally from Bray, Co. Wicklow, Maeve Galvin has worked as an international development worker across the United Nations and non-profit organisations for a decade and has lived and worked in Ireland, Cambodia, Nigeria, Myanmar and the United States. She currently lives in Temple Bar, Dublin with her partner. *The Saviours* is her first novel.

MAEVE GALVIN

THE SAVIOURS

A NOVEL

Merdog Books

Merdog Books
The Exchange, Castle Avenue, Buncrana, Co. Donegal, Ireland
Web: merdogbooks.com
Email: info@merdogbooks.com

First published 2020

2 4 6 8 10 9 7 5 3 1

ISBN 978-1-9165016-4-5

Set in 11/14pt Bembo
Typeset in Ireland by Merdog Books
Printed and bound in Great Britain by Clays Ltd, Elcograf S.p.A

For my mother, Deirdre, the greatest storyteller I know.

Prologue

Site 4 Refugee Camp, Thai-Cambodia Border, November 1991

Hours of sweating left Janice's t-shirt caught up in her armpits. Stealing a moment for herself between conducting dental exams, she itched under her arms, aware that it likely made her look as if she were impersonating a monkey. A sharp pain jabbed at her gut reminding her that her diarrhoea hadn't gone away. She had long since concluded that taking the anti-diarrhoea pills her doctor had given her before she left the States was about as effective as popping Tic Tacs. She winced at the thought of having to use the foul, hole in the ground toilet yet again. If it looked and stank like it was being used by hundreds of people on a daily basis, that was because it was.

She grabbed a sip of water. There was still a horde of people waiting in line to have her examine their teeth. The last time she had seen a line like that was a few months ago outside of the Crest movie theatre at home in Sacramento when she and Liam had gone to see the third Godfather movie. She had hated the movie. She had felt that it was overwrought and tedious and was frustrated by the convuloted Vatican plotline. What a complete let-down, especially after the first two movies had been so good. Liam loved it of course as the man had almost no critical filter. When they first got married, Janice had enjoyed that he was such an unfailing optimist, as if his warmth could melt her hard edges. More recently though, his unquestioning satisfaction with everything had been bothering her. That night at the movies, they rushed home as soon as the credits started to roll because they missed their little girl so much. They mocked one another for their newly-found parental neuroses and inability to enjoy a few short hours without her. How different her life was then, barely a year ago.

A little girl and her mother came forward for their dental check-up. The child was beautiful with caramel-coloured skin, big almond-shaped eyes and a fluff of jet-black hair. Her mother, not more than a child herself had her left arm amputated almost entirely. The vast number of amputees in the camp had been jarring for Janice when she first arrived there. Over decades of conflict, landmines laid by the Vietnamese and Cambodian armies, the Khmer Rouge and to her intense shame, the United States forces, were still causing dozens of deaths and injuries across the Cambodian countryside.

The young mother smiled at her shyly and spoke in the Cambodian language, Khmer. Janice's interpreter and guide, Vimol was a reserved, middle-aged woman who spoke English with a slight French accent due to a stint studying in Lyon. Janice had no idea how Vimol had ended up translating for Americans on volunteer trips, but her guess was that it wasn't a pleasant story, having learned quickly that almost every Cambodian bore some kind of staggering tragedy deriving from the genocidal Khmer Rouge time.

Vimol translated, 'Your blonde hair is fascinating for them. They have never seen that colour before. Can they touch it?'

'Of course.'

Janice crouched down in the dirt and removed her hair tie, letting loose the slightly matted hair she had forgotten to get cut before leaving the States that was now proving torturous in the Cambodian humidity. The mother patted her hair gently.

The child let out a high-pitched squeal of amusement.

'She's so beautiful,' Janice said. 'Vimol, can you ask how old she is?'

Vimol spoke again in Khmer and the mother beamed as she responded.

'She's three years old. She was born here in the camp,' Vimol translated.

'Wow. Three years old.' Janice held up three fingers and smiled at the mother and daughter. Her own little girl was two and a half and it was hard not to think of the contrast between her at home in a comfortable, rainbow-walled bedroom full of stuffed animals and this child who knew nothing other than life in a teeming refugee camp with a disabled mother.

'Vimol, can you ask the mother what her biggest challenges are in the camp?' Janice began to examine the child's teeth as her mother watched curiously.

Most of the refugees she was examining had never even seen a toothbrush and needed significant dental work. Janice felt frustrated at the limitations of what she could do for them with scant equipment and no one to help her. She only had a small supply of drugs and she hated having to select only the worst cases for procedures like extractions. But she was learning that they were curious about her and she told herself that may-be talking to the foreigner provided a small distraction from the misery of their situation.

'She says that she has nothing to do all day and that she is bored,' Vimol translated.

'What would she like to be doing?' Janice asked.

'She says that she would like a job. She says that she only has one arm but that she can still knit and make things. She would like to make money and to buy her daughter books and nice clothes.'

'She's absolutely right!' Janice responded enthusiastically as she flossed the little girl's teeth. The child's second molars hadn't come in yet which was very late for a normal three-year old but all too common here where the kids were stunted by a combination of trauma and poor nutrition. Janice was finding that whenever she asked about their lives, the refugees in the camp, particularly the women, many of whom were widowed were telling her that they were bored and wanted to work.

'Vimol, these people need some kind of activity. Some kind of skill-building. They need to be prepared for eventually getting out of here. Are the UN or any of the NGOs working on this?'

'I don't know, madame. I think they are focused on the emergency needs,' Vimol responded.

—

Janice's day ended a few hours later after seeing dozens more patients. Her head thundered with exhaustion but her mind was restless, and she found it difficult to sleep. Her time here was coming to an end and this made her feel apprehensive. The day after tomorrow she was due to go back to Cambodia's capital city for a few weeks before leaving. Phnom Penh was a mass of crumbling infrastructure with thousands of bicycles pedalling slowly down the main boulevards trying to avoid the giant potholes and a smattering of army tanks to remind you that you were basically in a war zone. It had seemed post-apocalyptic when she first arrived a few months ago. After what she had seen and experienced in the camp, it was going to seem like Paris in the summer.

Janice had lied to Liam about how close she was to the conflict. It wouldn't help him to know that she was only about thirty kilometres from where a weakened Khmer Rouge were still attacking, trying to claw their way back to power since being ousted by the Vietnamese. He was worried enough about her being there. She wasn't about to make it worse for him. She wasn't naïve enough not to be scared, though. There had been nights where she had lain in bed with the tension pulsating through her as she imagined being kidnapped. She had even deliberated over the details, such as whether she would say she had AIDS if she were captured, as a possible deterrent to rapists. But she had also never felt more alive. It felt so purposeful being there, being part of helping Cambodia. She didn't want to leave it all behind and go back to her old life. She couldn't leave now. She felt a responsibility to this country. How on earth was she going to tell Liam that she wasn't coming home?

1

Phnom Penh, Cambodia, April 2013

The irony of writing a proposal entitled *Empowering Vulnerable Cambodian Women* when a local prostitute had left his apartment only a few hours beforehand wasn't completely lost on Tom.

He reluctantly sat up in bed, wiping traces of tobacco, weed and cigarette papers from his laptop and opened it up. The air-conditioning in his room wasn't much use against the powerful combination of last night's whiskey and the insufferable Phnom Penh humidity. He pushed himself to do a little Saturday afternoon work knowing that he needed to show his colleagues how dedicated he was before he could relax for the remainder of the weekend.

How many people should he say would benefit from the work? The project plan was to train 500 women in basket-weaving but 500 was kind of a low number. He needed to make it sound more impressive for the donor.

He did the maths in his head. 'If rural Cambodian women have on average three children, let's assume all of them are beneficiaries of the programme too because their mothers are trained, plus husbands, plus the fact that they may have parents who live with them in the communities…'

He was in the middle of typing '3,000 beneficiaries' when Kerstin from headquarters began calling him on Skype. He readied himself to not sound hungover and was hopeful she wouldn't stick on the video function.

'Hello, Tom, Kerstin speaking. Can you hear me well?' Kerstin's German-accented voice sounded like it was coming through a megaphone.

'Yes, Kerstin. Loud and clear. How's all in Geneva?'

'Very good, thanks, Tom. I saw you online and wanted to ask you a favour. I was looking through our photos from the hand-weaving project for the conference in Vienna next month and I think we need some more compelling materials.'

'Sure, Kerstin,' Tom responded jovially. She hadn't turned on the video function which meant he could roll his eyes. 'What did you have in mind?'

'I think we need more photos. Showing that the women are weaving baskets and selling them is good, but we just need to show more of an empowerment story,' she said, emphasising the word empowerment. 'We need photos demonstrating that this programme has really had an impact on their lives.'

Tom inwardly groaned. His United Nations headquarters could never get enough of one-dimensional photographs of poor people smiling into a camera. How exactly was he meant to capture the abstract concept of empowerment? Make them clench their fists in the air? But Tom's hangover didn't afford him the energy to push back. Besides, Kerstin was far more senior than he was and to keep his career trajectory moving upwards he needed to keep her sweet. He agreed to get her the photos in the next week.

When they hung up, he figured that he'd done enough work for the day to spend the remainder of it leisurely sweating out his hangover on the spacious balcony of his French-colonial villa-style apartment sipping from a coconut.

Tom's move to Phnom Penh a year ago had cast him into the camp of the country's expat aid workers. Starting in the early 2000s, a Molotov cocktail of pent-up idealism had exploded onto Cambodia's capital city. There were more than 3,500 different charities, non-governmental organisations and UN agencies. One for about every 4,000 Cambodians. Expat jobs were plentiful once you had a university degree and some experience, and the aid-hungry Cambodian government doled out working visas to anyone with the right passports. Tom was one of a handful of Irish and quickly becoming a rising star at the UN.

A few hours later, after readying himself for a hedonistic Saturday night, Tom met his friends at a local beer garden, a short motorbike taxi away in Phnom Penh's plush Boeung Keng Kang 1 area which had turned much of its striking buildings from French colonial times into western-style bars and restaurants to cater to the influx of expats with disposable income. He arrived to find his friends already several beers in and in the throes of one of their usual dick-measuring conversations.

'How many times have you gotten malaria? I've had it three times,' Andre was saying. An animated Australian, Andre had been in Phnom Penh for six years. He was a journalist with loose credentials. At thirty, he was just two years older than Tom was but hard living had resulted in a red, pocked face that made him appear several years older. While he often talked about how much he wanted to leave Phnom Penh and how he was 'done' with the city, Tom couldn't envisage him living anywhere else given his refusal to pay more than 50 cents for a beer.

'I've only had malaria once, but I had giardia when I lived in Vietnam,' Joey responded. Joey was a polished, east coast American working for a local environmental NGO. Tom had deduced that he was some kind of rich kid given that a local salary could hardly fund his lifestyle of luxury beach resort weekends and frequent trips to visit expat friends in Bangkok and Singapore.

'Oh, giardia is nothing. That's just a tiny parasite,' Tom chimed in, sitting down and signalling a drinking sign at a beer-selling girl in a tight, red uniform to bring him a drink. He enjoyed goading Joey's competitive streak.

'Well, I had dengue last year. That really wipes you out,' Joey sounded defensive.

'Ah, dengue is nothing! While travelling across West Africa, I got this rare infection. Man, there were live maggots living under the skin of my thighs. I had to use a Swiss army knife to cut them out,' Andre recounted excitedly.

Andre's adventure stories often seemed well-stretched. His explicit account was interrupted by plates of barbecued meat and fried rice arriving at their table.

'Man, I'm about to eat half a pig here. Let me enjoy it without having to think about your thighs,' Tom interjected. The three men paused to squeeze limes into a bowl and mix it with black pepper to make a thick paste for the meat.

The night progressed in typical Phnom Penh fashion. While they chomped on barbecue, the beautiful beer girls ensured their glasses were never below midway full. From the beer garden, they crowded rowdily into a tuk tuk. Andre, a hardcore negotiator refused to pay the driver more than $1 for the short journey to a newly opened hipster-style bar where friends of friends were playing in a cover band.

The rooftop bar was getting crowded as the three men arrived. The double whiskey and coke that Joey handed him numbed Tom's revulsion at the beaver-sized rats that could be seen parkouring over the neighbouring tin roofs. He immediately scanned the place looking for possible work-related faces in the cluster of mostly white twenty and thirty-somethings.

He felt a relief at not seeing anyone he knew and not having to be 'on'.

The lead singer was a Dutch embassy official who had ditched his suit for ripped jeans and a flannel shirt. The band's set of covers included 'Don't Look Back in Anger', 'Living on a Prayer' and 'Sweet Child of Mine'. It was all a little generic for Tom's taste. Perhaps it was due to a combination of his western music-starved years in Cambodia and the copious amounts of booze they had already had but Andre was enthused.

'Fucking tune!' He pumped his fist in the air as they began to play the opening chords of Journey's 'Don't Stop Believing'.

'Same again?' Tom shouted to Joey. He was going to need to speed up his drinks to play catch up with Andre who was already looking sweaty and red-faced as he bounced enthusiastically to the music, his shoulder-length black curly hair swinging like he was a 1980s glam rocker.

Tom pushed through the swelling crowd clutching a round of whiskeys against his chest with precision. Joey was talking to two expat girls that he didn't recognise while Andre continued his solo dancing. Tom handed both boys their drinks and took a large gulp of his own. He was about to try to get a proper look at the girls Joey was with when the familiar opening croak of David Bowie's 'Space Oddity' caught his attention.

Tom was pleasantly surprised. The Dutch embassy guy could actually do a decent Bowie. The whiskey got the better of him and he began to sway alongside Andre. He forgot himself and sang along unselfconsciously.

He sensed that he was being watched and looked to his left to see one of the girls Joey was talking to was looking over at him in amusement. She smiled shyly upon his catching her watching him and looked away. Her friend and Joey looked to be deep in an animated conversation that she wasn't paying much attention to.

'Hi,' he approached her.

'I'm sorry to laugh but you're a terrible singer,' she told him, smiling a little. She had an American accent and her thick, waist-length hair was Jessica Rabbit red.

'Oh, I know,' Tom laughed. 'They used to ask me to just pretend to sing in the school choir so I wouldn't ruin it for the other kids. It's my greatest tragedy. I usually keep it under wraps but I just can't resist a Bowie classic.'

'That's totally fair,' she responded. She had a great mouth, Tom noticed. It was small but she had excellent pouty red lips the same colour as her hair. 'No one should be prevented from enjoying Bowie but I understand why you don't let that voice out often. Are you Irish?'

'Yup. At least we've established that you can identify accents better than you can musical talent.'

'Ha!' she let out a loud laugh in disbelief. 'I'm Irish-American actually. Thank your people for the red hair, my legions of cousins and my Catholic guilt about almost everything.'

'Oh, you're welcome.' His brain scanned itself for a witty response. 'Thank your people for Lou Reed, Big Macs and Rocky movies. I wouldn't want to live in a world without any of those things.'

'You're so welcome,' she laughed. 'Is there any chance that those things make up for our imperialist foreign policy and needless encouragement of consumerism?'

'Yikes. Well, let me give the rest of the world a call and let you know but don't bet on it.' Tom was enjoying himself.

'You do that. And if they decide to be little bitches, please remind them of how far-reaching our drone programme is,' she quipped.

'Oh, Ms America, such violent tendencies,' Tom put on a mocking tone. 'You could really learn a lot from the gorgeous, green little island your ancestors came from. We're totally neutral and more or less at peace apart from some problematic stuff up North.'

'Well, that's the thing. Your little island has a long history of terrible attitudes towards women's rights and bodily autonomy. Not so appealing for me'. Her animated face turned serious.

Tom was very impressed. He didn't think that the average American had been following the divisive discussions that were happening in Ireland around the country's abortion ban.

'Spot the feminist! I'm shocked and appalled,' he teased.

'And so, you absolutely should be,' she laughed a big, throaty American laugh. 'And anyway, Ireland doesn't meet my criteria. The thing is, I like my countries like I like my men; big, hot and a bit fucked up.'

'Oh really?!' Tom almost snorted with laughter, caught off guard by her candour. He hadn't been expecting that. 'You gotta love that American directness! Touché, Ms America, touché.'

Her friend beckoned to her.

'Hey, I think we are leaving now to go to a house party but it was fun shooting the shit with you.'

'Indeed, it was,' Tom tried to think of a good witty line but came up short. Unsure of how to conclude, he awkwardly gave her a military salute. 'Have a good night and try not to cause any international incidents!'

She flashed him a quick smile and left with her friend who had been talking to Joey. Tom instantly asked Joey who she was but he said he had only just met her.

'She may be private sector as her friend Ella works for the

Chamber of Commerce and I know her through work. I think she said that she's new here and her name is Katie or something like that,' Joey told him. 'She's pretty hot though, right?'

'Yeah, she's alright,' Tom feigned nonchalance. He hadn't been with an expat girl since he had arrived. He hadn't really seen the point given the plethora of locals who were as good-looking as they were available.

Sex was a plentiful part of Tom's Cambodian experience which had been a very welcome surprise. At 5' 10" with green eyes, hair the colour of milky tea and a cheeky smile, his looks wouldn't have been out of place on a background member of a 2000s boyband. He never had too much trouble getting girls but in Cambodia his black book numbers were rising significantly. Getting with local women and the occasional prostitute when it suited him was just such an easy process that he'd fallen into it comfortably.

Andre sauntered over and handed them both fresh whiskeys. 'What's happening, gents?' he grinned tipsily.

'Tom met a chick,' Joey told him.

'Oh, the ginger? Ha! Of course the Irishman wants a bit of fire crotch!' He slapped Tom on the back.

'Hey Tommy, I play tag rugby with the guy who's having the party that they are going to. We could stop by if you like?' Joey suggested.

'Could be a laugh. I'm easy,' Tom responded. The possibility of meeting the redhead again was certainly intriguing.

'Aw, man, who wants to be at a shitty house-party talking to UN wankers?' Andre protested while beginning to slur his words. 'We could head over to The White Tiger where everyone knows us, where whiskey sours are only $3, and we can have the finest local snatch in the city eating out of our crotches?'

'The man makes an eloquent point,' Joey laughed. He raised his glass at Andre, and they clinked and took deep slugs of their drinks. Tom felt a twinge of disappointment but knew he was outnumbered.

The White Tiger was a girlie bar in the heart of Phnom Penh's notorious party district. Street 51 consisted of six blocks of abundant nightclubs pumping out head-banging dance music and gaudy neon-lit fast-food joints. It was known for its bars with ironic names designed to appeal to Western backpackers such as the very popular Che Gue-Bar-A which was covered by murals of the Argentinian revolutionary's face, making it perfect fodder for Facebook photos. The district teemed with tuk tuk and motorbike drivers, food sellers and begging children trying to make money from hordes of drunk tourists. Where in many parts of the city it was common to see mismatched, silent couples made up of overweight, middle-aged white Western men and slim, beautiful Cambodian women in their twenties, around Street 51, it was particularly prevalent.

The three guys were given their usual heroes' welcome as they entered The White Tiger, a small and dingy establishment with sticky floors resembling an old movie theatre and a constant smell of toilet duck. Four Cambodian bar girls cheered and whooped upon seeing them come in and ran over to hug them. The boys got drinks and stood by the bar as they enjoyed watching the women shaking their tiny butts and child-like hips in bar uniforms of barely-there yellow shorts on the dancefloor, while David Guetta blasted from the speakers. Tom was savvy enough to know that it was all part of their performance but thought to himself that surely these girls must be happy to see young, attractive men who they could have fun with rather than the middle-aged beer guts they mostly had to endure.

The night began to smudge for Tom as the whiskeys continued. There was a prolonged and poorly played game of pool with Andre where each of them struggled to hold their cues straight. There were at least two rounds of tequila shots that Joey had insisted on buying for him, Andre and an indeterminate number of bar girls. There was some sweaty and spirited dancing to 'Gangnam Style' with Andre lifting one of the bar girls onto his shoulders. The sequencing of these events was unclear to him. Tom must have passed out as the next thing he could recall was the sound of Andre shouting at him.

'Mate! Mate! Wake up, you cunt!'

Tom opened his eyes with a jolt to the realisation that they were in one of The White Tiger's specially designated back rooms which consisted of little more than two worn brown leather couches and red painted walls featuring the bar's eponymous motif of a white tiger outline.

A bar girl with dyed blonde hair and thick black roots was next to him on the couch, nuzzling his neck and rubbing his unresponsive crotch. Across the room on the other leather couch, Andre was laughing maniacally.

'This is un-fucking-believable!' He roared. 'Look how far up I can get it!'

Andre's bar girl was naked from the waist down and lying on her back, her legs spread apart with a contorted, uncomfortable look on her heavily made-up face as if she was suppressing the urge to cry out.

Andre's left hand and half of his arm was inserted up the girl's vagina. With his free right hand, he was pointing to his obscured left arm.

'Look at this, mate. I can feel her fucking kidneys!' He shouted to Tom.

A hot spurt of whiskey bile shot to the top of Tom's throat.

'Aw, man, that's nasty,' he croaked. 'I don't need to see that.'

Where the fuck was Joey? Fuck it. He needed to get out of there.

'Mate, I feel rough. I'm heading home.' Tom slowly pushed the girl off him and felt around his pockets to make sure he had his phone, wallet and keys.

'Weak, mate, weak,' Andre yelled but he was too distracted to protest much.

Tom pushed through the backroom door and frantically made his way through the corridor to the bar's exit. He was relieved that the main bar door was easy to unlock. He steadied himself upon exiting as his eyes were scalded at the shocking brightness of the early morning sun. Street 51 was now deserted save for the many food wrappers, discarded bottles and dubious pools of liquid on the ground providing evidence of the previous night's debauchery. A lone, industrious motorbike taxi driver spotted Tom and called out a hopeful 'Moto-bike sir?'

The smell of marinating waste and stale urine hit Tom's nostrils as he began to vomit relentlessly on the side of the street.

2

A few days later, on a stewing hot Tuesday afternoon, Tom was in a jeep bobbing through the unpaved mud roads of rural Cambodia. He was on his way to Kampong Cham, a province to the North East of Phnom Penh to visit one of the basket-weaving projects he worked on. His unwanted companion for the day was Janice Steiner, the American founder of the NGO, Cambodian Hands which ran the project for the UN. Having found her intense and self-aggrandising upon first meeting her when he arrived in the country, Tom was careful to ensure his encounters with Janice were as brief as possible and typically made sure to deal with her deputies. However, today, to his irritation, she insisted on personally accompanying him and the trip was unavoidable if he wanted to meet his headquarters' deadline for the photographs of the project's women.

Tom was in no mood to stand in a rice field sweating his balls off trying to make everything look as heart-warming as if Walt Disney had personally curated it. His stomach was still not quite right from all the boozing at the weekend and the combination of the jeep ducking in and out of deep potholes and Janice criticising the driver made for a highly unpleasant journey. When she wasn't berating the driver, Janice was regaling Tom with stories from her time in Cambodia in the 1990s.

'Those blue beret fuckers set this country back years,' she fumed in an unprompted critique of the United Nations peacekeeping operation sent to Cambodia in the 1990s to help restore peace after the Khmer Rouge regime had killed about a third of the country's population.

'Those bastards,' she bore into Tom's eyes with intensity as she spoke so that eye contact was unavoidable. 'Coming in here and spending so much money on their fat cat expat salaries. You know they actually brought in AIDS and they caused thousands of Cambodian women to enter into prostitution. It ended up helping the Khmer Rouge and they had the nerve to call it a success.'

Tom doled out occasional 'reallys' and 'that's terribles' to appease her. While he had read that the mission had been controversial, he was fairly sure she was grossly exaggerating. Janice's longevity in Cambodia and her organisation's shining reputation among the UN, donors and others, meant that she was a powerful individual and he didn't want to get on the wrong side of her.

Tom had done his homework when he had initially learned that he was going to be working with her. The story went that she was originally a dentist and had come to Cambodia back in the day as part of a volunteer trip but had ended up staying in the country, setting up Cambodian Hands and essentially dedicating her life to helping Cambodian women gain skills and jobs beyond prostitution or unpaid farm work.

Some Googling had shown Tom that Janice's story had been lionised by several fly-in international television crews and newspapers over the past few decades. A particularly gushing magazine profile in 1998 had even gone so far as to call her, 'Cambodia's answer to Princess Diana'. The magazine photo-spread accompanying the text showed her as a thirty-something, big-haired blonde with a gleaming, toothy smile wearing double denim. If it wasn't for the Asian-looking backgrounds, it could have easily passed for a 1990s ad for Colgate. In one of these pictures, her diligent Cambodian 'daughters' as she called them in the piece were crouched alongside her like decorative accessories without any mention of their own stories or even a captioning of their names.

When at last they reached the project site, one of the managers from Cambodian Hands, Sophorn, a gentlemanly Cambodian in his late thirties came out to meet them at the jeep.

'Sophorn, how are you? How's the new baby?' Tom greeted him warmly.

'Good. Good,' said Sophorn shaking his hand. 'My wife tells me this is last one. But I want to have two or three more. If there are at least five of them, there is a good chance that one of them will become rich enough to buy me a beach house for when I'm old.'

'An excellent retirement plan,' Tom joked and they both laughed.

Janice interrupted them without greeting Sophorn.

'Sophorn, where are the women? Are they ready for the picture?' She heavily enunciated her words, making a picture-taking motion with her index fingers as she spoke. Tom inwardly cringed at her behaviour. Sophorn had been a teacher and had great English. He was fully capable of understanding them.

'We have five of them here and two more are coming,' Sophorn told her.

'Only seven?' Janice frowned and held up seven fingers as she talked. 'Why not more?'

'I called them but it's a Buddhist holiday today and many of them are going to the pagoda,' Sophorn told her. Tom could hear the anxiety in his voice.

'Did you tell them that this is important, and for our UN partner?' Janice raised her voice.

'Seven is not good, Sophorn. *Oht bahn, Oht bahn,*' she said in Khmer meaning 'not good, not good'.

Sophorn giggled nervously while Janice glared at him.

'Janice, it's fine,' Tom intervened. 'Seven is enough for us to work with. I think individual portraits are much more powerful than group shots anyway.'

'No, Tom, it's not good enough.' She kept her eyes on Sophorn who was lowering his head like a scolded child. 'He should have told them that it was very important to come today.'

'Okay, well let's begin to work with what we have.' Tom put on a chirpy voice in an attempt to diffuse his own discomfort as much as anything else.

Headquarters weren't willing to shell out for a photographer, so it was up to Tom and his ageing Nikon to capture the empowerment of the basket-weaving programme. The rice paddies were waist high and glistening green and Tom thought they'd make a perfect backdrop. Sophorn gathered together the small group of middle-aged women who had arrived at the project site and instructed them to stand in the field with each of them holding up a few of the woven baskets they had made. It took about ten minutes to get them settled in the field while Janice barked instructions at Sophorn.

The sunlight bounced off the wax sheen of the baskets and the women stood close to one another with their bright head-scarves in yellows and blues contrasting beautifully with the green of the rice paddy. Tom thought it was a great shot saving for the fact that none of the women were smiling. '*Nhnhum, nhnhum,*' he shouted loudly while readying his finger to shoot. *Nhnhum,* the Khmer word for smile was one of the twenty or so words that Tom had learned in his time there. The women looked at him questioningly without smiling.

'What are you trying to say, Tom?' Janice asked.

'Tom, you mean *nhnhum*, like smile?' Sophorn asked him gently, pronouncing it naa-nium.

'Yes! That's what I said,' Tom laughed exasperatedly.

'*Naa-nium!*' Sophorn shouted. The women burst into giggles, realising Tom's mispronunciation.

Tom quickly began to snap as they threw back their heads in merriment.

'Perfect! Amazing! Wonderful!' he exclaimed. The scene looked so naturally joyful as the women tittered with laughter. These were going to be great photos. Suddenly, almost out of nowhere Janice jumped into the middle of the shot.

'*Nhnhum*, ladies! *Nhnhum!*' she shouted, roaring with laughter.

She wrapped her arms around two of the women in the middle of the group and began posing right in the centre of the shot. Her Colgate smile from the 90s was very much still intact and contrasted greatly with some of the women who had gaps in their teeth as was common in rural Cambodia.

Tom was stunned at her barefacedness. He was here to photograph the women who were part of the project, not Janice. This felt wildly inappropriate. He didn't quite know what to do. He awkwardly continued to photograph while Janice put her hands on her hips and posed alongside the women. He glanced over at Sophorn who appeared nonplussed by her behaviour.

After a few moments, Tom told them that he had plenty of group pictures and wanted to focus on some individual portraits. It was a successful way of getting Janice out of the shots. He managed to get a few good ones of some women in their modest homes nearby with their children. By the time they began to lose the sunlight, he was hopeful that between those and the one or two usable group shots before Janice's bizarre intrusion, he had enough to send to Kerstin.

The day was gruelling and by the time they got back into the glorious air-conditioning of the jeep, Tom was hopeful that Janice would be tired too and that they would have a quiet trip back to Phnom Penh. To his dismay, she was eager to talk.

'Tom, did you read the new report by those liars at Save Cambodia?' she asked him as the car began to pull out.

'I must have missed it,' Tom lied hoping it would kill the conversation. The report had interviewed Cambodian garment workers and had been highly critical of the low wages and shoddy conditions in the country's factories which were producing clothes for big name European and American high street clothing brands. He definitely didn't want to get stuck in a discussion about labour rights with her.

'How dare they?' Janice got animated. 'They know how much the women here need those factory jobs. They shouldn't trash those jobs to outsiders.'

Oh Jesus. Tom didn't quite know where to begin. He didn't feel the report had said anything that hadn't been widely known. Outsiders? Did this woman realise she wasn't Cambodian?

Janice didn't need much of a response from him to continue.

'You know, I wanted to give Save Cambodia a chance. My daughter is even working with them at the moment, but if big brands leave Cambodia because of this, the thousands of job losses will be on their head.'

'You know, even talking about this is getting me so mad.' She smacked her hand on her thigh and looked into Tom's eyes intensely.

This woman is manic, thought Tom.

'Oh, I didn't realise you had a daughter. How old is she?' he asked in an attempt to steer her to a calmer topic.

'She's twenty-four. She grew up in the US with her Dad. She wants to do advocacy work and apparently we don't do enough of that at Cambodian Hands, so she just *had* to go to Save Cambodia,' Janice's voice was loaded with contempt making Tom reluctant to ask more.

'You know something,' Janice said excitedly. 'I'm just remembering that Save Cambodia's office is on our way home? Let's do a little detour!'

Tom was uneasy. 'Janice, I've got some deadlines back in Phnom Penh. I need to get back.'

'Oh, Tom, relax,' she told him. 'We'll just be a few minutes.'

Arguing with her seemed a useless exercise. After some redirecting of the driver, they pulled up outside a two-story building flanked by palm trees with large purple signage reading 'Save Cambodia'.

Tom was half-tempted to just stay in the car out of embarrassment but curiosity got the better of him. Janice was highly energetic. She practically bounded into the building while Tom quickened his pace to keep up with her.

'We want to see Pheary, your Director,' she told the young girl at reception.

'I'm sorry. Ms Pheary is not available. She has another meeting. But you can wait for thirty minutes,' she told them.

'We won't take long,' Janice smiled as she walked past her to the office marked 'Director' on the door.

'Lady, I'm sorry! Ms Pheary is not available yet,' the young receptionist cried out getting up from her desk and following Janice, but it was too late. Tom kept back as Janice opened the door.

A middle-aged Cambodian woman was sitting behind the desk mid-conversation with two younger women who were taking down notes of the instructions she was giving them.

'Pheary, I want to tell you that your report on the garment sector was disgraceful.' Janice shouted.

'Publically trashing the one industry that we have here that employs high numbers of women without being strategic about the consequences is just irresponsible. You should be ashamed of yourself.' The younger women in the office gasped as Janice pointed her index finger at Pheary while she spoke, a taboo in Cambodian culture.

Pheary looked stunned and slowly stood up from her desk. 'Janice, please ... calm down ...' She spoke in a gentle voice and tried to respond.

'If business leaves this country, it's on your head,' Janice interrupted her.

Tom was mortified. He couldn't believe he was witnessing this.

'Mom! What are you doing? Will you please stop shouting?!' A female American voice came suddenly from behind Tom and stopped Janice in her tracks.

Holy shit, he realised, recognising her. It was the red-haired girl from Saturday night.

3

'Dad, it was fucking humiliating. Having her barge into my place of work and yell at my boss like that. She was like a crazy woman. She seriously needs to work on her issues,' Caitlyn vented. It had been a few hours but the anger was still pumping through her. She could just about make out her father's concerned frown through the grainy Skype video.

'Honey, I'm so sorry. It sounds awful. You know your Mom is a very passionate person and she doesn't always remember her boundaries.' Liam Leahy never said a bad word about his ex-wife which Caitlyn found hard to understand.

'You should have seen her, Dad. She was completely obnoxious,' Caitlyn continued. 'I was so determined when I decided to come to this country that I wouldn't be defined by being Janice Steiner's daughter. A few weeks in and she's already fucking mortified me.'

'Sweetie, I'm sure it will blow over and you will be able to distinguish yourself from Janice by the good work that you do. What does that meme say? You do you,' Liam smiled while mispronouncing meme as 'meh meh'.

Caitlyn managed a laugh. 'Such impressive millennial referencing skills you have there, Dad. You know it's pronounced meeeem, right?'

'Haters gonna hate,' Liam quipped with faux sass.

Caitlyn laughed in spite of herself. It was her long-held belief that because she had so clearly been at the bottom of the line when they were distributing Moms, she had been given a gold-standard Dad as compensation.

'Seriously though, Caitlyn, I'm still worried about you there. Can you not just move in with your Mom?' Liam's voice turned serious.

'Oh, Dad, don't worry. I'm very safe here, honestly,' Caitlyn told him. She knew that it was hard for her Dad to see her in Cambodia of all places. Liam had visited Phnom Penh for one miserable week when Caitlyn was little, at Janice's insistence. He had been horrified by the state of the country which was then still recovering from the Khmer Rouge time and the subsequent conflicts. His negative feelings about Cambodia were then cemented by his wife leaving him and Caitlyn in Sacramento to move there and set up Cambodian Hands.

'Okay, but promise me you'll take good care. I hate that you've insisted on living on your own. Are you okay for money, hon?'

'I'm fine, Dad. It's so cheap here that my money goes a long way,' Caitlyn already felt guilty enough for taking an allowance from her Dad because her internship with Save Cambodia was unpaid. He never complained but the physicality of his job in construction was getting harder for him as he got older. He would probably be retired by now if she wasn't still relying on him for money.

She ended the call with her Dad feeling slightly calmer. Her boss, Pheary had been kind when she had apologised for Janice's bizarre intrusion but she was still mortified. Her one saving grace was that Save Cambodia's Deputy Director, Vic, an arrogant British guy who Caitlyn found intimidating had been out of the office when it had happened.

She filled up her only pot with water and began to prepare a money-saving dinner of boiled rice and egg. In college, Caitlyn had briefly seen a therapist who had equated all of her issues, even her stress over normal things like boys and college work, to Janice leaving. Irritated by the therapist's lack of imagination, she had refused to go to any more sessions. As if she was such a basic entity that her entire life's issues derived from having a Mommy-shaped hole like she was fucking Bambi.

Liam had invested so much into Caitlyn that it had been impossible for her to grow up feeling anything other than utterly loved. He taught her how to read before she started school and indulged her love of movies so much that by the time she was twelve years old, she could quote the Godfather movies almost verbatim. It had always been normal to her that her Mom was off in a far-away country helping people instead of being at home like other Moms. She had kept an okay relationship with her mother over the years equating her with a distant aunt who called at Christmas and her birthday. As she had gotten older, she had found it harder to relate to her mother but tolerated her calls and occasional visits out of habit. After seeing Janice's arrogance in showing up at Save Cambodia like she had, Caitlyn felt more distant from her mother than ever.

She cringed slightly recalling that she hadn't told her Dad about the Irish guy that was with Janice in Save Cambodia's office. It added to her humiliation that she had had a brief flirtation with this guy and then he ended up being there while she screamed at Janice. He had left with Janice when Pheary had politely asked them to and Caitlyn could only assume that he was working with her in some capacity.

She sat in her open-plan box of an apartment on the wooden two-seater which was in place of where a couch would typically be. It was more like a park bench than a couch but she had stuffed it with blankets to try and squeeze some comfort out of it. She chomped down on her bland dinner and piled soy sauce onto the rice to try and glean some flavour from it. She felt like she was carrying around a bowling ball in her stomach from all of the cheap rice she was eating. She was feeling lumpier these days and it niggled in the back of her mind. Healthier foods like salads were beyond her budget and the one time she had gone for a run around her block, she'd thought that she may collapse from heat stroke. She tried not to let the weight gain bother her, telling herself that she should be focused on her work and less shallow concerns.

She could hear small squeals coming from the kitchen and shuddered thinking that the large family of mice she thought had disappeared must have returned. She was hoping they would just go away as she didn't have the stomach to deal with traps or poison. Her apartment was definitely cheap for a reason. She flicked through the television channels looking for the one or two English language options to drown out the squeals.

—

The next day at Save Cambodia's office, Caitlyn's colleagues were happily treating her like nothing had happened. A prominent Cambodian land rights activist, Savat Nou had been arrested suddenly that morning on dubious charges and her colleagues were occupied with finding out the details and trying to get access to him.

Savat had been advocating for the rights of thousands of families who had been displaced from their homes without receiving any compensation following the government selling their land to a Chinese property developer in what was becoming an increasingly common problem. He and other activists had faced years of arrests and beatings from police for staging peaceful protests. Pheary had tasked her with writing a press release calling for his immediate release and Caitlyn was grateful for the opportunity to throw herself into a meaty task and remind herself of what she was really doing in Cambodia. This was exactly what she needed to get herself out of her own selfish little head. You have no real problems, she told herself.

To Caitlyn's delight, Pheary ended up approving the press release text with very few changes. They translated it quickly and sent it in Khmer and English to a long list of national and international media hoping that it would bring attention to Savat's case, especially outside of Cambodia as international attention was more likely to put pressure on the government. By lunchtime, Caitlyn was feeling good and decided to reward herself. Her budget limited her to getting a portion of $1 pork and rice from a street vendor. She splashed out on a Coke as a treat to herself which meant she spent $1.50.

Caitlyn was still ignoring Janice's calls but as the day continued, she was becoming more relaxed about the whole incident. She'd give it a few days and then maybe call her back at the weekend. By the end of the day, Caitlyn's usual motorbike taxi driver, Thoeun was waiting for her at the office gate. Her father had begged her not to take motorbikes but the remote location of the office meant that tuk tuks were nearly impossible to find after work. Besides, Caitlyn had found that she really loved the thrill of being on the back of a bike.

Thoeun was a careful driver by Phnom Penh's standards given that he used his arms to indicate in a city where giving prior warning of one's next direction was practically an alien concept. He even slowed down when approaching speed bumps. Caitlyn had come to trust him and felt relaxed as they whizzed through the streets. Speeding past ornate pagodas, old ladies selling coconuts and hipster Cambodian teenagers with quiffed hair on motorbikes, it was hard not to be intoxicated by this crazy and fascinating place. In some ways, she could understand how Janice had ditched a quiet life in Sacramento for it.

Caitlyn was lost in her thoughts as she watched an orange-robed monk approach some street sellers, holding out a basket for offerings in front of one of the city's many construction sites. Suddenly, she felt the laptop bag around her neck being pulled sharply and her neck began to bend with it. A young Cambodian guy on a motorbike next to her was pulling at her bag and hissing at her while his driver kept up with Thoeun. She cried out as her body began to slip off the bike. She tried to pull back and steady herself but in seconds her bag was gone and she could see the thief's motorbike speeding off ahead of them.

'Fuck, fuck, fuck,' Caitlyn screamed. 'I don't fucking believe this!'

Thoeun began to pick up pace and speed after them.

'Thoeun, go slow,' she shouted. Logic somehow crept in and she realised that it was pointless chasing after them. She asked Thoeun to pull over and she hopped off the bike shakily.

'You okay? You okay?' Thoeun asked her frantically.

'I'm fine. Just give me two minutes' she told him, turning her back to him to try and regain her composure.

They would have pulled her off the bike into the traffic. She could have been really hurt or worse. Her neck was cut and sore from the pulling of the bag but other than that she was okay. Her laptop was gone. Shit. How was she going to do any work? Most of her files were backed up but several pictures with friends in Sacramento that she hadn't saved anywhere else were now gone. She shuddered, remembering that some topless photos that she'd taken for her ex-boyfriend Nick were also on the laptop too. Her Dad was forever telling her to protect her privacy on technological devices but obviously, like an idiot, she hadn't taken him seriously.

Cash of about $15 was gone too, as were her apartment keys. Ugh. The money was one of the most frustrating losses. That was almost a week's budget for her and she was already well into her overdraft. To her relief, she hadn't her bank cards with her and her cheap smartphone was still safely in her skirt pocket.

She told Thoeun that she now had no money to pay him today but could reimburse him as soon as possible if he took her home. She knew he was probably dependent on her $1 a day fare and this was a loss for him but he was a kindly man and didn't let it show.

Back at her apartment, Caitlyn now had to wait for her landlord to arrive with a spare key. He had told her that he would be ten minutes but more than forty-five minutes later there was no sign of him. A tall white girl standing around alone outside a building at night looked an odd sight to the motorbike and tuk tuk drivers nearby who kept calling out to her in what she was fairly sure were sexual terms in Khmer. She ignored them and the familiar screeches of Phnom Penh's jumbo-rats as they scarpered around the street's garbage piles.

Her neck was sore and she needed painkillers. This was fucking miserable. She could call Janice. She knew she could. No, fuck that. She had never needed her Mom and today wasn't going to be any different. People get robbed in poor countries all the time. It was a bad day that was all.

When the landlord finally arrived with a spare key after another twenty minutes, her cockroach-ridden apartment with hideous green wallpaper the colour of boiled cabbage had never seemed so inviting. She didn't have the energy to wait for the rice to boil so she went to bed without any dinner.

4

By the weekend, Caitlyn still hadn't told anyone that she had been robbed. She didn't want her Dad to worry and the last thing she needed was to draw more undue attention to herself at work. She wore a light-blue silk scarf around her neck to cover the cut and friction marks from where her bag had been pulled. It was like being fifteen years old again and hiding her hickeys from her Dad.

She used her credit card to buy a new laptop. She wasn't sure how she would pay the bill when it came in but she would figure something out. Yet, her mood was still low and she couldn't seem to get back to feeling normal. At a weak moment on Friday, after ignoring another of Janice's calls, she was tempted to call her best friend at home. Lucy loved her and was excellent at providing comfort when Caitlyn needed it but she didn't really understand what Caitlyn was doing in Cambodia. She had a well-paid, stable job as an accountant and had no interest in leaving the United States for anything more than a two-week holiday to a luxury resort in Mexico. She would probably just tell her to come home, so Caitlyn decided against it.

She was feeling at a bit of a loss as to how to spend her weekend when she received a well-timed text from Ella asking if she was around to go for dinner and drinks on Saturday night. Ella had been in the same college as Caitlyn and they shared several mutual friends. She was a free-spirited and wonderfully foul-mouthed blonde who had been living in Phnom Penh for two years and had an impressive job at the International Chamber of Commerce. They didn't know each other very well but Ella had reached out to her when Caitlyn made a Facebook post about coming to Cambodia and they were quickly becoming close. Socialising felt like the distraction Caitlyn needed after the week she had just had.

She dressed up a little, as much for the psychological uplift as for the fact that on its website the stylish French bistro they were due to meet at looked far more upmarket than the cheap noodle shops Caitlyn typically went to for Phnom Penh dinners. She blow-dried her hair rather than letting it dry naturally and wore purple lipstick, dark blue jeggings and a purple high-necked strappy top which slightly covered the marks from where her bag had been pulled.

She deliberately arrived at the restaurant a little later in the knowledge that she wouldn't know anyone at the dinner other than Ella. Caitlyn squeezed herself through the line of oversized cars parked on the footpath blocking the entrance to the restaurant. She couldn't understand why gross SUVs were so popular in Phnom Penh. The restaurant had small candlelit tables situated in the leafy courtyard of a charming old building covered by overhanging, elegant string lights. Caitlyn found herself wondering not for the first time how so many high-end restaurants could survive in a place as poor as Phnom Penh.

Ella was sitting at a gazebo style table with three other women. Caitlyn was reasonably adept at meeting strangers but there was always a twinge of nervousness whenever she had to make a first impression. She went around the table shaking hands and catching names. There was Danielle, an Australian who worked for the World Bank, Nina, a Scottish lawyer, and Singaporean Sara who worked in child protection.

Both Nina and Sara had legs so long that Caitlyn would have given her left boob for them. It was not hard to notice that alongside how impressive they were, all four women were exceptionally beautiful. She felt a little frumpy by comparison.

'Sorry I'm late,' said Caitlyn sitting down and placing her napkin on her lap. 'What have I missed?'

'Not a lot,' said Ella. 'Nina is just filling us in on a terrible date she had last night.'

'What she means to say is *another* terrible date,' Nina quipped in a rhythmic Scottish accent.

'It was fucking godawful. The guy was a cretin.'

'Don't scare her too much. Caitlyn's new,' Ella was laughing.

'How long have you been here, pet?' Nina asked her.

'Just a month so far but I'll be here until early next year,' Caitlyn responded.

'Well, as someone who has been here for two and a half years. Let me tell you …' Nina fixed her golden-brown eyes across the table at Caitlyn. 'Finding a decent man in Phnom Penh is like finding a freckle-free arse in Scotland.'

Caitlyn laughed, 'It can't be that bad.'

Danielle jumped in, 'Nina's exaggerating but she's not entirely wrong. I've been here eighteen months and every guy I've dated has turned out to be an arrogant asshat.'

'What makes them so bad?' Caitlyn was amused.

'Ooh! Ooh! Look at the table at 3 o'clock. This makes for a perfect visual aid.' Danielle got excited and gestured unsubtly at a corresponding table.

Caitlyn looked to her left to try to get a sense of what she meant. There was a couple at the table. She was tall and stunning and dressed in an elegant sundress with long, enviable dark curls. He was significantly shorter and more average-looking with a thick waist and a depleting hairline.

'Oh, this is perfect,' Danielle continued. 'See Danny DeVito over there on a date with Jennifer Lopez? There is no way that these two would get together outside of Phnom Penh. It's a numbers game and the numbers work in his favour. See, if you are an expat guy, you have your pick of beautiful locals as well as tons of gorgeous, accomplished expat women to choose from who outnumber expat men by odds of about, like six to one. So, Danny DeVito finds that in this town, he's George Clooney. Meanwhile, Jennifer Lopez who is used to having so much attention elsewhere realises that here, her options are very fucking limited. All of a sudden she's quite interested in Danny DeVito!'

Danielle made a mock-bowing motion and they all laughed loudly.

'What Danielle has forgotten to add,' Sara jumped in. 'is that after dating a Jennifer or two, Danny becomes an asshole. He realises he can get any girl he wants. Suddenly, no woman is good enough for him and he's terrible to the women he once would have been dying to go out with.'

'Case in point, the human wankstain that I had drinks with last night,' Nina added. 'He's an Aussie journalist who has been here for years. He's been after me for months. I finally agree to one drink and he turns up hammered and then gets pissed off with me when I won't go home with him after less than an hour.'

Their food came and Caitlyn lapped up her chicken stew. At $11, it was the first luxury meal she had allowed herself since she had arrived, but it was worth every penny. She put thoughts of her credit card limit to the back of her mind.

The women continued to order bottles of wine and the

conversation flowed between work and life in Phnom Penh, with men remaining the theme of the night. By dessert, each of the women described the qualities that their ideal men would possess. It was obvious to Caitlyn that the 'inventory' as they called it had been a conversation topic for the group in previous discussions as each woman was quick to recite hers.

Ella's criteria were – 'entrepreneurial, speaks more than one language, dark hair, over 5 foot 11.'

Nina's were – 'close to his family, big arms, outdoorsy and must want kids.'

Sara's were – 'must be an avid reader, must earn good money, be a great cook and have no Mommy issues.'

Danielle's were – 'must be funny, a great dancer and be in possession of a big cock and the ability to use it.'

After the laughter at Danielle's inventory died down, they asked for Caitlyn's contribution.

'Oh, god, I have never actually thought about it,' Caitlyn said honestly. 'Definitely someone quick-witted who likes movies and music.'

Caitlyn enjoyed the humour and the warmth of her new friends immensely. As the bottles of wine continued arriving at their table, Caitlyn lost count of the drinks she had and the amount she would have to charge on her credit card. She was feeling giggly and carefree by the time Sara suggested they go dancing.

'Ladies, let's go to Wild. It's 90s night'.

They made it to Wild, a darkly-lit basement nightclub of the tackier variety full of rich Cambodians drinking champagne straight from the bottle and smoke being pumped onto the dancefloor. To Caitlyn's dismay, 90s night was less Smashing Pumpkins and more Spice Girls but she soon embraced the nostalgia and began to enjoy herself. Ella handed her a tequila and she happily gulped it down while shaking her butt to Destiny's Child.

Shit, she realised after a while. Everyone else had bought rounds of shots and it was her turn. They would have to go on her credit card too but she could worry about that in the morning. She ambled her way through the sweaty crowds up to the bar and squeezed into an empty spot to order.

'Ah would you look who it is?' A loud, Irish, male voice came from behind her. She groaned inwardly. Of course, it was him. She knew it without turning around but when she did, the sandy-haired Irish guy from the other week was grinning broadly at her.

'Hi,' she said. He was definitely attractive but in a wholesome sort of way. The kind of guy that would look perfect on an election poster as a Republican Party candidate.

'Look,' she began, emboldened by the wine and tequila. 'I don't know how you know my Mom but I'd appreciate it if you didn't make a thing about telling people that I'm Janice's daughter. It's not a secret or anything but I'm just happier being quiet about it and making my own way here.'

'I get you.' He grinned again. 'Actually, I don't think we've officially met. I'm Tom, Tom Fenton'. He took her hand and gave her a gentle handshake which lasted a little longer than necessary.

'Ah Major Tom, of course, like in "Space Oddity,"' she grinned. 'I'm Caitlyn, Caitlyn Leahy.'

'Caitlyn Leahy, a great Irish name! Can I buy you a drink?' He let go of her hand and placed his hand on her shoulder affectionately.

'It's actually my turn to buy my girlfriends tequilas but

thanks anyway.' Caitlyn knew that her embarrassment was making her behave a little curtly.

'No worries,' Tom gave her a lopsided grin which she suspected was an affectation but still found cute.

She turned from Tom and ordered five shots.

'How do you know my mother anyway?' she asked as she waited to get served.

'I work for UN Poverty and Cambodian Hands runs our hand-weaving project.'

The barman came back to her, 'Your credit card isn't working.'

She was mortified, 'Can you try again? It should be fine.'

The barman rolled his eyes.

'I have cash. Let me get this.' Tom handed the barman a $50 note before she had a chance to intervene.

'You didn't need to do that,' Caitlyn protested.

'Don't worry. The card machines never work in this place. It's a total pain,' he smiled again.

'Okay, but I'll get you back. Thank you.'

She was almost too humiliated to feel properly grateful and knew she needed to get away from this guy. She lifted the tray of shots and moved quickly to join her friends.

The next hour or so passed in a blur. She and Ella were enthusiastically belting out the lyrics to Coolio's 'Gangster's Paradise' on the dancefloor when she felt a hand on the small of her back. She turned around and saw him, smiling at her. One of them leaned in and the next thing she knew she was greedily kissing Tom Fenton.

Her head was hazy and she wasn't clear how it had started or whether or not it was a good idea. All she knew at that point was that he smelled amazing and she was melting into a truly great kiss. She put her hands in his hair to get a better grip and realised that her crotch was locked against his and there was a warm, firm sensation pushing against her. His hands lowered to just above her butt and she felt a tingling in her underwear. Fuck. It had been a long time.

One of them broke away from the kiss and realising that they were in the middle of a packed dancefloor, they moved wordlessly to a ledge behind one of the smoke machines. Tom began kissing her neck and Caitlyn closed her eyes and moaned gently as he slipped his thigh between her legs. Her hands found themselves lightly fingering the belt at the top of his jeans. He ran his hands down her face and traced the outline of her bra-straps. He moaned a little and she felt his unmistakably full erection dipping into her. She angled her chest upwards, willing him to touch her boobs. It could have been hours of kissing for all she knew. It was probably the booze and the insane week she had had but she knew what she wanted.

'Can you take me home?' she whispered.

He broke into a wide grin and nodded, 'Absolutely.'

5

Janice's built-in alarm clock woke her up at 5:30 a.m. It hardly mattered what time zone she was in or when she had gone to bed, her body was wired to wake up at the same time every morning. A call with a donor in California the night before had ended at midnight but she had been restless afterwards and it had taken her hours to get to sleep.

That was the thing about being the head of an organisation like hers. It was a never-ending treadmill. You could never truly switch off. She made herself her first green tea of what typically ended up being eight cups most days and she began to write down her to-do list. She had become an obsessive list writer over the years. Her lists were full of things that she needed to do and people she needed to contact, of potential funding opportunities for Cambodian Hands, ideas for new projects, possible risks and threats to their work and ways to counter them.

That morning, the *New York Chronicle* was sending a journalist to visit the hand-weaving project and giving him her full attention was likely to take up her entire day. Dealing with the press came as second nature to Janice after so many years and she didn't feel confident that her staff could manage it without her.

It had been a while since a big US media outlet had come to do a profile of their work. Americans were still her biggest individual donors but she worried about their short memories. She invited every opportunity to remind them that the US had dropped more tonnes of ordnance on Cambodia during the Vietnam War than the allies had dropped during the entirety of World War II and that the country and its challenges hadn't gone away. It wasn't easy keeping Cambodia in people's consciousness when it wasn't considered a particularly newsworthy or important country. It was especially difficult when you were competing with so many worthy causes sprouting from all kinds of conflicts and disasters globally. These days, the war in Syria was the big one that Westerners were donating to. It was bleak thinking of these awful challenges as their competitors in some kind of tragedy Olympics, but Cambodian Hands had suffered a big knock to donations following the 2004 tsunami in the Indian Ocean and then again during the 2008 financial crisis. Having deftly steered her organisation through vulnerable times and come out resilient, Janice knew all too well that opportunities like the *New York Chronicle* couldn't be squandered.

Her driver collected her at 8 a.m. and they went straight from her house to pick up the journalist from his hotel. It struck her as odd that he was staying in Raffles, one of Phnom Penh's swankiest hotels. So much for all that talk of newspapers losing money. The French colonial, art deco hotel remained a living showcase of Phnom Penh's cultural and intellectual 1960s heyday and had housed high profile visitors like Jackie Kennedy just a few years before the Khmer Rouge had obliterated the country's intelligentsia.

Janice sat waiting in the hotel lobby admiring the original tiles and decided to use the time to give Caitlyn another call. She was getting worried that Caitlyn still hadn't returned her calls after several days. She waited anxiously as the phone rang twice before transferring to voicemail. That girl was so fucking stubborn. It was maddening.

'Hi. I'm Parker Atkins,' a cheerful voice interrupted her. The journalist was a cherubic young guy who looked like his Mom still wiped his nose.

Jesus, he's only a kid, Janice thought. Everyone from the UN officials she met to ambassadors and donors were increasingly younger these days. She was having to get used to having meetings with people who had never seen fax machines and thought they knew everything about how to fix Cambodia's problems because they were fresh out of master's degrees in development studies.

'I have to admit, I'm a huge fan of yours so forgive me if I'm a little starstruck,' he told her as they got into the jeep.

'That's very sweet,' she said. 'We have a good day planned for you. We're going to take you to meet the women in the weaving project for some interviews. Some monks are also coming today to conduct a blessing ceremony of our new workshop.'

'Sounds absolutely wonderful. Thank you so much for arranging it,' Parker gushed.

Gotta love that youthful enthusiasm. Had she ever been like that? she wondered. Maybe for about five minutes.

The driver trudged down pothole-filled roads on the way to the weaving project location out near Kampong Cham. He seemed to be deliberately driving into the potholes instead of away from them causing Janice's fragile, sleep-deprived body to heave with nausea. He did this every time, she thought irritably. He was a sweet guy and she didn't want to have to replace him but he sure as shit wasn't making it easy for her.

'Please avoid the potholes, Boran!' she called to him.

'I have to ask,' Parker began, taking out his notebook and poising himself to write. 'I've read lots about your life and it just sounds completely fascinating. You grew up quite poor in Sacramento but you managed to put yourself through dental school, then you came to Cambodia when it was total chaos here and you started this incredible organisation. It would make a phenomenal book. I mean I would totally read that book and watch that movie. How have you never written it?'

'Thank you. People have asked this question but I try not to make the story about me. If I ever was to write anything it would be about the amazing women you are about to meet,' Janice responded.

It was true, well kind of. She didn't mind being the story occasionally if it helped to bring funding and attention to Cambodian Hands, but a book was something very different to a short newspaper article. A book would probably need to look at some of the sacrifices that she'd made including moving away from Caitlyn. She knew that people didn't understand that about her and she wasn't going to put herself in a position where she had to try and explain her choices.

They arrived at the new workshop which essentially looked like a small factory made from sheet metal in the middle of the rice field. Inside, a group of twenty or so women were sitting on chairs in front of desks weaving baskets by hand. Janice was proud that this was likely the first time that these baskets, which had been woven for hundreds of years, were being made in a place even slightly resembling a factory.

Without asking for permission, Parker began to take photos. He enthusiastically moved in to take close ups of the women's faces and their working hands. The women had gotten used to having to be on display occasionally and didn't let the presence of a boisterous American distract them from their work.

After a short while, three orange-robed monks came in

and silently sat themselves facing the crowd of women who stood up from their desks and began to gather themselves expectantly on the workshop floor. Janice beckoned to Parker to come and sit down with them. She could see that he looked uncomfortable and was struggling to get his chubby legs into a cross-legged position in an imitation of the pose taken by the women. She doubted that his expensive-looking cream pants would emerge unscathed from the dusty workshop floor.

'Sorry,' she whispered to him apologetically. 'It's traditional.'

'Oh, it's totally great,' he smiled at her through obvious discomfort.

The monks began sombre, repetitive chanting. Parker, Janice and the others closed their eyes in concentration. The monotone chant continued for about twenty minutes while they sat patiently cross-legged looking enraptured. Janice peeked at Parker and could see that he was wriggling into new positions wherever he could to try and get more comfortable on the floor. The monks stopped chanting suddenly and stood up and began to douse the participants with small buckets of cold water. Janice and the women who had been expecting this and experienced it several times before had little reaction.

Parker jumped up, soaked through his shirt. 'What the hell?' he exclaimed.

'It's a traditional water blessing,' Janice told him, trying to guard her amusement.

'Okay,' he sat down wordlessly and flinched as the monks poured a smaller vessel of water over his head.

When the ceremony was finally over, Parker was dripping wet but nonetheless got to work interviewing the women. Sometimes, it was easier when they just wanted to talk to her and she could shield the women from this bullshit but getting the story out was a necessary part of keeping their work going. Janice privately disliked having to allow strangers to pry into the women's lives and mine them for material. At least Parker hadn't brought his own translator, and the Cambodian Hands manager, Sophorn, who the women knew very well could translate. Sophorn had worked for Janice for a few years and although he had a tendency towards laid-backness which often frustrated her, she was in no doubt about his dedication to supporting the women.

Parker's first conversation was with Pagna, a pretty woman in her early thirties with an almost permanent, toothy smile. She was one of the veterans of the hand-weaving programme having participated over several years.

'So, how has your life changed because of the programme?' Parker started by asking her. Janice internally groaned at the clichéd question while Sophorn translated.

'I worked on my family's farm for most of my life and took care of my husband and our kids but over the years it got harder for us to make money from the farm. My husband would get stressed and he would beat me. I heard about this project from a friend and I came to learn. Now, because of the money I am making from the baskets, we have bought some chickens for the farm and I am saving to buy a pig. My husband is calmer now and he is much happier,' Sophorn translated.

It still got Janice a little emotional hearing these stories. To the average *New York Chronicle* reader, maybe getting chickens and no longer having the shit beaten out of you by a scumbag husband wasn't much and it definitely wasn't enough but she felt proud that her organisation was able to eliminate misery in ways that were significant for these women.

'That's great. Wow,' Parker responded while swatting

furiously at non-existent mosquitos. He was clearly used to more urban settings.

'How would you say that the programme has empowered you?' he asked.

Jesus, how is this kid working for the *Chronicle*? Journalism really is a dying industry, thought Janice smiling encouragingly at him while Sophorn translated.

'I now keep the money in my house,' Pagna explained. 'My children see that I am in charge of the money, not their father. This means I have the power.'

Parker continued to interview and photograph other women but remained most interested in Pagna; the youngest and most vibrant of the participants.

'Can we see her house and visit her family?' Parker asked Janice when he had concluded with the other interviews.

'I think that's up to Pagna,' Janice told him.

Sophorn translated and Pagna agreed to allow them to come home with her. Sophorn, Janice, Parker and Pagna piled into the jeep as Pagna directed the driver to her house which was more than a twenty-minute journey from the workshop.

'Wow, she lives far away,' Parker exclaimed when the car finally stopped outside a small wooden farmhouse with little surrounding it. 'How does she get to the workshop every day?'

Sophorn translated the question to Pagna who answered quietly.

'She says she likes to walk,' Sophorn translated.

Janice glanced at Pagna who had a slightly uncomfortable look on her face. Janice felt a sinking feeling come over her. Something wasn't right here but she knew that now wasn't the time to address it. Not in front of Parker.

'God, how do they live like this?' Parker whispered loudly to

Janice upon entering the shabby but neat house. He took some hand sanitiser from his pocket and began to apply it liberally on his hands and arms.

'It must be so difficult,' he said quietly as he began to click away with his camera.

Parker talked to Pagna's husband who told him via Sophorn's translation that he had learned how to be a better husband. He also got several adorable photos of Pagna and her husband as well as their cute young children with their chickens. He even insisted on them all taking a selfie together including Sophorn and Janice. When it was time to leave Parker seemed thrilled with his photos and interviews.

'You are doing such amazing work,' he enthused to Janice. 'I think it's going to be a great story. Thank you so much for being so generous with your time. I'll probably just need to interview someone from UNP and then I can get this written up.'

Janice thanked him appreciatively, feeling relieved that the day was over. She sent Parker back to the city with her driver and asked to speak with Sophorn in the small office back at the workshop.

'Sophorn, I'm worried about Pagna,' Janice started. 'Her story doesn't add up. Why on earth is she walking to the workshop every day? It must take her hours.'

'I don't know, Janice,' Sophorn answered apologetically.

'Please call her and ask her again about why she walks to the workshop. It doesn't make sense to me,' Janice instructed.

Sophorn took out his phone and spoke in Khmer on a call for a few moments.

'Her husband answered the phone and said she was asleep,' he told Janice after hanging up.

'Sophorn, I really don't like this.' Janice felt nauseous again.

When Boran the driver came back, she insisted that he bring them back to Pagna's house.

'It's getting a bit late to just call to them,' Sophorn protested.

'It's only 6 p.m.,' Janice snapped at him. 'We're doing this.'

They arrived back at the house just as the sun was setting and the evening sky had broken into ribbons of colour. Pagna's husband answered the door topless and looking ill-tempered. He blustered something in Khmer at Sophorn. Sophorn responded asking where Pagna was.

'Pagna!' Janice called into the house from the doorway. 'Pagna!'.

Pagna emerged looking frazzled with a fresh reddish mark surrounding her right eye which was slightly closed. Janice's stomach plunged.

'Did he hit you?' Janice screamed. 'Shit! Sophorn, ask if he hit her!'

Sophorn translated but Pagna refused to answer and looked frozen in the doorway.

'Sophorn, please tell her that I want her to get her things and the children and come to stay with me in Phnom Penh. They aren't safe here.'

Sophorn translated and Pagna looked pained and stayed silent. Her husband began to shout at her.

'Don't you dare shout at her!' Janice yelled at him.

Clearly unsure of how to respond to a screaming white lady on his doorstep, he stopped shouting and glowered at both Janice and Sophorn and whispered some kind of Khmer slurs under his breath.

'*Mok! Mok!*' Janice called to Pagna. *Mok* was the Khmer word for come.

Pagna began to move slowly, taking a plastic bag and filling it with random clothes and food from the kitchen. She grabbed the two small children by the hand and awkwardly left the house with Janice and Sophorn while her husband scowled at her but did not stand in their way.

Janice began to erupt as the car pulled away.

'Sophorn, how did this happen? Why do we have women saying that the weaving project is helping them when it's not true?'

'I don't know Janice. We only know what they tell us,' Sophorn stammered.

'Ask her then!' Janice demanded.

Sophorn spoke to Pagna in Khmer and translated her response.

'She says that her husband was good when she first started coming to the weaving project and that's when she told us her story. She says that when she wanted to buy a bicycle to come to the workshop, he said no and started to keep control of the money that she was making and soon he started to hit her again. She didn't want to say anything, so she just kept to her original story and repeated it whenever she was asked. She wants to continue to come to work and didn't want to disappoint us because she thought that we were so happy to hear her story.'

Janice cursed loudly as Pagna broke into deep sobbing and clutched her daughter. This was fucking despicable, she fumed to herself. How could she have missed this?

Her own father had been a domineering asshole possessed with a real resourcefulness for turning regular household items into objects with which to beat the shit out of Janice, her Mom and her elder sister. A phonebook, an ironing board, her mother's rolling pin. The slightest smell of vinegar still made her retch recalling the time that he had smashed a bottle of cider vinegar over her head when she was eleven.

Janice had smoked her first and only cigarette, at her father's gravestone on the day of his funeral when she was 18 years old. She had refused to go to the ceremony but fuelled by a bottle of wine, she had gone to the graveyard that evening and told him what a twisted, sick, tormentor he was and how she felt nothing but gratitude at his passing. Liam, her new boyfriend at the time, had gone with her and silently watched her scream at the newly erected headstone for more than an hour. When Janice's anger broke into unrelenting sobs, he had embraced her and pulled out a packet of Marlboro Red from the back pocket of his jeans and said, 'Let's have a smoke in a tribute to the vice that killed the bastard.' They smoked the entirety of the packet together wordlessly through spluttering coughs and occasional tears. That was the evening that had confirmed her suspicions that she had let herself fall in love with Liam Leahy.

Janice felt utterly defeated about Cambodian Hands having not helped Pagna and her children. She turned to Sophorn.

'We need to set up a system to catch issues like this and really make a difference for these women rather than just having them say it does. Tell her and the children they can stay with me in Phnom Penh for a while and soon we'll get some accommodation sorted for them.'

6

Tom's dick was awake before he was. In fact, he wasn't even sure that it had gone to sleep. He grabbed his phone from the bedside locker and checked the time; 9:19 a.m. They had only gotten to sleep a few hours earlier. He took a sip of water and turned around. Caitlyn was fast asleep on her side. Her masses of red hair were splayed all over the pillow and looked partially matted from their exertions a few hours ago. He couldn't resist lifting up the bedsheet and taking a look at that perfect porcelain ass of hers. His dick throbbed harder reminding him of what he wanted. Usually it was totally dead after a night like the one they had just had. He had no idea where this energy was coming from. He spooned into her, positioning his dick at the curve of her ass, tracing his hands gently over her belly and beginning to kiss her neck.

'Mmmm,' she grumbled sleepily. 'I know what you're doing.' She smiled without opening her eyes, backing her ass into him.

'What? What am I doing?' He began to kiss her ear softly and reached his hands down below her belly. He was delighted to find that she was warm and wet, and he began to gently explore.

'Keep doing that,' she moaned.

'Can I taste her?' he whispered.

'Oh, if you must,' she giggled, turning around on her back delightedly and opening herself up for him.

—

'Okay, I need to go get some kind of liquid,' Caitlyn

announced sitting upright in bed once they had slept for a few more hours.

Tom grinned at her. 'You can drink my …'

'Don't!' She tossed a pillow at him. 'Don't be such a sleazy cliché to say I can drink your come. It's gonna make me seriously regret having all that sex with you.'

She smiled broadly at him as she stepped out of bed and began searching for her clothes. She was fully naked but didn't seem to have an ounce of shyness as she pulled the sheets around and started putting on pieces of clothing.

'I should really go home and conquer this hangover,' she said pulling her top on over her head.

'No, don't go!' Tom said with an eagerness that caught him by surprise. 'I think I should at least make you breakfast.'

'Breakfast? It's like 1 p.m.'

'Let's call it brunch then. I'll make it worth your while. Let's go see what's in the kitchen.' Tom pulled on his boxer shorts and jumped out of bed, holding in his stomach as he could feel her eyes on it.

His colonial era apartment was full of warm rattan interiors and Buddhist art he had picked up in various local galleries. The kitchen had been remodelled by the French-Cambodian architect who owned it with art deco black and white tiles complimenting the natural light from the full-length windows. The maid had come the previous afternoon so the place was spotless. She was paid alongside his rent which his work covered. Tom had adjusted so easily to having someone pick up after him that he dreaded the prospect of having to go without it again at some point in the future. Making herself right at home, Caitlyn went straight to his pride and joy, a large American stainless-steel fridge he had gotten shipped in for a cost that far exceeded the average Cambodian family's monthly income.

'I'm not seeing much to work with here,' she said opening the fridge. 'Lots of beer, eggs and protein drinks. Jesus, this is such a jock fridge. I bet it bullies the shit out of other fridges.'

It was a silly joke but he found himself laughing. She was certainly quite funny. He didn't often find women that funny.

'Ooh, I found tomatoes and a bell pepper. We could make omelettes?' She looked at him expectantly.

He was very much enjoying the sight of her in his kitchen in nothing but the strappy purple vest thing she had been wearing last night and her knickers.

'I am an excellent chef. You! Couch!' He steered her through the archway to his large round rattan sink chairs and flat screen television.

'Oh, okay then,' her cute smile made him melt a little as she tucked her feet up and turned on the television.

Jesus, what was wrong with him? He was clearly getting soft. But he was enjoying himself. He put Van Morrison's *Astral Weeks* on his iPod and began to crack the eggs.

'Coffee, dear?' he called into Caitlyn.

'Yes, dear,' she shouted back. 'Black and strong please, like my men!'

'Today, it's white and sweet or nothing, dear,' he laughed peering in at her. She was now fully lying down on his couch. He took a mental image of how appealing she looked all white legs and messy, red hair.

After they had eaten, in his quest to get more time with her, Tom suggested they watch a film. He had a decent collection of Cambodia's finest bootleg DVDs and gave her full decision-making power.

'Oh my god! *Edward Scissorhands*! This is one of the greatest movies of all time,' she whooped enthusiastically opening up the DVD case. 'We're watching this. If you don't love Tim Burton's unique brand of gothic sentimentality, you have no soul!'

'Yes, ma'am!'

He poured them some red wine given that it was already afternoon and they settled next to each other on the couch. The natural sink in the couch drew them close together and given that neither of them had anything more than underwear on their bottom halves, his left thigh was pushed up against her right thigh.

They weren't long past Edward Scissorhands starting to give the townswomen eccentric hairdos when Tom realised that he was paying far more attention to the warmth of Caitlyn's thigh than anything that was happening in the film. She moved her head from his shoulder and gave his neck a quick kiss. He lightly touched her big bottom lip with his thumb and the next thing he knew her lips were on his. *Edward Scissorhands* was soon abandoned. They lay in bed together afterwards, him on his back, sitting slightly upright, her on her belly with her legs sticking up in the air.

You're perfect, he thought with a visceral urge to tell her so. Jesus, what was wrong with him? he thought again. 'You're lovely,' he settled for.

'Luuuuuvly,' she mimicked the deep U pronunciation in his Irish accent. 'Sorry. I can't take a compliment, so I use humour as a defence mechanism. I blame the Irish heritage. My Dad is the same. Anyway, you are quite lovely yourself.'

She rested her head on his chest and they lay wordlessly, not quite sleeping but with their eyes closed. It felt to Tom strangely more intimate than anything sexual they had done in the past 24 hours.

She looked up at him suddenly and groaned. 'Oh god! I just remembered that you work with my friggin' Mom. This is a bit incestuous.'

'Don't worry about it,' he told her. 'I honestly don't know her that well. I mostly deal with her staff who run the project.'

He was still struggling to reconcile with the fact that the fun, sexy woman in his bed was Janice Steiner's daughter. She didn't even look like her. Well, maybe there was a similarity around the blue eyes. Better not to think about that too much though.

'I don't like that you've seen my family insanity in action but I know so little about you. Tell me about your family,' she sat up excitedly.

'Well there's really not that much to tell. They are all back in Galway. I'm the youngest of three boys. Parents are still together. Very vanilla childhood. Very little to complain about.'

'Sounds really tough,' Caitlyn quipped. 'So, given that you had such a healthy, normal upbringing, how did you end up in this crazy line of work?'

'I really wanted to do something meaningful with my life and have always felt passionate about helping communities in need. The UN seemed like the ideal place for me.' This was Tom's well-worn line for questions about why he did what he did.

'You see, I just don't fully buy that,' Caitlyn started getting animated. 'There are many ways to help people but not all of them come with the excellent salary and smug self-satisfaction that working for the UN provides.'

'Whoa! So pretty but so cynical!' He laughed. 'A little anti-UN, are we?'

'Na, I'm not anti-UN at all. I think it's healthy to be critical about it though and not get seduced by the superficial stuff.'

'I'm not seduced or superficial,' Tom could hear a smidge of defensiveness in his own voice.

He continued: 'I don't think people should apologise for wanting a good salary. But it's more than that. Think of how many more people you can reach by working for an influential UN agency versus working for a small local NGO, however well-meaning.'

'But it's not just about the numbers of people! This is the problem with this sector, everyone is so obsessed with numbers and not enough about the substance behind them,' Caitlyn's eyes flashed as she spoke.

'I don't disagree with you but it's a matter of creating an enabling environment for systemic change. Imperfect as it may be, outside of governments, and maybe a few major corporations, the UN and only the UN has the resources, clout and mandate to truly make change happen at a scalable level in a way that is actually sustainable,' Tom was getting into his zone. It wasn't the first time he had made these points.

'"Enabling environment for systemic change." Seriously? Jargon much? What does that even mean? I can see that you've drunk the Kool aid,' she poked his stomach.

Typically, Tom avoided anyone who came close to making him feel intellectually inferior but this was different. While it was possible that he was blinded by his intense physical attraction to her, he found that he was enjoying her company immensely. He was suddenly dying to download her opinion on every subject under the sun.

'Well, enough about me ...' He transgressed. 'Your motivations are far more interesting. What's your plan and why, pray tell, are you not working for your Mum's organisation?'

'Ugh, that old chestnut,' she rolled her eyes. 'Of course, I respect Cambodian Hands and my Mom, pain in the ass that she is, has done some genuinely impressive things. But I need to do my own thing. I mean what self-respecting person wants their career defined by charges of nepotism? Who do you think I am? Sofia Coppola?'

Tom laughed, feeling a rush of admiration. 'I respect that massively. Very cool. So, what's the long-term goal?'

'I don't really have one,' Caitlyn's face turned serious as she took a sip of wine. 'I mean I just wanted to do impact-ful, interesting work, really. But it's hard to find the right place to do that. Obviously, I have a lot to learn but I'm not sure if Save Cambodia is doing more than being on the sidelines, pussy-footing around a shitty government that has no interest in listening. Then again, I don't want to become cynical either.'

'Oh, no fear of that,' Tom teased.

'What about you?' She asked him. 'Is there a cushy head-quarters job in the near future?'

'Well, I don't know. For sure, I'm ambitious. I want to learn what I can from the UN system and if I happen to rise through the ranks a little. It wouldn't be the worst thing.' He winked at her.

'Oh god,' she laughed. 'I can so imagine you living the perfect senior UN life. You'll have like, a hot Scandinavian wife. You guys will have a gardener, chef and three nannies while you faff about in $800 suits holding workshops in fancy hotels, pretending that you care about poor people.'

'Ouch! So cold!' Tom clasped his hands over his heart in mock dramatics. 'Yup. Pretty much. You have me all figured out. Except, I'm not into blondes. But I'll take a feisty redhead any day!'

He nuzzled into her neck. He was again surprised at his

own stamina and probably could have attempted a round or two more but it was getting late and they both had work the next day so reality started to seep in. Caitlyn said that she had to leave.

'Thanks for the … um hospitality, I guess.' She seemed a little shy all of a sudden and he felt awkward too.

'Anytime, dear,' Tom winked at her.

They gave one another a slightly uneasy hug and she left.

I should have kissed her goodbye! What happened to my game? He instantly chastised himself after the door closed. He felt a sudden feeling of loss when she was gone which surprised him. Oh well, all in all, a very enjoyable Sunday. By far his nicest hangover day in quite some time.

He was still grinning to himself as he got into bed a few hours later. He could smell her perfume on the sheets and had no immediate plans to change them.

7

Tom's headquarters in Geneva was very pleased with the photos he sent in from the project. They had been well-received at the Vienna conference and they had even been posted alongside a lengthy story about the basket-weaving programme on the UNP website, quoting him. Of course, he had less selection to choose from among the photos that didn't have Janice needlessly jumping into them, but he was still rather proud of his photography skills after the addition of a few filters.

A journalist from the *New York Chronicle* newspaper who was visiting Cambodia had even requested an interview with him about the project after spotting the piece online. Tom walked around the office feeling a buzz of self-achievement. He was certain that influential people within the organisation were paying close attention to him and he fully intended to keep it that way.

In his time working for UNP, Tom had only done occasional interviews with journalists from the English language media in Cambodia which hadn't provided him with much of a challenge. They would ask inane questions which in Tom's eyes unearthed their lack of understanding of Cambodia and the UN's work. The journalists working for these local publications were often overconfident twenty-somethings, fresh from completing English degrees from universities in America, Australia or the UK, for whom Cambodia was their first real job. In their home countries, Tom felt many of them would be lucky to write stories about unpaid parking fines but being native English speakers willing to work for wages not far from those of the country's sweatshop workers meant that the cash-strapped Phnom Penh newspapers let them report on complex issues without them needing to have much reporting experience behind them.

But this was different, this was the *New York Chronicle*. Tom felt excited and prepared himself for a grilling. He had written down some bullet points that he felt were especially quotable about how the weaving project was bringing 'sustainable impact'. He wanted to weave 'systemic change' into at least one of his answers too. Talking about systemic change was very in right now.

The journalist had wanted to meet him at Phnom Penh's Foreign Correspondent's Club on the riverside. Tom was momentarily amused at the choice of venue. The FCC, as it was known, was a beautiful, yellow colonial era building with a long history as a war reporter hangout back in the Khmer Rouge days, when Western journalists didn't have the ample selection of bars that Phnom Penh had since accumulated. Today, adorned with black and white photography from various reporting that occurred at that time, it made for a romanticised place for tourists to get rooftop cocktails.

The reporter's name was Parker Atkins which Tom thought was a preposterously American name, more appropriate for a pharmaceutical company than a person. It gave Tom an image of a wizened, cynical American hack like an older version of Dustin Hoffman's gutsy, fast-talking Carl Bernstein in *All the President's Men*. Disappointingly, Parker Atkins turned out to be a thickset guy around his own age with a 1990s step haircut.

'You must be Tom. Thanks so much for meeting me.'

Parker was earnestness personified. He seemed to Tom to be so bland and wholesome as if he were the human equivalent of a box of cornflakes. He told him off the bat that it was his first time visiting Cambodia and that he wanted to write 'something that makes a difference.'

Parker told Tom that he'd been to visit the hand-weaving project and had already interviewed Janice.

'She and her work are just so incredible. To think that those poor women could be sex workers if it weren't for her ...' he trailed off.

Jesus wept, Tom thought. Once again, Janice, the white saviour dominates the narrative.

'Did you interview the participating women themselves?' Tom asked. 'Many of them have really compelling personal stories going back to the Khmer Rouge time.'

'Oh, yes, I absolutely did.' Parker beamed and began showing Tom pictures of the women that he had taken.

'Think of the awareness that these photos will raise. Isn't it wonderful how visuals really engage the intellect but also engage the heart?'

Tom inwardly groaned. He was irritated by Parker's almost theatrical levels of sincerity. It didn't appear that his limited intellect had any goals for publishing a story about poor people beyond the vague parameters of 'raising awareness'. He proceeded to ask Tom a series of mundane questions about why the UN was supporting Cambodian Hands and their work. It seemed like a complimentary exercise for what was very likely another fluffy story about how wonderful Janice was.

Tom managed easily to dish out his pre-planned quotes at Parker who eagerly jotted them down. A Google search later that night in his apartment would show him that Parker Atkins was the son of a wealthy New York senator and on a much-coveted internship with the *Chronicle*. His social media was full of travel photos accompanied by 'inspirational' quotes. A selfie that Parker had taken with Janice, Sophorn and a weaving project woman and her family accompanied by a copy-pasted quote from Hilary Clinton's 'Women's Rights are Human Rights' speech was particularly cringeworthy to Tom.

He said his goodbyes to Parker after writing down a few titles in response to his request for book recommendations on recent Cambodian history. Although the interview had not proved as stimulating as he had hoped, any disappointment was overridden by his excitement at the prospect of seeing his name in the *Chronicle*. He was mentally planning out the wording of a suitably humble Facebook post sharing the article once it was published when he spotted a familiar greasy head at a table on the other side of the Foreign Correspondent's Club typing at a laptop. He hadn't seen Andre since that eventful night in The White Tiger.

'Maaaate!' Andre looked up and spotted him. 'What brings you down to these parts?'

'Hey, man,' Tom tried to repress the vile images etched into his brain from the last time he had seen Andre. 'I've just been meeting a guy from the *New York Chronicle* who is doing a piece on our project.'

'The *New York Chronicle* are in town?' Andre was suddenly all business.

'What exactly are they working on?' He gestured to the seat in front of him and Tom sat down.

'They're in town doing a few cultural pieces. They want to cover our hand-weaving project because it's mostly indigenous women,' Tom responded.

'That's the Cambodian Hands project, right? Did he tell you if he's talking to Janice Steiner?' Andre had an urgency in his voice.

'Yes, he's talked to her already. Andre, man, what's all this about?'

'Oh, nothing. Just a story I'm working on. Top Secret, I'm afraid.' Andre winked at him.

Tom felt uneasy, 'Andre, are you working on a story about Janice?'

'Can't say, mate. Can't say. Jesus, I fucking hope the bloody *Chronicle* haven't scooped me. Did the guy give any specifics about what he was going to ask Janice?' Andre ran a hand through his dark curls, looking agitated.

'Mate, you are kind of freaking me out here,' Tom was getting irritated. 'The guy was a nice young guy. It seemed like he just wants a feel-good story. He'd never even been to Cambodia before. What are you writing about Janice? You know my project is with Cambodian Hands.'

'Okay, maybe he's not after the same story but I'll look into it anyway to be on the safe side. I can't say anything else but this story is gonna be big for me and I don't want anyone fucking with it. Thanks mate.' Andre began typing on his laptop again indicating that the conversation was over.

'Wait,' Tom persisted. 'Can you at least tell me if this story you are working on might be negative for my work?'

'Mate, I can't fucking say anything but just keep an eye on Janice.' Andre made a loop with his index finger as he talked, as if to symbolise the word *crazy*.

Fuck, fuck, fuck. Tom had a bad feeling about this. He suppressed the urge to punch Andre for putting him in this position.

'Be careful with this, mate. You need to have real substance here,' Tom told him.

'I am, don't worry,' Andre winked at him. 'This has been in the works for a long time and I'm gonna get it as tight as a fish's bum.'

Shite, thought Tom. He wanted to leave Cambodia with a five-star reputation and begin his ascent up the UN ladder. He couldn't be associated with some kind of media scandal. There was also the complication that he had had a tonne of sex with Janice's daughter this past weekend. What if Caitlyn was part of Andre's story? Wait, did Andre even know Caitlyn was Janice's daughter and that she was in town? Maybe not. He certainly wasn't going to tell him.

Later at home, he contemplated his dilemma as he sat on his balcony and drank a beer while watching the Phnom Penh sky slice itself into chunks of orange and purple. This town could do a sunset like nowhere else that he had ever known and the beauty of it calmed him slightly. Should he tell his headquarters in Geneva that Janice was about to be involved in some kind of scandal so that they could deal with it? But what if Andre's story came to nothing? Andre was kind of a bullshitter after all. Should he try and talk to Janice? Jesus, maybe he should try and talk to Caitlyn.

His phone beeped interrupting his thoughts. It was Parker Atkins telling him the story would be on the *Chronicle*'s website by the weekend. He felt a flutter of excitement rush through him. He couldn't wait to tell his family. His father, in particular didn't understand Tom's work very well but got such pride from bragging about his 'son who worked for the United Nations'.

At home in Galway, Tom had learned to become a bit of a performer. He found it easy to twist himself into different shapes depending on the scenario to disguise how out of place he truly felt. He became so good at feigning his opinions and preferences that he sometimes forgot his real feelings on a subject. To this day, he avoided bananas out of habit and had no idea what they tasted like because as a child he had pretended to dislike them, copying a kid in his class who refused to eat them.

Schoolwork had come easily to him but back then it wasn't cool to be smart. Being popular had been a far greater priority for his teenage self. He had smoked John Player Blue cigarettes and worn Adidas three stripe tracksuits; the indisputable uniform of cool kids in early 2000s Galway, in spite of not having an athletic bone in his body. He had learned to amp up the working-class tinge in his accent by drawing out his syllables and cursing more to make himself sound edgier. Once he talked, acted and looked like they did, it was easy to become a popular kid. He took well to the lifestyle of drinking cider in fields, fingering girls at teenage discos and ignoring his schoolwork.

The indisputable leader of the cool kids in Tom's school was Rob Kelly. Rob had a charisma that fifteen-year-old Tom would have given his left nut for. With his sallow-skin and dark hair, girls said he looked like Johnny Depp. He didn't speak very often but when he did, everyone listened. When he complimented you, like the time he told Tom he liked his new Nike Air Max runners, it was like being in the sun.

Tom wanted to be Rob but because he couldn't be, he settled for being his best friend and more or less copying everything Rob did. When Rob spiked his hair with Brylcreem, Tom did the same. When Rob began to listen to Eminem, Tom did too. When Rob started getting into amateur DJing, Tom got his parents to buy him an expensive set of DJ decks for Christmas that went largely unused.

At some point around the time that Tom and Rob were smoking weed and mitching off school, Herpe started coming along uninvited. Jovial, skinny and awkward with a mullet of curly hair that he used to say was 'African sunset' rather than red, Herpe took naturally to being the butt of many jokes. His real name was Stephen Herbert but Tom had christened him Herpe because he was 'impossible to get rid of' and it had caught on so well that their entire school soon came to know him as Herpe. Tom had been so proud of himself for that nickname at the time but now whenever he heard others use it, he felt a gnawing guilt remembering how much Herpe had hated it but had given up protesting against it. He sometimes worried that that stupid nickname had contributed to the way things had turned out for Herpe.

When they were seventeen, both Rob and Herpe dropped out of school. Rob to do an apprenticeship in carpentry and Herpe to work in a long succession of retail jobs. But by that time, being cool wasn't enough for Tom anymore. He wanted to be impressive and he wanted to get the fuck out of Galway and he realised that he couldn't do that without going to college. He didn't want to have a life like his brothers who had boring jobs, went to the same pubs every weekend and only travelled to places where ordinary people went on holidays, like cheesy resorts in Spain. He wanted to see the world and do important things. The summer before his last year in secondary school, Tom started quietly reading his school books and catching up on all of the things he had been ignoring.

Rob got a girl pregnant around the time that Tom got his Leaving Cert results which were high enough to get him into politics and law in University College Dublin. These days, Rob had three children and was still living in Galway, with a gut and a receding hairline. He had peaked in life at sixteen years old. There was no way Tom would have let that happen to himself.

As he finished his beer, Tom realised that there was some-one outside of his family that he'd love to share his *New York Chronicle* success with and that someone was Caitlyn. Would she crack jokes or would she find it genuinely impressive? He was suddenly dying to know and had an urge to see her. Andre's bullshit could wait. It would probably turn out to be nothing anyway. He hadn't even gotten her number when she had left his place on Sunday night. Idiot.

Thank fuck for Facebook. It was a little creepy to reach out to her there but fuck it.

He typed Caitlyn Leahy into the search box. There were more of them than he had anticipated. There were Caitlyn Le-ahys in Ireland, Scotland, Australia, the Philippines and various spellings of Caitlin, Katelyn, Kaitlyn. Ugh. He wasn't even sure how she spelled it. Where was she? Finally, after several pages of searching there was a profile of a Caitlyn Leahy who had gone to Sacramento State University. The profile was a picture of the actress Talia Shire in a wedding dress in an image from 'The Godfather'.

Of course, he grinned to himself, pop culture reference on point. This had to be her. He typed her a message. *I found where you were hiding! Let me make you an offer that you can't refuse. Tapas, wine, you, me, Friday night?*

8

Caitlyn liked casual sex in the moment it was happening. She liked the split-second shift change when she'd know that kissing had broken into something more. She liked the negotiation of 'how do you want to do this?' and 'is this good for you?' Above all, she liked the gamble of it all. Where in most areas of her life, she was disciplined and 'responsible', sex was an area where she allowed herself to indulge when the mood struck her. In the moment she would be resolute and determined, but afterwards the emotional hangover would come and she would subject herself to hours of analysis on whether it had been justifiable. As if any kind of justifiability criteria existed. An internal conflict would ensue between feminist principles which taught her that her sexual agency was her own and societal conditioning which made her worry about whether she should have 'made him wait', as if sex was something sacred for women to preserve and reward men with. Intellectually, she fervently disagreed with the latter mindset but it didn't mean that she didn't torment herself about whether it may have some truth. It was exhausting.

There wasn't time to brutalise herself too much after she slept with Tom, as Pheary had given her the most substantial bit of work that she had thus far been given at Save Cambodia. Save Cambodia had convinced the country's Minister for Communications to speak at an event they were having the following week to mark World Press Freedom Day, and Caitlyn was tasked with writing the minister's speech.

She approached the speech as a way for the government to

show a leadership role on press freedom. She enthusiastically typed about how governments should protect journalists, how the media was a necessary tool to increase the health of a democracy and encourage informed citizens to take action, not just for themselves but on behalf of their societies. Meticulously reviewing and replacing words with stronger equivalents, she typed for hours until she had a decent draft. She concluded with a Gandhi quote that seemed tailor-made. 'Truth never damages a cause that is just.'

Time had sped past and it was already pitch-black outside. She was the last one in the office. She quickly emailed her draft to Pheary and Vic before leaving. She was breaking yet another promise to her Dad about not taking motorbikes home after dark again, but it felt worth it. She steadied herself on the back of Thoeun's motorbike as he sped through the streets, miraculously knowing when to turn corners in spite of the absence of street lighting. She should have been nervous about the slightly death-defying journey home but Caitlyn felt too content in her sense of productivity to worry. It was amazing to have written something meaningful and powerful that someone important was going to deliver in public. She was really doing something.

Too exhilarated to bother cooking, she bought a feast of eight pork dumplings for $2 from the Chinese noodle shop on her street. It was a dingy restaurant that had dogs hanging around near the kitchen but she figured that given the dumplings were fried, they couldn't make her sick.

—

A few mornings later, Vic stopped by Caitlyn's desk as she was opening up her laptop to start the day. Vic had been in Cambodia for years, spoke fluent Khmer and had a permanently disgruntled look on his face. Caitlyn hadn't had much interaction with him but she sensed that he was easily irritated so she typically tried to keep out of his way.

'Caitlyn, let's have a quick chat about the speech you wrote for the minister,' Vic started, pulling up a chair to her desk. Caitlyn moved her laptop aside and readied her notebook and pen expectantly.

Holding a printed copy of the speech that she had written covered in red biro markings and yellow highlighter pen, Vic bore down at her with creased brown eyes.

'Firstly, let me say that I'm aware that you are new to Save Cambodia and to this country. But you need to understand that this speech would never work here.'

Oh shit, Caitlyn's stomach knotted.

'Okay ...' she responded.

Vic continued, 'I would recommend that you do some real research on the Cambodian government's record on press freedom. This government's control over the media is getting increasingly worse. It's becoming one of the most dangerous places in the world for journalists to operate. It would, quite frankly be totally naïve to think that the minister could make statements like what you have in here without looking like a hypocrite.'

Caitlyn was mortified. She definitely didn't know all of the details in the way that he did but she had worked hard on the speech and she couldn't help but feel defensive.

'I'm aware that there are these challenges but I saw the speech as an opportunity. I thought it was a chance to get the minister to say the right things.' Caitlyn could hear her voice cracking.

'Be careful about using phrases like the "right things" in this country, Caitlyn.' His tone quickened indicating his irritation.

'Imposing your American ideas of what's right could be construed as cultural imperialism. It's huge that we've gotten the minister to even come to this event. The speech is meant to be a few light remarks acknowledging the day. I'm sorry if you thought otherwise.'

What the fuck? Cultural imperialism? Caitlyn felt attacked and her face began to boil up with humiliation. Later on, she would replay the conversation in her head for hours and have a million articulate responses but in the moment, she felt somewhat feeble.

'But … how are a few light remarks meant to change anything?' She managed to spit out.

'We need to develop a relationship with the minister over time. Flatter him by having him speak at our events and get a few headlines. Later on, the tough conversations can be had behind closed doors.' Vic stood up from his chair indicating that the conversation was ending.

'I'll send you some reading. Please revise the speech to make it more appropriate.'

'Yup. Got it.' Caitlyn managed to muster up a half smile.

Vic went back into his office wordlessly and Caitlyn put on the appearance of getting back to work as if nothing had happened. She stared at her laptop without the ability to focus on the screen. After it seemed like a reasonable amount of time had passed, she went to the bathroom and shut the stall door behind her, before allowing herself to cry. She slowly let out controlled sobs into a folded-up wad of tissue paper under the pretence of blowing her nose. She wanted to get into a proper baby wail cry but choked it back knowing that it would possibly be overheard.

Caitlyn felt humiliated but more than that she was flooded with self-doubt. She had always been an excellent student. Studying and retaining information came naturally to her curious mind. She had maintained that as long as she worked hard and thoroughly prepared, she could take on anything. But she clearly didn't know what she was doing in this job, and in Cambodia in general.

On the night that they broke up, her ex-boyfriend Nick had fumed at her: 'You think that just because your Mom left you, it makes you deep. It doesn't. You know nothing about the real world and it's going to slap you in the face when you realise that you are not even close to being as smart as you think you are.'

He was hurting at the time but she knew that he believed what he was saying. It had stayed with her, squashed under a pile of other insecurities like her weight, her abandonment issues and how she had fucked things up with Nick. Each insecurity was just waiting for a chance to resurface and make her feel like shit.

That speech had meant something to her, and she felt robbed of the opportunity to do something meaningful. She felt a surge of homesickness and realised that more than anything she wanted desperately to be waking up in her childhood bedroom while her Dad made pancakes for breakfast and Talking Heads' greatest hits played on his ancient CD player.

'Give less of a shit, honey.' Her Dad's words came to her.

Okay, get your shit together and give less of a shit, she told herself. The nonsensical mixing of shit metaphors slowly began to serve their motivational purpose. Her face looked red and blotchy in the bathroom mirror in spite of her best efforts with water and tissue paper. She cursed herself for not being the kind of organised woman who brought makeup to work.

If her colleagues outside in the open-plan office noticed that she had been crying they were too polite to say so. Back at her desk, she began to dismantle the beautiful, impassioned speech that she had been so attached to. She copied and pasted sentences from the texts of several other dull governmental speeches that Vic had emailed and made light word changes so that the plagiarism was less obvious.

Later that night, at home, she continued to work towards filling the 2000-wordcount with long, platitudinal sentences. She was typing 'Now more than ever, we must put our differences aside and join hands to work on this important issue' when a message from her Facebook account flashed onto her computer screen. Reading Tom's words gave her a hit of joy, the kind that only a bona fide crush could provide.

—

The date was more than likely to be nothing special, she mentally prepared herself. It was certainly a welcome distraction from dodging Janice's calls which she had now been doing for weeks and feeling disillusioned about whether the work she was doing was making any kind of difference but she couldn't help but feel ripples of nervous excitement at the prospect of seeing him again.

Upon arriving, Caitlyn checked herself in the elevator mirror. She was already regretting wearing her jeggings which were feeling buttered onto her legs by a layer of sweat. Phnom Penh didn't seem to cool at all at night. Tom had asked to meet at a new rooftop tapas restaurant. She had taken to avoiding the city's tourist-riddled riverside at Ella's advice but the place was a pleasant surprise. The restaurant was playing Frank Sinatra and had sparse turquoise rattan tables and chairs overlooking the Mekong river which were hidden by black sun umbrellas giving diners their privacy.

Tom was freshly shaven and looking handsome in a plain dark blue shirt. He had gotten a haircut since she last saw him which made him look younger.

'Hello, friend,' she greeted him cheerily as he gave her a kiss on the cheek. 'So, you went big with the restaurant? Not too shabby.'

'Oh, this old place? Total shithole.' He gave her that lopsided grin of his.

'I'd think you were trying to get into my pants but we both know it's a bit late for that,' she quipped.

'Oh, we both know those pants are absolutely worth trying to get back into.' He looked straight at her with a glint of want in his eyes which took her by surprise. Caitlyn felt her thong panties tighten excitedly.

'Drinks!' Caitlyn hastily jumped on the cocktail menu to cut through the sexual tension.

The conversation poured easily as they drank cocktails and shared tapas. Tom was on a high at the prospect of the *New York Chronicle* article coming out featuring his interview. She thought that it was very cool that he was getting featured in the *Chronicle* and told him so. He beamed at her flattery and she was pleased to see that it was clearly something he had wanted to receive.

He revealed more about himself than he had previously. She got more of an insight into his upbringing in Ireland which sounded fairly wholesome and uncomplicated. He painted a picture of himself as a music and politics-obsessed oddball who contrasted greatly with his two sporty, alpha-male older brothers. She laughed loudly as he re-enacted in great comedic detail a story about his 12-year-old insistence on picking Kurt as his Confirmation name in tribute to his beloved Kurt Cobain from Nirvana and how it resulted in his parents having a lengthy conversation with a horrified local priest because it wasn't a saint's name.

He asked her all about her own upbringing and she found herself talking unguardedly about her childhood in Sacramento with her Dad in a house full of movies, with hordes of loving but overbearing cousins, aunts and uncles living close-by.

'So, you could work for the UN anywhere. Why Cambodia?' she asked him popping a salty green olive into her mouth.

His voice straightened itself up as if adjusting to work mode.

'I think it's a fascinating country to have as my first developing country posting given the UN's history of essentially bringing peace and democracy here. Obviously, there are still a lot of challenges but if you look at how far the country has come since the Khmer Rouge, it's very inspiring.'

The post-cocktail wine was beginning to take hold and she could feel herself getting animated.

'I get that things have improved since that awful time but it's been what? Thirty-five years? The Khmer Rouge time is such a low threshold to compare to. Don't you think things should be improving here more quickly?'

Tom became more animated too.

'I don't disagree with you' he told her. 'But we're talking about building up from a place where nearly a third of the population including its intellectual heartland were wiped out. The starting point for that kind of devastation isn't even at zero. It's at like minus 10. Real systemic change takes time.'

Caitlyn filled her water glass with the objective of pacing her drinking. He seemed so docile about it all. It made her want to challenge him.

'I'm aware of the history. Believe me. I've grown up getting master classes from my Mom. But don't you think there's any room for critique of the operational pace of the UN, NGOs and so-called 'international community'? Doesn't it feel like we're working too slowly and cautiously and just hoping that things will somehow get better?'

She could hear herself sounding more like a depressive activist rather than a charming date. Former boyfriends had always said in the early stages of being with her how much they loved how opinionated she was but it usually graduated into them liking this quality of hers far less over time.

Tom shook his head. 'Of course, there are organisations doing amazing work and those who are coasting along and some who are even making things worse but you can't lump them all into one. It's not that simple.'

'I think what frustrates me is the lack of visible impact,' she interrupted him. 'It's been more than twenty years since the UN came in and the country has NGOs working on every cause imaginable but something like only 23% of Cambodians have toilets, one in five of this country's men say they have engaged in rape, a quarter of the country can't even read and plenty of other stats that I'm not even aware of.'

She paused and then started up again.

'This is cocktail talk and I've had a rough work week but don't you ever worry that we may be totally misguided flying in here thinking that we can be the saviours of this country?'

Tom grabbed her hand and looked at her with an expression that fell somewhere between sympathy and amusement.

'Firstly, let me say that I'm sorry that you've had a rough work week.' He kissed her hand.

'Secondly, let me say that there are major things that have improved. HIV rates, women's rights, infrastructure, job opportunities for poorer people to name just a few. Thirdly, in terms of being misguided, I would ask you what's the alternative? Stay at home with all your education and privilege in your middle-class life and get an unexciting job where you don't ever have to think about the fact that nearly half the human population lives in poverty?'

Caitlyn felt her earlier irritation at him wash away. He had a point. She liked it when he was less scripted and UN-ish, when she could hear glints of real passion in his voice.

He continued: 'Look Caitlyn, Cambodia's fucking complicated. You aren't going to fix this country. But you can learn a lot here and get better at what you do. Plus, the lifestyle is decent and there's a lot of fun to be had.' He winked at her and the cheeky smile returned.

'You are hilariously shallow,' she laughed at him.

'And speaking of important issues, we need some more wine … *Som Bong! Moi Tet,*' Tom called out to the waiter asking for another bottle of wine.

'Oh, how impressive. How's your Khmer?' Caitlyn had been meaning to take lessons to enable herself to be able to communicate more than hello, but languages were not at all her strong point and the Khmer pronunciation seemed so alien. Even Janice had given up on learning it.

'I can order drinks fluently,' Tom quipped.

'You can take the boy outta Ireland … '

'A wild national stereotype, my dear and only partially true,' Tom smiled.

'Sorry about stereotyping. It's just easy to do. I've never even been to Ireland but my Dad is a bit consumed with all things Irish. He's obsessed with Sinéad O'Connor and has pushed several authors like Colm Tóibín on me.'

'Oh, you poor American, you've totally mangled that pronunciation. It's pronounced "Collum Toe-Been"', he laughed at her.

'Ah, you guys have some seriously messed up names that are tough to pronounce. My Dad always emphasises that Irish-Americanism is its own subculture and very divorced from actual Ireland-Irish culture.'

'He's absolutely right and I think a lot of Irish people would appreciate his awareness of that,' Tom sipped from his wine.

'It's a weird one,' he mused. 'Whenever I've been to the States, I'm so appreciative of the reaction I get when I tell people I'm Irish. It opens doors for you and gets you such a warm welcome. But I've found Irish-Americans often have an idea of Ireland that's based on outdated views, inaccurate history and irrelevant stereotypes. You don't want to ruin people's idea of their heritage even if it's kind of false. We all need fairy tales. So, you find yourself going along with things like St Patrick's Day and ignoring your disgust at leprechaun tattoos even though as an actual Irish person you don't recognise your own culture in it.'

'Okay, so help me out and be my cultural guide.' Caitlyn definitely felt tipsy at this point. 'As an American and even, God forbid, an Irish-American, how can I avoid getting it wrong? What are my dos and don'ts?'

'Hmm, let me see. Okay right off the bat, don't make jokes about excessive drinking, don't say "top of the morning". That stuff should be obvious. Don't, and I mean don't, ever copy our accent. We fucking hate that. No one can get it right and it's almost certain to be offensive.'

'Okay, duly noted,' she laughed. 'What about the do's?'

'Do acknowledge the difference between Irish and Irish-American as you've just done and another definite do is … *do* have wild, unhinged sex with an Irishman tonight!' He looked at her expectantly and wiggled his eyebrows in mock-suggestiveness.

'God, the things I have to do for cultural sensitivity!' Caitlyn laughed heartily. 'Should we get the bill then?'

9

Caitlyn woke up in Tom's bed and glanced at her phone. It was nearly midday. Shit. She had eight missed calls from Janice and five missed calls from her Dad including a text message.

Where are you? Your Mom is at your place and you aren't there. Please get in touch honey.

Tom was still fast asleep next to her and she looked at his handsome face and messy hair with regret. It was tempting to turn her phone off and nuzzle into him. But she couldn't have her Dad worrying about her. Ugh. She threw on her clothes and left his place without waking him up. She could message him later.

Janice was sitting on the steps outside Caitlyn's apartment when she arrived. She looked tired and agitated and was clutching her phone in her hand anxiously.

'Jesus, Caitlyn, where were you? I thought that something had happened to you!' Janice pulled her involuntarily into a hug. Her white musk perfume was overpowering.

'I'm completely fine. I was out last night and stayed with a friend. There's no need to be this dramatic.' Caitlyn could feel the irritation rush through her.

'Caitlyn, this is not Sacramento,' Janice blustered. 'You can't ignore my calls for weeks and stay out all night. Bad things happen all the time here. You have to be in touch with me.'

Caitlyn felt her head pound from the previous night's wine and couldn't be less in the mood for Janice's bullshit. What right did this woman have to interfere in her life?

'I'm tired and I need to ring my Dad now because you made him worried. Thanks for your concern but I'd like you to leave.'

'Caitlyn, we're not done talking. You are in a dangerous country that you don't know. I was fine with you saying that you don't want to live with me but you can't cut me out.' There was an almost wail-like quality to Janice's voice which gnawed at Caitlyn.

'Me, cut you out. Seriously? Can you fucking hear yourself?' Caitlyn felt blinded by rage and the words tumbled out of her mouth. 'You abandoned me when I was three years old. How can I cut you out?'

Janice looked pained. 'Caitlyn, I know you are upset about what happened with Save Cambodia, but you have to understand, the report they did could be so damaging for this country. I've no problem with critique if there's some kind of strategy involved but that report was sensationalised and irresponsible to put out. 500,000 women workers could be affected. I had to confront Pheary and stand up for Cambodian women.'

Caitlyn felt her throat block up. Of course, Janice hadn't even addressed what she had said about abandoning her. It was too late to hit the brakes on her anger. They hadn't actually had a proper fight since Caitlyn was a teenager, in recent years, Caitlyn had just been politely responsive to her, but not today. She felt herself hungering to tell Janice exactly what she thought of her.

'You probably did stand up for Cambodian women at one point in time but none of them asked you to go and attack Save Cambodia's work. You were completely out of line and your ego just can't accept it,' she fumed.

'You are still very young, Caitlyn. You can't possibly

understand these issues properly. We'll talk another time when you are feeling more together.' Janice sounded so calm suddenly. She stepped away from Caitlyn as if to leave.

'Well, that's patronising. Fine, fuck you. God forbid you have to listen to someone actually tell you the truth.'

Janice left the apartment complex without turning back. Caitlyn thought about calling after her but instead hurried inside and sat on her shitty, uncomfortable couch and burst into tears.

She was so angry at Janice but she was more angry at herself. What the fuck was she doing? Why was she even in this country? She could have gone and interned somewhere else where she didn't have to deal with her Mommy issues. Maybe she was just out of her depth with all of it.

She could call her Dad. Ugh, she didn't want to upset him. He would only worry about her. Mary. She could call Mary. Caitlyn was close to her Dad's sister. She had been like a surrogate mother to Caitlyn and the main female role model she had when she was growing up. It was Mary who had first bought Caitlyn tampons when she realised that she had been using pads for the first few months of her period because that's all Liam had known to buy. It was still late Friday night in Sacramento but Mary was at home with her kids and her husband.

'I'm so sorry, hon,' Mary told her when Caitlyn filled her in on all that had happened. 'I think she's probably trying to be a mother now that you are right there but maybe she forgets that you are twenty-four years old and will need space. Don't forget that this is new territory for her too. It's a big deal for you both to be in the same place.'

'Maybe,' Caitlyn agreed.

Mary continued, 'Safety-wise though, you absolutely need to stop ignoring her messages and just keep her posted that you are okay. I understand why she got so worried and how she got a bit hysterical. I would be the same way. You need to be more responsive to her.'

'I know I do,' Caitlyn reluctantly agreed. 'It just feels so hypocritical, her wanting me to be in touch all the time. It irritates me so much that I don't want to respond to her. It's just so hard to understand her, Mary. I don't get her at all.'

'All I can tell you is that Janice was never the easiest person. Your Dad adored her but she didn't want the 'normal life' in Sacramento. It wasn't enough for her.' It had long been clear to Caitlyn that Mary wasn't a big fan of Janice's. She had always been much more candid with Caitlyn about her than her Dad was.

Caitlyn sighed, 'I understand that a little I think, but seeing her that day in that office showed me that she clearly doesn't know her boundaries. She wants to control things and I don't want to let her control me.'

'I don't know much about how things are in Cambodia,' Mary replied. 'But it looks like she's really done some great things there and now people have put her on a pedestal. Being around people who refuse to ever criticise you has an impact on how you do things and treat people.'

'That would explain some of her behaviour but it doesn't excuse it,' Caitlyn said. 'I know I've asked you this before but what was it like when she left?'

'Oh, goodness. It was awful. Very, very hard,' Mary recounted. 'Your Dad was a wreck. But he had to get up and go to work and get through life because he had you.'

'It's so hard to think of him in that situation. He wasn't

much older than I am now. I don't know how he coped,' Caitlyn contemplated. 'Do you think I'm crazy for moving here?'

'Hmm. Maybe a little,' Mary chuckled. 'No honestly, Caitlyn, I think you are incredibly brave. You are putting your talents, education and heart to good use and I admire it greatly. But I think that part of being in Cambodia is that you need to figure out how to manage the relationship with Janice on your own terms. On some conscious level that must be why you went there.'

'I really don't think so,' Caitlyn told her. 'I wanted to come here for the work. Obviously, I've learned a lot about it through her but it wasn't consciously anything to do with her.'

'Look, you are in the same place after all this time. Now is the ideal time to look at the relationship and try to make it one that works for you,' Mary insisted.

'I get the logic of what you are saying, Mary, but mostly I just feel irritated by her,' Caitlyn felt tired.

'You are probably very hurt by her, Cait, and you've never really had a chance to deal with it, so it is clearly rising to the surface. I wish I was there to give you a hug.'

'I wish you were too.'

'If it gets too hard, call your Dad, get on a plane and come home.'

'I don't think I need to do that but I feel a bit better after talking. Thanks, Mary.'

'No problem, hon.'

'Give my hugs to Greg and the kids.'

'I will, Cait. Keep me updated on how things go.'

Caitlyn felt calmer but was still in need of a comforting distraction. *Clueless* was the movie that she always watched whenever she was sick or sad. It was silly in parts but also warm, funny escapism. She found a working link and willed the glacial Cambodian internet to download faster. She was boiling water to make herself some tea when Tom text her.

Lovely lady, where did you disappear to? #abandoned
Sorry! Family insanity. Raincheck?
I've honestly never understood what that term 'raincheck' means. I think it's a US thing. Whatcha up to for the evening?
Not a lot. Not in a great mood to be honest.
Would Phnom Penh's best-rated pizza and some decent-ly-rated company help?
Tom, I had fun last night but I honestly could not feel less in the mood for sex right now.
I get it and that's honestly not at all what I meant. Look I know how it is being far away from home and not having your usual friends and family to rely on. I hate the thought of you being upset.
How good is Phnom Penh's best-rated pizza?

Caitlyn didn't bother to change out of her simple black cotton pants or clean her apartment. She probably could have been embarrassed at how much dingier and smaller her place was than his and about the two dead cockroaches in the kitchen that she hadn't bothered to sweep away but she decided not to care.

Tom turned up at her door with a large pepperoni pizza, garlic bread and a bottle of red wine. She didn't even have wine glasses but he found two coffee mugs in her cupboard which had probably seen better days. She hadn't realised how hungry she was, she gulped the wine and gobbled the pizza and her headache began to subside.

They sat on her uncomfortable couch and silently watched a slow buffering version of *Clueless*. As usual, he smelled amazing. She rested her head on his shoulder. It was nice just having him next to her. The link for the movie stopped working just as Alicia Silverstone was about to realise she was in love with her ex-stepbrother who was played by Paul Rudd.

'Oh god. This internet is the worst,' Caitlyn groaned clicking to refresh the link.

'Leave it,' Tom told her. 'We've both seen it before. She ends up with Paul Rudd and it's all gloriously nineties. Listen, do you want to talk about the family stuff?'

Caitlyn didn't. 'It's just my Mom being a dick but thank you. I think I'm just going to take a nap or something. Sleep will help.'

'Okay, let me clean this up and I'll leave you in peace.'

Tom got a paper towel from the kitchen and wiped the garlic bread crumbs from the coffee table that they had been eating on. Caitlyn was touched by this small, considerate gesture. He got up to leave and they sank into a long hug. He kissed her lightly and affectionately and then looked at her intently.

'Look Caitlyn, I like you. I think you are brilliant and beautiful and sexy as fuck. I'd like to spend more time with you. What do you think?'

'Okay. Sounds like fun,' she grinned at him. 'Thank you for coming over and taking care of me.'

'That's what I'm here for.'

He winked at her before closing the door behind him.

10

Janice fixed herself a black coffee in the knowledge that today, her usual green tea wasn't going to cut it. It was still only early afternoon but after arguing with Caitlyn, she felt depleted. She carried pain about Caitlyn. Of course she did. But until now, it had always seemed like she was doing so well and she hadn't felt real cause to worry too much about her. It was still quite common to hear stories about young NGO workers getting robbed or attacked. She had gotten so frightened when Caitlyn wasn't at home in her apartment. It was such a relief that she was okay, even if she was terribly angry with her. Caitlyn was so clearly completely naïve about Phnom Penh and deliberately not checking in with her just to be spiteful. Janice was upset but conceded that it was probably best to give her space and anyway, she had work to do which would be a welcome distraction.

Janice was grateful not to be working in an empty house. Pagna and her children, a six-year-old girl, Bopha, and a four year old boy, Leap, had been staying in Janice's home, a small but very comfortable villa that she had spent years restoring to its pre-Khmer Rouge glory after buying it for a steal because it had been so badly decimated in the conflict. None of them knew how to swim but the three of them enjoyed sitting out at her rarely-used pool and dipping their feet in the water while eating steamed pork buns which were Janice's housekeeper, Tevy's speciality. Typically, Tevy only came once or twice a week but since Pagna and the kids had been there, Janice had been paying for her to come every day. She and Pagna still struggled to communicate and Tevy, a warm, hard-working woman who had worked for Janice for many years was a much-needed ice-breaker and translator.

Janice took her laptop and coffee out to the pool and sat on a sun lounger working while Pagna played nearby with her children and chatted with Tevy. She was so tired that it was hard to give her full attention to work. She had been having angry nights lying awake in bed wondering how she had failed to keep the women she was meant to be helping from domestic violence. She was furious with herself for allowing such a glaring gap in Cambodian Hands' work. Anger at herself was a powerful motivator for Janice. When she couldn't sleep, she had started working on an outline of how Cambodian Hands could really tackle domestic violence in the community. She had put together a sketch of her dream programme that included a media awareness-raising campaign, community ambassadors, an alert hotline, discussion groups with men and training on non-violent behaviour aimed at them.

As she tried to work, she noticed to her dismay that the chatter in Khmer had died down a lot around the pool since she'd come out to join them. It felt a little awkward. Pagna was still very shy and guarded in her presence. Janice concluded that if she worked from the office it would be more comfortable for everyone.

Although it was Saturday, she called Sophorn and asked him to come in and meet her at the office to help her crunch the numbers on how much the domestic violence plan would cost. She could sense his reluctance to come to work and it irritated her. She knew that he had little kids at home but this was really important. Janice's tolerance for any kind of lax behaviour among her staff had completely eroded over the years. Initially, she'd been carefree about being a boss and not said anything if people arrived late or took a longer lunch but she soon learned that whenever she was laid-back, people soon took advantage of her. If she wanted to get things done, she needed to push people.

By the time she had walked to the office, Sophorn was already there and grumpily pouring over some printed out spreadsheets.

'Looking at the activities that you want to include, my estimation is that this domestic violence work would cost us about $50,000 to do,' he informed her.

'Hmmm,' Janice pondered. 'That's probably still a little bit high to get funding without having to revert to a big grant application process. Can you look at the numbers again and try to get it down to $30,000?'

'Yes, I can try. It's getting a little late but I can do this first thing Monday morning,' Sophorn offered.

'I'd appreciate if you did it now, Sophorn, so I can get moving on this. You know, it is really important that we are looking at the women's needs in a real way and trying to address weaknesses in our programme,' she told him.

She knew that she was being a little bit manipulative but if he'd wanted to have a nine to five job with no weekend work, he should have gone and worked in a bank.

While Sophorn worked wordlessly, Janice sat at her desk and wrote a lengthy email to a contact at AIDAmerica headquarters in Washington DC. In order to get extra funds to do something new, Janice knew she would have to work around the system a little. AIDAmerica were Cambodian Hands' biggest donor and had been giving them their core funding since the late 90s. Marianne Goldberg, now a senior figure in AIDAmerica in Washington, was an old friend of Janice's who had lived in Phnom Penh in the early 2000s. They had known one another a long time but Janice had never called in a favour before. It had been about a decade since they had last seen one another but Janice remembered Marianne as having a work–life balance that was just as poor as her own. She felt confident that Marianne would be responding to emails on a Saturday.

Cambodian Hands has managed to bring more money into thousands of women's lives and that of their families and help to reduce their poverty but it has not been enough to counter the power dynamics against women and reduce domestic violence, she typed.

She told Marianne about her ideas to tackle the issue and asked for AIDAmerica to grant them $30,000 in funding. Marianne would get it, she thought. She was someone who cared about getting things done. Besides, $30,000 was so little for AIDAmerica. It was probably less than their annual budget spent on balloon-releasing ceremonies.

To help her make her case stronger she needed to talk to Tom from UNP and get their backing too. She called him but got no response which didn't surprise her. He was probably hungover or something. He seemed like that type.

'Hi Janice, is everything okay?' He called her back after a few minutes. His voice sounded throaty. He was definitely hungover.

'Hi Tom, everything's fine. I've sent you an important email this morning. Have you had a chance to look at it?' she asked.

'No, I'm sorry I haven't been online yet today,' he told her.

'I want to add a new domestic violence programme to the weaving project. It's a real problem for the women participating in the project and we need to tackle it. I'm asking AIDAmerica for the funds. It would be great to have UNP's support to help us make our case,' she explained.

'Oh, okay, that sounds interesting,' he croaked. 'I mean for us as UNP, our mandate is really around economic empowerment. For gender-based violence, that would fall under other parts of the UN like UN Female.'

'Well, that's fine. The economic parts of the programme will still be there. We're just adding to them,' Janice told him.

'Okay, that's good,' Tom began. 'But you know, the weaving project is seen as so successful. You've won awards for that project. Maybe you should be careful not to shake things up too much?'

Jesus, what an idiot he was.

'We are trying to make the programme better by addressing this important issue. There's limited value in making the women less poor if they are still getting the shit beaten out of them,' she blustered.

'Okay, I hear you. I really would need to check with headquarters. I imagine they may not be comfortable adding their name to something that isn't in UNP's field of expertise though.'

Janice sighed audibly.

'There's nothing that you'd really need to do other than let me tell AIDAmerica that you support us expanding to address domestic violence issues. Being in favour of the programme expanding doesn't exactly need expertise. The whole point of asking for funds is to bring in new expertise. Are you not in favour of ending domestic violence, Tom?' she challenged him.

'Of course, I am, Janice,' Tom stammered a little. 'But I don't speak for the whole organisation. I need to talk to my HQ.'

'These women can't wait too long, Tom,' she told him. It was a cheap shot she knew but he just sounded so irritatingly passive about it all.

'I don't think we'd object in any way,' he conceded a little. 'As long as the basket-weaving work is continuing and the new work you are doing doesn't distract or change it in any way.'

'The only change will be the bigger impact we have on these women's lives,' Janice insisted.

'Let me talk to Geneva and get back to you.'

Janice finished the call with Tom feeling frustrated. How hard was it for him just to say he was in favour of the programme addressing the domestic violence issues in the community? In the meantime, she saw that an email had come through from Marianne. Wow, that was quick. Good old Marianne. Janice read excitedly.

Dear Janice,

It's wonderful to hear from you after all these years. I've been following your career and am always encouraged to see that you are still so committed to empowering Cambodian women and at the forefront of change. Sadly, I'm sorry to say that I think it would be impossible for us to fund something like this. Speaking to you frankly, the powers that be here are increasingly frustrated with the lack of progress that Cambodia has made. They are tired of throwing millions at a country and not seeing enough impact. It's become quite acrimonious between those of us still believing that change is possible in Cambodia and those who have given up, many of whom wish to refocus the American tax payers' money elsewhere. We are of course continuing our existing funding commitments to Cambodia and I don't see that changing any time soon but when the question of new funding for Cambodia comes up, things become tricky. Your annual grants from AIDAmerica are safe of course, based on Cambodian Hands' reputation but I think it would be hard for us to take a risk by funding the organisation doing something it hasn't done before and from everything I've seen in your reports, Cambodian Hands has no experience in gender-based violence so this would be a difficult case to make. I would encourage you to try elsewhere. The French, of course are still a good source for the region. In other news, I would love to grab dinner next time you are passing through DC and talk about the old times and catch up on all of the inspiring things …

Oh, fuck it anyway. Janice was too irritated to continue reading. Her teeth clenched. She was a lifelong clencher. It was a habit that she had long given up trying to break. Being a dentist in her former life, she wasn't blessed with any ignorance about the damage that this nasty habit was causing her. She was slowly eroding her own teeth until eventually they would have about as much strength as lumps of wet flour. At the very least it had been a kind and quick turndown she supposed, but if she went to the French government or any other donor, they would make her send in a proposal and go through a whole process. Getting the $30,000 could take months or not happen at all. She had really been hoping to avoid all of that insane red tape with Marianne.

$30,000 was only about half of a mid-level UN worker's salary in Cambodia and she was having to go around begging for it. Jesus, it wasn't even the cost of flying someone like that kid Tom to Phnom Penh and putting him up in a villa for a year. She was getting so fed up of seeing money wasted on lifestyles and silly conferences instead of real work. The hypocrisy of it all. She herself only took a salary of $3,000 dollars a month. She had only recently gone up from $2,000 in order to put more money aside for Caitlyn. It was easy to get by on such a small salary in Cambodia. She needed to think of a plan B on how to get the funds but her head was pounding too much and she couldn't think clearly. She closed her eyes momentarily and felt her head droop as she drifted off to sleep.

—

Janice woke up to hear her phone ringing. It was her housekeeper, Tevy.

'Tevy, what is it?' Janice answered. She rubbed her cheek and could feel the small square outline marks where she had been facedown on her laptop keyboard. She wasn't sure how long she had been asleep for.

Tevy sounded anxious, 'I think Pagna has gone back to her husband.'

Janice cursed loudly.

'I went to the pagoda and the supermarket and when I came back, she and the kids were gone,' Tevy continued.

'Wait, Tevy. Why do you think that they've gone back to him? I thought she was doing well. Maybe they just went out somewhere?' Janice asked.

'She said that she was missing her home and she told me that she wanted to go back to him. All of their things are gone too,' Tevy explained. 'I had a bad feeling. I shouldn't have gone out and left her. I'm so sorry, Janice.'

'It's not your fault Tevy,' Janice told her. They couldn't even call Pagna, Janice realised recalling that her husband was the one who kept their mobile phone.

She should have gotten her a new one when she had the chance, she scolded herself. Her first instinct was to get a car and go to Pagna's home and insist that she come back to stay with her. Tevy pleaded with her not to.

'I tried to talk to her, Janice, but I don't think she is ready to leave her husband. I hope that she will change her mind, but it is her decision and no one can force her.'

Janice trusted Tevy. In many ways, she'd been the closest person in her life for the past twenty years.

'You are right about Pagna but what about the kids?'

'But she's their mother. If she wants to go back, you can't do anything.'

'I can't just sit and do nothing,' Janice cried.

'I think you have no choice, Janice,' Tevy said quietly.

She finished the call with Tevy deciding to make her way home. Janice felt shattered. From Caitlyn to Pagna to UNP and AIDAmerica not giving her the support she needed, everything was spiralling out of her control. She considered herself a resilient person but Janice felt beaten down.

Her phone beeped and she instantly jumped to it thinking that it may be a message from Pagna. Instead it was from a woman called Gillian from an NGO that worked on hunger reduction. Janice didn't know too much about their work except that they seemed to have an events budget the size of Jay Gatsby's and were forever inviting her to conferences and launch events.

Hi Janice, I'm so sorry to text you on a weekend but just wanted to double check that you are still speaking at our event this month. Everyone at Hunger Stops Here is so excited to have you onboard.

Oh shit, she'd forgotten about that entirely. Janice usually tried to keep her conference participation to a minimum believing that most conferences were far more focused on people looking like they were doing good work rather than those who actually did good work. She couldn't recall if she'd ever officially said yes to speaking but Gillian had been so damn persistent. Ugh. So much for going home. Now, she had a speech to write.

Typically, whenever she had to give a speech, she used it as an opportunity to get across specific messages about what Cambodian Hands was working on. She always tried to be inspiring and motivational and to try to make whoever was listening care about the issues facing Cambodian women if they didn't already. But today, inspiring was the last thing she felt. Maybe this conference is an opportunity to call out some hypocrisies, she thought as she began slowly typing.

She put on her iPod and stuck on her favourite album, Alanis Morrissette's *Jagged Little Pill*. She had fallen in love with it when Caitlyn had played it on repeat during the summer vacation she spent in Phnom Penh with her as a teenager. When she initially heard it blaring from Caitlyn's room, it had just sounded like shouty noise but soon Janice came to find the unbridled anger and resilience put forward by Alanis, meaningful and even nourishing. She switched to her favourite song, a track called 'You Learn'. The familiar tune calmed her a little. She smiled to herself as the contents of her speech began to form in her head.

11

Tom wasn't used to being this distracted by a girl. At work, he was finding himself looking up things he knew she loved like Sinéad O'Connor's reggae album, Tim Burton movies and Chimamanda Ngozi Adichie's books and speeches so that he could later recite nuggets of information back to her when she talked about them. He had also done an intensive Google dive of Caitlyn Leahy and found everything that the internet was willing to show him. As soon as she had accepted his Facebook friend request, he had gone back through every picture ever posted of her since her account had been set up in 2008. The earlier photos were mostly of her in bars and at parties during her college years. Every time she was pictured with a guy, he found himself wondering if she had ever slept with him. One guy, Nick Holmes, a jock-ish type straight out of an American high-school movie was pictured a lot with her and clearly an old boyfriend. A picture of him lifting her up into his arms in 2010 made Tom feel a twang of jealousy. Of course, this led to him doing a deep search of 'Nick Holmes Sacramento' to learn everything he could about the guy. He was still built like a shipping container but was now a manager in a sushi restaurant and still in Sacramento, so Tom felt better about him no longer being viable competition. He was doing more of this stalking than his actual job but felt that he had done enough work lately to coast a little.

It helped that Tom had gotten pretty good at giving the right level of email input without thinking too deeply about what he was going to say. 'Just to give my two cents' was a favourite opening line of his before questioning the sustainability of an idea or suggesting that they ought to have a robust monitoring and evaluation strategy. In his world, even the most mundane of documents had to be checked by twenty people to get their input and all twenty of those people had to give some form of comment to justify their pay check. The substance of what he said mattered far less than whether it was in line with the UN spiel and thankfully he was fairly fluent in UN spiel at this stage.

Tom had quickly learned how to play the UN game in Geneva. He had arrived as a fresh graduate on a three-month internship to the first UN opening that had accepted him after multiple applications. Working for no salary in one of the most expensive places on the planet and for one of the most prestigious organisations imaginable and only being able to afford Subway sandwiches for dinner hadn't deterred him at all. He had fallen in love with the United Nations from the first time he walked down the spacious avenue flanked by giant flags from all around the world leading up to the famed UN Palais des Nations.

In Geneva, Tom didn't view his lack of experience or knowledge as an impediment. He took it upon himself to approach people, introduce himself and ask questions. He learned how to feign wide-eyed interest, nodding intently while they were speaking as his brain rapidly scanned itself for intelligent follow up questions. He regurgitated word for word sentences that he had heard other people use which sounded smart, passing them off as his own.

His boss at the time was Caroline, a Canadian lady close to retirement age. She was attractive in a buttoned-up, blondey, grey-haired sort of way. She had worked in several war zones before ending in up in Geneva in a leadership role. Like many women of her stature in the UN, Caroline had had to work harder to get to the top. Sixty-five-hour working weeks for thirty years across many countries hadn't left her time to have a personal life.

Tom knew that Caroline took her job far too seriously to have an indiscretion, but he wanted her to think that she could have him. Even back then, he had known the real power of sex was not in the act itself but in knowing you could. He was subtle with small comments and strategic glances. Just enough to flatter her and to get her thinking he was interested but not brazen enough to warrant being unprofessional. When Caroline mentioned in passing that her sister was visiting, Tom put on his best earnest face. 'Does she have eyes as amazing as yours?' he had asked, giving her his perfectly crafted lopsided grin.

When his three-month internship was up, Caroline gave Tom a contract as a junior consultant while the other interns he had started with were thanked for their time and sent off to do years of more unpaid internships. After three years in Geneva, Tom ran out of hands to shake. When a position came up in Cambodia, Tom leapt at the opportunity and Caroline's recommendation had sealed it for him.

That Saturday, Caitlyn had invited Tom to a boat party that some of her friends were going to. He was enjoying the fact that in the past few weeks since he had turned up at her place with pizza, she was reaching out to him and inviting him to dinner or to stay over. He was quite sure that she liked him a lot. When his *New York Chronicle* article got released, she had even shared it on her Facebook page. Sure, it featured her Mom quite prominently but that was still a sign that she was really into him. There was something about her that made him feel the need to please. He felt the need to say only the cleverest things that he could think of which was kind of exhausting. He would even sometimes think of witty observations to tell her when he wasn't with her and then pretend that he had come up with them on the spot like the one about the Egyptians and social media. He had read it somewhere but thought it was good enough to amuse her and pass off as his own. They had been lying in bed in her place one morning before going to work when he had come out with it.

'People say that social media shows how shallow our society has become in the 21st century but think about it, what did the Egyptians paint on walls? Pictures of themselves and pictures of cats. What do we post on social media? Selfies and pictures of cats. People's values are just as vacuous as they always have been,' he said.

'That's fucking brilliant and so true,' Caitlyn had laughed loudly.

He loved feeling that he had her approval and craved more of it.

Phnom Penh's boat parties were notoriously debaucherous. Tom had been to many of them but this was Caitlyn's first. He met her at her place. She was looking hot in a striped navy and white dress which hugged her ass and her red hair was piled up on her head.

'Like my look, sailor?' she posed cheekily with a hand on her hip.

'Very nautical,' he nodded approvingly grabbing her into a kiss.

'I was going for nautical but nice,' she quipped.

They hopped in a tuk tuk down to the riverside area where

the boat was docked. It was still bright on a Saturday evening and the city was bustling with hipster Cambodians on motorbikes, scantily-dressed tourists stumbling out of bars and food sellers calling out to people on the sides of the streets waving unidentifiable fried objects on sticks. They sat in a contented silence taking it all in as they sped by Phnom Penh's golden roofed palace with hundreds of birds perched outside on its manicured front lawn. He felt a wave of happiness wash over him. Shuttling through Phnom Penh with Caitlyn Leahy when the sun was about to go down was a damn good place to be, he thought.

The boat was a packed haze of familiar Phnom Penh expat faces. It was clear that most of the partygoers had done some hard-core pre-drinking and were already loud and tipsy while getting onto the boat. Caitlyn introduced him to her friend Ella whom he remembered that Joey knew and a few other girls. They were all quite hot and Tom felt relieved he had a clean record of not having had sex with any expat women prior to Caitlyn as it would definitely have worked against him now.

There were fridges full of beers and wine on the boat and in a genius move, someone had taken big empty drums of water and refilled them with whiskey so that people could pour their own measures to incredibly liberal amounts. Blur's 'Country House' was blaring through speakers as the boat pulled out of the dock out into the Mekong river. If there was a party theme, it wasn't apparent to Tom beyond nautical and attention seeking. A couple of beefy looking Australian guys were topless and wearing captains' hats and pirate eye patches, and a few girls had skimpy bikinis with costume pieces like Hawaiian leis and arm bands. They had hot bodies but Tom felt proud the girl he was with had kept her outfit far classier than they had.

The boat pulled along the Mekong and people began to dance and sing along loudly to Blur. When he had first arrived in Phnom Penh, at parties like these Tom would wonder what the politely smiling Cambodian boat staff must think of this loud group of white idiots jumping around half-naked and spending more money than the average local person earned in a month, getting themselves polluted drunk. But the expat way of living had become so normal to him that these days he forgot to even question it.

'Let's go on top of the deck where it's quieter,' Caitlyn suggested. She squeezed his hand and he carried her beer. It was indeed calmer upstairs with far less people. She pulled him in for a kiss and he could feel his dick hardening as she pressed her body up against him. Jesus, this girl could keep him stiff for days.

'You know what you are doing,' he murmured as he bit her lip gently.

'I have no idea what you are talking about,' her blue eyes flashed with mock-innocence. 'This is pretty nice though, huh?'

The sun was setting into a purple sky and they could see the city lights in the distance with new construction sites dotting along both sides of the river. The familiar jaunty opening chords to the Stone Roses's song 'Sally Cinnamon' began to blare through the speakers providing him with a rush of joyful nostalgia.

'Oh, man, I love this song. I haven't heard it in years,' he exclaimed.

'I don't think I know this song,' she responded.

'The Stone Roses? Seriously?'

'Never heard of them,' she looked disappointed.

'Ah, I suppose they may not have made it in the US. You've missed out. Their first album is one of the most singularly perfect albums of all time. I'm gonna have to educate you.'

'Okay, you've made some big claims. I'm intrigued.'

Tom grabbed Caitlyn again for another kiss and was feeling the joy of the music, the moment and the girl when his bubble was burst by a familiar voice.

'Alright, mate!' It was Andre, who was joined by a pretty Cambodian girl in a tight, yellow dress.

Tom broke swiftly from the kiss with Caitlyn.

'Hey, man. How're things?'

'Good, good, man. Plenty of booze downstairs so I can't complain. Who's this lovely lady then?' Andre was slurring his words.

'Andre, this is Caitlyn, Caitlyn this is Andre.'

'Hi!' Caitlyn warmly shook his hand.

'Hi, I'm Caitlyn. What's your name?' Caitlyn also shook hands with the Khmer girl who Andre hadn't bothered to introduce.

'I'm Sokunthea,' she said. Tom shook hands with her too and introduced himself.

'So, what's all of this then? Are you the reason that this guy has been abandoning his mates?' Andre directed himself at Caitlyn. Tom's teeth clenched as he observed Andre looking up and down at every inch of Caitlyn, practically licking his lips.

'If he's ditching his friends, that's nothing to do with me but yes, we've been spending time together,' Caitlyn smiled tightly, clearly aware of being visually undressed.

'For some quality time in the sack with you, darling, I would happily abandon all of my nearest and dearest. What are you doing with this cunt?' Andre's eyes were bloodshot and Tom realised how drunk he was.

Caitlyn looked at him in disgust, clearly bristling at the use of the word 'cunt' as well as Andre's general demeanour. She edged her body as far from Andre as the confined space would allow.

'Calm it down, mate. We're still on our first beers,' Tom put his hand on Andre's shoulder using every ounce of his mental restraint not to punch him. 'Caitlyn and I are having a quiet chat here. We'll catch you guys later, downstairs on the dance-floor.'

He ushered Caitlyn further down the deck, cursing the boat for not being bigger. Andre turned his attentions to Sokunthea and was now draping himself all over her tiny body.

'So, that guy is a friend of yours? He seems totally sleazy.' Caitlyn had a rigidity in her voice he hadn't heard before.

'He's not that bad. Just a drinker. Sorry if he was a pain,' Tom responded.

'How do you even know him?' Caitlyn wrinkled her nose in disgust.

'Ah, you know, it's a small town and he's a reporter for the *Phnom Penh Herald*. We have some mutual friends like Joey, who Ella knows.'

'I didn't like how he talked to me. He was gross.' She sounded quite haughty, Tom thought.

'I wouldn't worry about it, Caitlyn. He was hammered.'

Tom was keen to move on and get back to the nice evening they had been having.

'He was still gross ... And you were so ... passive.' There was more than a hint of irritation in her voice.

Tom felt defensive. 'What was I meant to do? Start a fist fight on a boat? Be realistic.'

He wondered if punching other guys publicly was the kind of thing her ex Nick had done.

'Of course not. It just felt like you were quite accepting of his behaviour,' her tone heightened again.

'I didn't like how he spoke at all, but I've been around drunk people enough to know that it's easier to just move away.'

'Yeah, I get it. It was just somewhat … unexpected,' she said quietly.

'My behaviour was unexpected?' Tom challenged her.

'Yes. A little,' she sounded defiant.

It didn't feel like a full-blown fight but he felt irritated by her for the first time. He had dealt with the Andre situation effectively and any disappointment she may have in him felt like an overreaction on her part. They distracted themselves with whiskey as the boat turned and went around the Mekong for a second time. Andre was slumped in a corner with Sokunthea and Tom strategically made sure to be as far away from him as possible.

He wanted to get the fuck off the boat but was forced to make obligatory conversation with Caitlyn's friends and others at the party. One girl in the group was talking about how difficult it was to get a trustworthy maid in Phnom Penh.

'I mean you don't want to have to count every stray dollar that you have in your home but that's what you have to do to make sure they aren't stealing from you.'

'I had this problem when I lived in Hong Kong. Sometimes you just need to keep their passports or identification cards as an insurance policy,' someone else responded.

Tom nodded through their conversation mindlessly. He willed the night to be over. He was probably going to have to confront Andre about whatever he was writing about Janice at some point but tonight was clearly not that night.

Caitlyn came home with him. He didn't ask her to, but she

assumed so he didn't argue. She sidled her underwear-clad body up to him in anticipation in a way that normally would have driven him wild but he wasn't up to it and blamed the whiskey.

As they were starting to go to sleep, a text message from Andre bleeped through.

Best of luck with Firecrotch, mate. Me and Joey are down at The White Tiger if you fancy something a bit more exotic ☺.

12

A few days later, the weather should have been cooling down but Phnom Penh still had the humidity of a human armpit and the smell of rubbish marinating in the hot sun was a constant. Tom had a ten-minute walk to work every day but he had taken to bringing a second shirt with him in the knowledge that his first shirt would be soaked through with sweat by the time he got to the office.

His colleague Harold, a chubby, humourless South African who led their peace building programme had gotten into the habit of having his driver drive his UN jeep a five-minute distance to his regular Japanese lunch restaurant. He would make him leave the car on with the air-conditioning blasting while he was inside eating imported sushi platters just so that he could have a cool ride back to the office when he was done. Disgusted as he was by the wastage and hypocrisy of this, Tom was finding himself so exasperated by the heat that he was more than a little jealous.

That day, there was a big conference in the Raffles Hotel on poverty reduction run by a prominent hunger alleviation NGO. Phnom Penh had some kind of conference or workshop held almost every other day and the novelty of sitting in windowless hotel ballrooms full of little round tables, handing out business cards to strangers who may or may not prove useful to him had mostly worn off for Tom. But he particularly liked Raffles.

Tom was already mentally planning his food selection from the Raffles buffet when he got there. He would definitely start with fresh seafood, have the roast lamb for a main if they had it, and finish with a cheese plate full of imported cheeses of which Raffles had the best selection in Phnom Penh. He was pulled from these thoughts when he was signing in at the registration table and saw Janice's name on the agenda. He hadn't realised she was speaking. Ugh. There really was no such thing as a free lunch.

He joined a table of people he vaguely knew from other UN agencies and various NGOs. Networking had come easily to him since his Geneva days. He enjoyed the feeling of self-satisfaction it gave him knowing that someone important would walk away having been impressed by him. But after a year in Phnom Penh and seeing the same faces at everything, it was beginning to lose its lustre.

As they waited for the event to get started, an Argentinian woman who worked for an education NGO, whose name he was pretending to remember was boring him with the same spiel that she had given him a few months ago at a similar conference about the 'pressing need' to make Cambodia's education system more 'experiential and interactive for students'.

He nodded fervently belying his true feelings; that it was a nice idea but miles from the top of the priority list in a country where teachers only got paid $50 a month and kids needed to bribe them to even get them to correct their homework.

A text came through from Caitlyn, giving him a welcome excuse to turn his attention to his phone.

I'm bored. Entertain me. How goes it? Have they served the caviar yet?

He felt a stab of irritation. Of course, she was taking swipes at the event. Maybe it was the weather getting to him but he hadn't felt quite as charmed by Caitlyn since the night of the boat party. Of course, the sex was still unbelievable. The girl could control his dick like a snake charmer but her little quips and comments which he originally found witty and sharp were seeming increasingly sanctimonious.

He responded: *Not yet, it's a disgrace. I don't even have a personal butler.*

She responded: *Ha! Keep me posted on the speeches. I guarantee someone will throw out a Malala or a Kofi Annan quote.*

Will do. Your Mum's speaking at it by the way.

She didn't respond.

Janice was introduced as the first speaker. Dressed in a long cape-like navy blue dress, with over-eyelinered raccoon eyes, she looked like a Disney villain. When she started to speak, her voice was full of theatrical bluster.

'As many of you know, I first came to Cambodia in the 1990s. Back in those days, life and work here was very tough. It was violent, dirty, incredibly poor, had zero infrastructure and getting the most basic of good work done was difficult and time consuming. But I was seduced. Seduced by the country's natural beauty and fantastic culture and the tenacity of Cambodian people, particularly Cambodian women. I was seduced by the need to rebuild the country following the despicable devastation caused by the American bombings, the war with Vietnam and the Khmer Rouge. Like it has for so many others, Cambodia got into my heart and it has never left.

'In the early days, I, like everyone, believed that our community; that is NGOs and the United Nations, were doing their best for Cambodia. But today, I have come to think that while some good work has been done, we have not done nearly enough. My real fear, my friends, is that we have become too complacent and have fallen short of being the leaders that we profess ourselves to be. Here we are thirty years later and what has been achieved? I've heard all the statistics about poverty reduction. The World Bank says that the poverty rate is now only about 20%. But I ask you, how real are these hard-won gains? And how secure are they?

'Many people who have apparently escaped poverty in the statistical sense are still at high risk of falling back into poverty if there were even the slightest of economic shocks. What about the so-called "near-poor"? Those who live on less than $2.30 per day per person.

'It's important for us to acknowledge that statistics and the categorisation of who is poor and who isn't is highly flawed. 40% of the population are living on less than $2.30 per day but only the 20%; those living on less than $2 per day, are actually classified as in poverty. There is a stage managing to this. The difference of 30 cents per day makes it so that the number of people who are apparently poor is halved. 3 million people in poverty sounds a lot better than 6 million doesn't it?

'Why would the reality of the poverty in this country be stage-managed? Who could gain from that? There is an obvious truth here that must be spoken as we sit in Phnom Penh's most glorious hotel, where rooms can cost $300 a night.

'By exaggerating the improvements that have been made, this despicable government can continue its corrupt and dictatorial regime and the major corporations who exploit this country's natural resources can claim that the country is improving because of their actions. But we, the UN and NGOs also benefit from this. If Cambodia is becoming less poor, we can continue to justify our status quo existence under the pretence that our methods are working. I'm told there are eighty people at this workshop. Most of you are expats and your salaries are between $40,000 and $100,000 per year. The average Cambodian doctor earns $14,000 per year if they are lucky.

'How can we justify that? How are we walking around thinking that this is okay and convincing ourselves that history will judge us kindly? Many of you before me here today are smart and passionate people and know that I am speaking the truth, but it will be uncomfortable for you to acknowledge this because it's about you. None of us want to believe that we may be profiting from poverty but it is our reality. This country has an infection. It has been festering in the pit of its belly since the 1990s. It's called hypocrisy. We are, my friends, massive hypocrites. Many of you are well-meaning hypocrites but hypocrites nonetheless.' She paused for dramatic effect and looked out at everyone.

Oh, Jesus fucking Christ, thought Tom. He scanned the room and all eyes were locked on Janice. The Argentinian woman's face looked flushed with shock at what she was hearing. A reporter he knew from one of the Phnom Penh's English language papers was sitting across from him scribbling furiously. But Janice wasn't done yet.

'This country has provided wonderful incomes and enviable lifestyles for foreigners while poverty for Cambodians persists. There's a cure for poverty, it's called jobs. We need to be putting our energy into creating good jobs for Cambodians, real jobs, particularly for Cambodian women because when women are employed, entire families benefit.

'What we need is courage.

'We need the private sector who are profiting enormously from this country's natural resources to be held accountable for the damage they cause.

'We need donors and foreign governments to demand more accountability for the billions of aid that they pour in annually.

'We need the government to start serving the people instead of lining its back pocket.

'And we ourselves, the NGOs and UN agencies, we need to rethink how we operate and stop avoiding the hard questions about our role in this country.

'Addressing poverty is not something we can do alone – it requires all of our effort and a realisation that we must call out hypocrisies and make some uncomfortable changes to a system that may benefit us personally. Thank you.'

She had a look of almost maniacal joy on her face as she left the podium to a few lone claps. The MC took the microphone and announced that there would be a coffee break. A rumbling of angry conversations broke out around the room. Tom was flummoxed and it sounded like others around him felt the same way. Janice wasn't wrong about the government and she probably had a point about the hypocrisy but calling out these things in a room full of NGOs and UN people just wasn't how things were done.

The Argentinian woman turned to Tom, looking as disgusted as she would if Janice had defecated all over the stage.

'What rubbish!' she said. 'I know we are meant to respect her because she was here before anyone else but the woman clearly knows nothing about how international aid actually works and all of the things that diplomats are doing behind the scenes.'

'I think she's finally fucking lost it,' he heard a British guy from a labour rights NGO behind him say loudly.

Tom felt viscerally uncomfortable. He wasn't bothered hanging around for the rest of event having to hear the difficult reactions to Janice's speech. He wanted to get out of there. He left the ballroom without saying goodbye to anyone and headed out to grab a tuk tuk.

As the tuk tuk pulled away from the Raffles courtyard, he called Caitlyn.

'Hey, what are you doing calling me from the conference?' she answered.

'I have a crazy idea. Please don't say no,' he started. 'It's hot as fuck, you are hot as fuck. Tomorrow's Friday, let's get a cab to the beach tonight and stay there for the weekend. We can call in sick tomorrow.'

—

Tom was surprised that without too much nudging, he managed to convince a somewhat cautious Caitlyn to ditch work on Friday and come to the beach in Sihanoukville, a coastal city to the south-west of Phnom Penh. They had thrown their things in bags and he had gotten his favourite taxi driver, Dara to pick them up. Dara was a former monk with great English. Tom always tipped heavily and in turn, Dara was always available to pick him up at a moment's notice. It was about a four-hour drive to Sihanoukville and Tom managed to get them a room at one of the beach's high-end hotels, complete with private beach.

This was exactly what he needed, he thought. Caitlyn was in great form when he picked her up. Wearing a lacy green top and short skirt and bright red lipstick matching her hair colour, she looked like Poison Ivy.

'So, how was the conference today?' she prompted.

'Oh, it was the usual blah blah.' He didn't want to kill the holiday mood by telling her about Janice and the speech. 'I'm so glad you are up for this. You are going to love Sihanoukville.

Wait 'til you see the beach!'

'No, I'm so glad you instigated it.' She put her arms around him and he tingled at her closeness. 'Work has been a drag and to be honest, I was a bit worried that you were losing interest in me … '

She kissed his neck softly.

'Jesus, no,' he told her. 'Hey, does this feel like losing interest?' He placed her hand onto his hardening dick in his shorts.

She moaned quietly and began to rub him as they sank into a kiss. He began to reach under her skirt and to his delight he could feel that she was deliciously wet through her knickers. Tom mentally willed Dara the driver not to turn around as he began to go to work. His damn phone rang loudly and jolted him from the moment.

'Sorry, it may be work.'

It was a number that he didn't recognise so he answered with his professional tone. 'Tom Fenton speaking.'

'Hey, mate, it's Andre. How are you?'

'Not bad, mate. Just in the middle of something. What's up?'

'Okay, I won't bother you for long. It's a work thing. I'm working on a story about Janice Steiner and I'm wondering do you have anything you'd like to share?'

'You are going to need to tell me more about the actual story,' Tom prodded.

Caitlyn looked at him quizzically and Tom switched the phone from his left ear to his right ear which was furthest away from her.

'All I can say is that Janice Steiner is being accused of some behavioural issues and the piece is coming out tomorrow. I wanted to give you the opportunity to provide any comments on your experience working with her. It can be anonymous if you like.'

'I have nothing to contribute.' Tom hung up the phone, adrenaline pumping through him.

Fuck, fuck, fuck.

'Is everything okay?' Caitlyn inched back into him.

'Yes, it's fine. Just an idiot intern in work bugging me.' He was sure his voice sounded crackly. 'Where were we?'

He launched into kissing her again and thankfully she didn't press any further.

13

Caitlyn had never in her life stayed somewhere as luxurious as Sihanoukville Beach Resort. Tom insisted on paying their bill claiming that he had gotten a great deal because it was so last minute but she was adamant that she would pay him back when next month's allowance came through from her Dad. She tried not to dwell on the money too much as whatever the cost, it was worth it. They had a round-shaped bed, a jacuzzi in their bedroom and a balcony leading on to a private terrace with a dipping pool flanked by palm trees. It looked like somewhere the Kardashians would stay.

The cab journey to get there had essentially provided four hours of intense foreplay and they had jumped each other as soon as they had checked in. She had woken up after a gorgeous sleep to him making her a coffee to have on the terrace where he had arranged for their breakfast to be served.

Over the past number of weeks, she had felt her walls come down regarding Tom. He was warm, witty and the sex was wonderful. It had been a while since Caitlyn had felt anything beyond fleeting sexual attraction for anyone as her feelings for her ex were still a little raw.

Nick wasn't long back from serving in Afghanistan when they first met while majoring in journalism in Sacramento State University. She had fallen deeply in love with him very quickly and with the intensity, came a deep insecurity that her feelings weren't fully reciprocated. He was extroverted and jovial until he got to a certain level of drunk at parties and would turn silent and distant. He refused her efforts to get him to see a therapist about his time at war. They talked about him becoming a music journalist and her becoming a foreign correspondent. However, when they graduated, they both faced the reality that a major global recession was still underway and neither of their chosen fields were exactly doling out good jobs. While she decided that she wanted to work for NGOs and started doing a masters in human rights, he endeavoured to give up on his career ambitions and work in a restaurant. To her, this was infuriating. He had only joined the military and gone through the emotional mutilation that was Afghanistan in the first place to get his college tuition paid for so that he could get a good job and make a better living than his mechanic father did.

It had only taken about 30 seconds for her to decimate their three mostly-happy years together. For months, Nick insisted that he 'needed space' and 'time alone' but that it had 'nothing' to do with Caitlyn. He had refused to go with her to a Halloween party her best friend Lucy was having. Caitlyn loved Halloween and was tired of staying in with Nick while he played video games and gave one-word responses to her attempts at conversation. In previous years, they had gone all-out for Halloween, donning couples' costumes as Axl and Slash from Guns N' Roses and Wayne and Garth from *Wayne's World*. She knew their costume would be highly anticipated by her friends and she dreaded having to make excuses for his not attending yet another social event. She haphazardly pulled together a medusa costume by covering herself in neon blue body paint, donning a black ballet leotard that she'd found in a thrift store and putting toy snakes in her hair. She felt shit under the blue paint but the costume alongside the charitable vodka and orange juices that Lucy kept handing her gave Caitlyn a lift. She enjoyed herself at the party, dancing to music she would normally deride like T-Pain and 50 Cent.

That night, Lucy's elder brother, Travis was home from New York where he had an overpaid job in some kind of management consulting firm with a name that impressed people but Caitlyn could never remember. Barely dressed in an Aladdin 'costume' which acted as a fantastic excuse to show off his perfect abs in their entirety, saving for a tiny purple waistcoat, Travis was evidently still as much of an object of desire as he had been in high school, when Caitlyn had last seen him. She had never even had much of a thing for Travis. He had always been a bit too obviously good-looking and conventionally eligible for her taste. People were dazzled by him and Lucy adored him but Caitlyn couldn't recall ever hearing Travis say anything notable enough to make her think that he was worthy of his considerable hype. Physically, he looked to Caitlyn like an exact sketch of what she would draw if someone had a gun to her head and asked her to draw a handsome man as quickly as possible without giving her time to think about any potentially interesting details.

But when a drunken Travis ambled up to her at the beer pong table towards the end of the night and told her he thought she had the best costume at the party and made for 'a sexy fucking medusa', Caitlyn's battered confidence felt nourished by the attention. She let him kiss her. She estimated that it lasted about half a minute before she pulled back and told him it was a mistake. The image of his mouth smeared with her blue paint as she broke from the kiss triggered the most visceral sense of guilt that she could have possibly imagined.

Caitlyn couldn't even get through the next day before

cracking and telling Nick what had happened. She convinced herself that she was telling him out of honesty but it was obvious to her now that she had been subconsciously hoping that a healthy dose of jealousy would revitalise their flimsy relationship.

Nick's reaction had been cold and resolute. Any warm feelings he had for her were chopped off in a single swoop. He told her that he was '100% done' and that under no circumstances would he be interested in talking about it any further. Within days, he left every photo, gift, birthday card, borrowed item or shared purchase from their relationship at Lucy's place and refused to answer Caitlyn's calls or texts. It had been excruciating but time helped and she slowly managed to wean herself off checking his Facebook page more than once a day.

Her budding relationship with Tom was slowly painting a new coat of paint over her lingering Nick feelings. It felt new and shiny and unsullied by bullshit, as if she had flipped her pillow over to the cooler side making her feel more relaxed and at ease. She was starting to imagine a future with Tom. She found herself daydreaming about them travelling the world together, working in different developing countries. Having seen her heartbreak after Nick, her Dad had been so excited when she told him that she had met someone new. He had been particularly impressed that she was dating an Irishman and had jumped about ten steps ahead insisting that she and Tom go on a trip to Ireland so that she could meet their distant relatives there. Even Ella and the girls had been impressed with him after the boat party and had told her what a cute couple they made which had given her a nice glow. She and Nick had been the kind of couple that others envied in college too and she liked the feeling of others admiring her relationship.

They spent the weekend lounging on the hotel beach, reading. Ella had lent Caitlyn the first of Elena Ferrante's Neapolitan novel series and she was blissfully transported to 1950s Naples while Tom read a weighty looking biography of Aung San Suu Kyi. The hotel's private beach was practically deserted with the exception of a few expat couples and families. They ordered fresh crab and fruit plates from the hotel which they served right on the sand.

On Saturday, after a mid-afternoon nap which of course led to some jacuzzi sex, a first for Caitlyn, Tom insisted they go into the town centre and get a drink down by the pier and watch the sunset together. Sihanoukville town was a departure from the opulence of their resort. Caitlyn was put off by the prominence of gaudy hotels and beach bars teeming with loud backpackers who were practically naked saving for cheap local market vests advertising South East Asian beers.

Caitlyn had learned from Ella and her friends that mocking backpackers was a popular expat pastime but the contempt at the heart of the jokes was unquestionable. The backpacker tendency to cram Cambodia into a quick two days of temples as part of a broader trip to South East Asia before declaring having 'done Cambodia' incited an energetic hatred from expats. Expats derided backpackers' lack of knowledge about the 'real Cambodia' and were offended by their 'lack of respect for local culture'. Upon seeing them in their droves in Sihanoukville playing with street children and posing for the ideal Facebook photo, Caitlyn was inclined to agree.

Tom must have read her mind. 'We're getting out of here. I promise. There's a gorgeous place just up the road I want to take you to.'

They went to a beautiful Italian bistro tucked away on the pier and it suddenly seemed like an entirely different city. Tom insisted on ordering a bottle of prosecco.

'To our first trip away,' he toasted her. It was a cheesy move but she was too happy not to enjoy it.

'I'm sorry, this is so tacky of me but you look so pretty, and this moment is too perfect.'

He took out his phone and took a picture of the two of them against the pink sunset holding up their glasses of prosecco. They had never taken a photo together before and Caitlyn knew that it was something meaningful for him to do. He had gotten a little burned in the sun and his nose was peeling, the new layer of skin under the burn was the exact same shade of pink as the sky behind them.

'Oh, look at that, you are the same colour as the sunset,' she laughed.

He looked a little embarrassed and her heart swelled. 'It's going to turn brown, just you wait,' he exclaimed.

I love you, she thought suddenly. She realised the words were practically on the tip of her tongue and swallowed them whole. Oh fuck.

After dinner, they went dancing at a beach-side bar which played several 2000s rock hits. Caitlyn went easy on the liberally poured vodkas and coke that Tom kept placing in front of her. She could see that he was getting drunk and enjoying himself. She watched him do a fist pump in the air as they danced enthusiastically to The Killers's 'Mr Brightside'.

He was pretty goofy when he let his guard down and her cheeks were practically sore from laughing at his dance moves. As the bar started winding down for closing time, they heard the familiar opening chords to David Bowie's 'Space Oddity'.

Tom scooped her up and lifted her into the air.

'This is our song!' he yelled enthusiastically.

She laughed as he awkwardly put her back down and continued to embrace her.

He shouted to others on the dancefloor, 'My girlfriend and I first got talking because I was singing along to this! It's our song. Woo! Thank you, Bowie!'

They laughed back in amusement at the sight of the rambling, sunburnt, drunken Irishman. He turned his attention to her again.

'Caitlyn, it's definitely our song isn't it?' His drunken face looked at her with earnestness. It was nothing short of adorable.

'Yes, it is, Major Tom.'

She rested her head on his sweat-drenched shoulder as they swayed to the music.

—

The next morning, Caitlyn's head pounded. She couldn't quite remember how they had got back to the resort the night before.

'Good morning, starshine,' Tom grumbled at her across the pillow. His eyes were bloodshot and his straw-coloured hair was mussed up.

'Good morning,' she groaned reluctantly. 'I have no memory of the last few hours of last night. Damn you and your vodkas! I didn't do anything embarrassing did I?'

'You were fine. You desperately wanted to have sex with me but that's normal.' He was getting out of bed. 'I'm going out for a quick swim before breakfast to help cure me. Want to come?'

'I'm too fragile. I need more sleep,' she groaned.

He kissed her forehead quickly as she snuggled back into the expensive sheets, appreciating how much more luxurious they were than the cheap market ones in her apartment in Phnom Penh, that practically exfoliated her skin every night. She glanced at her phone to check the time and saw that she had missed calls from Janice and her Dad.

A text message had come through from Ella.

Hey Caitlyn, just wanted to check in on how you are doing with the reports about your Mom. I'm here if you need anything. Ella xx.

Reports. What the fuck? She quickly sat up in the bed and called Janice.

'Caitlyn, where are you?' Janice skipped any form of greetings.

'Hi Janice, I'm away at the beach. It was spontaneous. What's going on?'

'There's been some vicious things about me in the *Phnom Penh Herald* these past few days. I'm not worried but good to make sure you were clued in.'

'I don't understand. What's it saying? Will you be okay?'

'I'll be fine. Come see me when you are back though.'

There were two articles about Janice in the *Herald*. The first one had Friday's date.

Prominent Human Rights Activist Criticises 'Hypocritical' Expats
By Chloe Bennett

Janice Steiner, the head of leading women's NGO, Cambodian Hands has hit out at Cambodia's expat community in a blistering attack.

Speaking to an audience of mostly foreign NGO and UN workers at a conference in Phnom Penh on Thursday, Ms Steiner, a long-term rights campaigner, described Cambodia as being 'infected' with 'hypocritical' expats 'who earn between $40,000 and $100,000 a year.'

She also levied harsh words at the Cambodian government.

'By exaggerating the improvements that have been made, we, the UN and NGOs can continue to justify our status quo existence' and 'this despicable government can continue its corrupt and dictatorial regime,' she said.

Gillian Hicks-Goodwin, a representative from the organiser of the event, NGO, Hunger Stops Here said that Ms Steiner's remarks were not planned as part of the conference programme.

'The theme of the conference was "Catalysing Civic Action to Reduce Hunger in a Digital Age". Janice Steiner was asked to provide remarks on this topic,' said Ms Hicks-Goodwin.

One conference attendee who spoke to the Herald on the condition of anonymity said that Ms Steiner's remarks were 'grossly inappropriate' and that people in the room were 'shocked'.

'I'm not sure what she was hoping to gain as the speech was utterly lacking in solutions. Frankly, it came across as quite rambling. It's unclear how levying these accusations at an audience of highly skilled professionals who just happen to be paid decent remuneration is a productive means of resolving Cambodia's challenges.'

Ms Steiner could not be reached for comment.

The second article was a lengthier feature piece with numerous pictures of Janice throughout the years. Caitlyn recognised the by-line image as belonging to Andre, Tom's sleazy friend from the boat party a few weeks ago.

Exclusive: Cambodia's Saviour Unravels
By Andre King

Downtown Phnom Penh in one of the city's newly opened American-style cafés, Sokha* (31) sips an iced coffee. These days, she's working as a bank teller in her hometown of Battambang but just a few months ago, she was a project manager at one of Cambodia's best known and most respected NGOs, Cambodian Hands, under one of the country's most prominent human rights activists, Janice Steiner.

So, what led to Sokha's sudden change of career? She, like several other former Cambodian Hands employees spoken to for this investigation over the past several months, tells the same story of a Janice Steiner very different from her glittering public image.

They talk of a megalomaniac bully who undermines her staff and treats them so poorly that they eventually can no longer stand to work for her.

'Not many people stay working for Cambodian Hands for longer than a year or two. It just becomes too hard,' says Sokha.

Several of Ms Steiner's former employees make the same claims of poor treatment.

Sokha says that Ms Steiner was never physically abusive with any of the staff but that name-calling and screaming were common practice.

'She talks down to you and blames you for things that aren't your fault,' she says.

Today, Sophea's hair is long and glossy but she says that when she worked for Ms Steiner it began to fall out with the stress of working for her.

'She would call me up at crazy hours of the night and over the weekends complaining about different things. My husband

would tell me not to answer the phone but I was terrified of her,' she says.

Another former employee, Mony*, now working for another NGO told the *Phnom Penh Herald* about Ms Steiner's less than orthodox ways of expressing discontent with her employees' work.

'I submitted a report about one of our projects which she wasn't happy with and she made me clean the office toilet for two weeks. The organisation does great work but her management style is impossible to put up with over the long term.'

It's unclear whether Ms Steiner's behaviour and treatment of staff dates back to when she first set up Cambodian Hands in 1992. Many former staff of Cambodian Hands got their start there in the 1990s and are still working in the sector. Several of these refused to speak to the *Phnom Penh Herald* on the record.

Rithy* who worked for Ms Steiner in the late 1990s says that 'she's a very passionate woman and cares a lot about Cambodia but it's true to say that she can sometimes be very difficult.'

Ms Steiner's reputation in Cambodia and beyond has not been cited to as anything other than in favourable terms before now. Starting Cambodian Hands in 1992 with a small portion of her own savings, she has built the organisation to be one of the biggest NGOs in the country. One that is supported by UN agencies, numerous donors and has become a favourite of celebrities and prominent international visitors. Helped by a media savviness that has brought the organisation significant publicity, she has raised millions in support of Cambodian women and encouraged the UN and others to make significant investments into women's livelihoods. She has also been awarded several accolades including the prestigious UN Humanitarian of the Year in 2002.

Those who have worked with Ms Steiner say there is a vast difference between the image she puts forward in the media *spotlight and the one that she shows in the workplace.*

'With donors, she's very polished and nicer to the staff,' says Sophea. 'It's all about image.'

'I think she's a little bit crazy and probably should get help. She shouldn't be managing people,' says Rithy.

It was reported yesterday in this same paper that Ms Steiner spoke out against Phnom Penh's expat community at a conference this week calling them 'hypocritical'.

Many government, UN and Cambodian Hands board members have been contacted for this piece but have refused to comment.

*Names have been changed to protect identities.

Caitlyn was stunned. Janice was difficult. Of course, she knew that. She had known that for as long as she could remember. But had she really been treating her staff so badly? Could these claims really be true? And what was she doing lashing out at the UN and NGO expats when she so clearly needed their support? Caitlyn didn't know which emotion to prioritise. The shame at Janice's behaviour and her own unwitting association with it, the anger at Janice for not treating people decently, or the strange sadness that the idea she had built in her head for so long of the Mom who was off helping people being shattered.

'Hello beautiful,' Tom came back into the room. His hair was slicked back with pool water and he had a towel around his shoulders.

'What's wrong, babe?' He said upon seeing her downcast expression.

She started to fill him in and then interrupted herself. 'Wait, you were at the Raffles conference. Why didn't you tell me that Janice had gone crazy at everyone?'

'I honestly didn't think it was a big deal. I mean you aren't close, and I didn't think it was my place to say anything.' Tom sounded so casual about it.

'But it's still a bit fucking weird. I asked you about the conference and you chose not to say that my mother had said these things that had offended a room full of people?' Caitlyn blustered.

'Caitlyn, it's a tricky situation to navigate. You don't talk about her much and when you do it's negative. I had even texted you that she was there, and you didn't respond. What was I meant to do?'

'I feel like you cheated me and weren't transparent though. The other bigger story is by your creepy friend from the boat too. Did you know about this too?' Caitlyn could feel her face getting hot as she spoke.

'He's not a friend. He's barely an acquaintance. I swear, Caitlyn. I didn't know that Andre was writing a story about Janice,' Tom looked at her earnestly.

'Did you know about the bullying stuff? Tell me truthfully,' she asked with sincerity.

'I didn't. It's the truth,' he stressed.

She paused. She wanted to trust him but she felt stung by his behaviour.

'Okay, thank you,' she told him. 'How bad was the speech?'

'To be honest, Caitlyn. I don't know your Mum well but what I will say is that saying those things is not how things are done.'

'I agree. But, is she really that wrong? There is hypocrisy don't you think?'

'I don't disagree with you,' Tom said. 'But as I said, it wasn't the time or place.'

His complacency seemed so weak to her. He was just so unwilling to question the system.

'When would be the time or place?' she challenged him.

'Caitlyn, what's happening with your Mom sounds difficult and complex. Picking on me isn't going to help the situation.'

'Okay, fine.'

She got up out of bed and got into the shower and scrubbed her hair furiously, her irritation at Tom preventing her from enjoying the waterfall shower. They needed to check out of the hotel soon and her priority was getting back to Phnom Penh to figure things out. Their little paradise break was well and truly over.

They shuffled around each other awkwardly for the rest of the morning, making strained small talk as they packed and ate a quick breakfast before a driver friend of Tom's regular driver, Dara, picked them up.

They sat in silence in the car. She was dying to get home and think things through. The cab was dirtier and far stuffier than Dara's had been on the journey down and the driver was honking loudly as he sped indiscriminately over the roads without indicating or even appearing to check any mirrors. Caitlyn had become accustomed to death-defying driving in Cambodia and was too preoccupied in her thoughts to notice it too much. Tom had politely asked the driver to slow down but gave up after several of his attempts were ignored and was now silently glued to his phone.

Out of what seemed like nowhere they suddenly heard a massive bump followed by a smash.

14

The car jolted Caitlyn forward so suddenly that she scarcely had time to realise the crash was happening before it was over and they had veered to a halt.

'Fuuucccckk!' Tom shouted over the noise of the blaring alarm. 'Caitlyn, are you okay?'

'I'm fine. I think.' She felt the adrenaline pumping through her but nothing seemed to hurt.

'Shit! You're bleeding!' Tom touched her shoulder where the seatbelt had sliced through her skin.

'You are too.' He had a cut above his eyebrow.

The window at the front of the car had cracked into large pieces but had somehow managed to avoid shattering entirely despite the impact. They got out of the car carefully and started checking each other for injuries. Miraculously, they had a smattering of oddly-placed cuts and marks between them but nothing really worrying. The driver was okay too, save for a deep cut on his hand.

'You were going too fucking fast!' Tom screamed at him. Caitlyn had never seen him so worked up.

'Not my fault. Not my fault. The guy in front went too slow,' the driver was shouting hysterically while gesturing with his hands causing his gushing wound to drip blood on the ground.

'It's okay, it's okay,' Tom steadied himself and spoke more calmly. 'We just need to call an ambulance.'

'No ambulance! No ambulance!' The driver pleaded.

'He's worried the police will come with an ambulance and

he'll get into trouble,' Caitlyn guessed.

They were at the side of a deserted road with nothing nearby other than a few houses amid the rice paddy fields. The driver sat on the ground against the car and began to sob. A few locals came out of a nearby house and started to talk to him in Khmer. Caitlyn recognised that he was saying the word *louy* over and over again which was one of the few Khmer words she was certain of. It meant money. This accident was clearly going to mean a huge financial loss for him.

Tom went straight into action-mode, phoning up every cab company and driver whose number he could find to try and get someone to pick them up. Caitlyn awkwardly tried to talk to the small group of people who had gathered around but it was impossible with her terrible Khmer. None of them spoke a word of English. Many of them appeared more interested in staring silently at her rather than offering help, causing her to desperately wish that her black beach dress was covering more of her body. A smiling elderly woman in a large straw hat handed her two warm cans of coke. She paused and awkwardly wondered if she should pay her. The lady beckoned her away making it clear that the drinks were free and Caitlyn was touched by the kind gesture.

While Tom continued his dogged pursuit of a cab, Caitlyn sat on her bag at the side of the road sipping her practically boiled coke and debating with herself about whether or not she should call Janice. Janice would probably have contacts out near Sihanoukville and someone would be able to help them. But telling Janice meant Janice telling her Dad, and then Mary and everyone else would find out. They were worried enough about her being in Phnom Penh. It would be this massive deal which was the last thing she wanted. Ugh. What time was it?

1:12 p.m. Okay, she told herself that if Tom didn't get a taxi by 1:30 p.m. she would call Janice.

'Okay, I've rang like fifteen different drivers in Phnom Penh and they are all telling me they will call their Sihanoukville friends and get back to me as soon as they can.' Tom was red-faced and his forehead was dotted with beads of sweat. She could hear the stress in his voice.

'It's okay,' she said, handing him his can of coke. 'Sit down and drink for a second. We just have to wait a little while.'

He looked pained. 'It's amazing that you are so calm. I'm so sorry about this, Cait. Dara is usually so safe and reliable. I wish he'd been driving us instead of this idiot.'

'It's okay. It's not your fault.' She really did feel calm somehow. Maybe the panic hadn't sunk in yet. She rubbed his back affectionately as he sat down beside her.

'I'm sorry. I'm a fucking idiot.' He looked almost teary. 'I really fucked up that stuff with your Mum too. I'm so sorry, Cait'.

'It's okay. I'm sorry too. It doesn't matter,' she told him and she meant it. It just didn't seem important any more.

He reached over and held her tightly. His phone rang interrupting their hug and they both jumped excitedly. A driver arrived within thirty minutes. Tom must have offered him an exorbitant fare to get him there so soon.

Their initial driver was still slumped against his car by the time they were leaving.

'Tom, should we give him some money?' Caitlyn asked. 'He's going to need to fix the car and he's losing money on our fare and he's probably out of work now too.'

They pieced together the remainder of their cash which was about $70. The vast majority was Tom's money and although he looked slightly put out, he didn't argue. Tom gave it to the driver while scolding him.

'Buddy, you really need to learn how to fucking drive. Not so fucking fast next time. You could kill someone.'

'Thank you, thank you. Sorry, sorry.' The distraught driver eagerly took the wad of cash.

Tom and Caitlyn wordlessly folded into a hug in the second taxi home. Caitlyn felt overcome with tiredness. She wasn't ready to think too much about what could have happened to them in that accident. Life was cheap in Cambodia. People died in needless accidents all the time. Maybe she'd been thinking that being foreign and white somehow protected her. She turned to Tom.

'Let's not tell people about this. I feel like I'm going to have to deal with the stuff that's happening with my Mom and I don't want to bring on more drama.'

'Of course. I totally get it. Let's just put it behind us,' said Tom. 'But I want you to know that when I heard that smash sound, my first thought was of you. I'm so sorry.'

'It's not your fault, Tom, really. I'm fine. It was scary but we're okay.' She leaned her head into his chest and inhaled the faint combination of sweat, aftershave and fabric softener.

'I'm here for you with the stuff with your Mum and anything else you need, Caitlyn,' he told her before hugging her so tightly that her sore shoulder stung.

They kissed deeply before the cab dropped her home.

That evening, Caitlyn called her Dad in Sacramento and felt instantly emotional upon hearing his voice. She couldn't tell him about the accident, but she badly wanted his input on what was happening with Janice.

'Do you think it's true, Dad?'

'I really don't know, hon,' Liam said sounding downcast. 'She can be difficult as you know but she's so committed to the work. If there's any truth to it, I'm sure she had no idea that she was upsetting people so much.'

'This is a serious attack on her reputation, Dad. I don't know how she'll come back from this.'

'I'm worried about her, Cait. She puts up a tough front but she's not made of stone. Will you go and spend some time with her and see if she's okay?'

Caitlyn recoiled slightly at the idea of spending time with Janice.

'I swear, Dad. I'll never in a million years understand how you are so kind about her after how she treated you.'

'Your Mom is a very good woman. Spend real time with her and you'll see that, hon. You are a lot like her in fact.' She could hear the smile in his voice.

'I'm nothing like her, Dad.' Caitlyn told him seriously. 'I would never abandon my kid or bully my staff.'

'Oh, that fire-tongue of yours!' He exclaimed. 'Life's short, Caitlyn. You are going to have to let go of your anger towards her at some stage … Now, tell me the latest about your lovely leprechaun. How big is his UN pot of gold?'

'Oh, Jesus, Dad,' Caitlyn groaned as she laughed. 'Are you seriously making an awkward sex joke while also being offensive about my boyfriend's nationality?'

'I was asking about how much money he earns. I'm an old-school Dad who wants a young man to be financially-worthy of my daughter. Get your mind out of the gutter, kid!'

'You are so inappropriate!' She laughed. He was right about life being short though, she thought. Surely today had reminded her of that.

—

Caitlyn took the next day off work. She texted Pheary and Vic that she had some family issues to attend to. She didn't feel the need to provide any more detail and they didn't ask any questions. They knew who her Mom was and it was too small and gossipy a town for them not to have heard about what was happening.

When she called Janice, she was surprised to learn that she was in her office working as if nothing had happened. Caitlyn hadn't been to the Cambodian Hands office since the summer she had spent in Phnom Penh as a teenager. At the time it had been the only place where she could get online and she had spent many hours there writing long, juvenile emails to Lucy about how bored she was, how shockingly poor Cambodia seemed and how she wished she could go back in time and marry Jim Morrison; her obsession at the time. Back then, it didn't even have air-conditioning but today, it was far bigger and more impressive than Caitlyn remembered, having been extended and revamped over the years as Janice attracted more donor money and grew the organisation.

When she came to Janice's personal office, she was struck by how chaotic looking it was. It had written-on flipcharts with lists hung on most of the walls, post-it notes stuck on the window panes, and piles of notebooks and papers and cups of half-drank green tea on Janice's battered teak desk. It reminded Caitlyn of the movie, *A Beautiful Mind* where Russell Crowe plays a math genius who writes equations all over his windows.

'Jesus, Caitlyn, what happened to your face? You have some kind of bruise on your cheek,' Janice greeted her.

Fuck. Caitlyn had thought that her long-sleeved top and her lasagna-like layering of concealer and foundation had covered up any evidence of the crash but clearly her skills as a make-up artist were lacking.

'It's nothing. I just fell off a motorbike,' Caitlyn lied.

'Caitlyn, you promised your Dad you wouldn't take motorbikes. Was this in Sihanoukville? That place is full of drugs and disgraceful behaviour,' Janice fumed.

Jesus, she was irritating. Caitlyn tried to speak calmly. 'Yes, it was there. But I stayed in a nice, safe place, away from all of that.'

'How can you afford those fancier places? Who were you in Sihanoukville with?'

'It's not your business but my boyfriend brought me.'

'What? You have a boyfriend. Nobody told me.' Janice sounded scornful.

'Actually, you know him. It's Tom Fenton from UNP.'

'That Irish kid?' Janice raised a thin eyebrow.

'Yes, him. What's wrong with him?' Jesus, Janice knew how to push her buttons.

'He's fine, I guess. Just seems like your typical UN-er. No original thoughts in his head.' She looked wholly unimpressed. 'To be honest you could do better, sweetie.'

'Who the fuck asked you? He's actually very brilliant.' Caitlyn could feel her temper flaring but she knew that she needed to get onto the real reason she was there. 'Look, who I'm seeing is not your concern. What's happening with these bullying allegations?'

'It's nothing to worry about. Really. It's just some disgruntled people. There's a reason no one used their real name. It will die down.' Janice sounded defiant gesturing as if to brush the allegations away.

'I don't get it though. Why would they say these things?' Caitlyn asked.

'Oh, I don't really know,' Janice said coolly. 'Maybe there's someone behind it. I've been calling out things as they are a lot lately. People don't always want to hear the truth when they have vested interests in lies. There's a lot of people here that wish I'd shut up.'

'But wait, will you be okay?'

'I'm fine, sweetie. I promise.' She looked at Caitlyn calmly. 'You think I haven't gotten some bad shit said about me before? This is not my first rodeo. It will blow over, Caitlyn.'

'But how are you going to respond? Are you going to keep a low profile for a while?'

'I'll do no such thing. I haven't killed myself for this country for more than twenty years and made the sacrifices that I've made to get scared now. It will all be fine.'

'What is it about you that makes you think you are so invincible? You know that …' Caitlyn stopped in her tracks, distracted. She noticed for the first time that behind Janice's head was a framed picture of a child's handprints with one hand in royal blue and the other in light green and the name 'Caitlyn' written on it with an adult's handwriting that she recognised as Janice's.

'Wait, what's that picture behind you? Did I do that?' She asked.

'Yes! Of course!' Janice spoke excitedly. 'Don't you remember how amazing your paintings were as a kid? Your Dad and I thought you were going to become the next Frida Kahlo because you were so obsessed with finger painting and you were always painting and colouring while sitting in your bed.'

It was true. Caitlyn had loved painting as a child. She hadn't thought about it in years but some of her happiest memories as a child were when she would spend hours at their kitchen table at home or on her bed dipping her hands and fingers into differently coloured pots of paint. She had refused to use brushes or sponges and as a result she was forever leaving hand-painted marks around the house and in her bedroom. Her Dad had eventually put cover sheets on her bed because of her insistence on painting in bed.

'You designed our logo. Look!' Janice picked up a notepad on her desk featuring the Cambodian Hands logo to show her. The graphic image was of two overlapping handprints one in royal blue and one in light green in an unmistakable copy of the child's picture on the wall.

'I know you are angry with me, Caitlyn, but I've never stopped being your Mom.' Janice smiled at her somewhat sadly.

Caitlyn could feel a lump rise in her throat. 'I guess not.'

15

Janice felt a bolt of happiness seeing that Caitlyn was clearly moved to hear that the Cambodian Hands logo was taken from her childhood painting.

'I suppose I've felt a little abandoned over the years,' Caitlyn said softly.

'I'm so sorry that you've felt that way,' Janice told her apologetically. 'It was never meant to be like that. I never intended to be away for as long as I have been.'

'Then why didn't you just come home?'

'I always meant to at some point,' Janice explained. 'But then as you got older, it seemed like you needed me less. I'd call you at home and you were often too busy with your friends or watching a movie or whatever to come and speak to me. It felt like it would be wrong of me to go back to Sacramento and disrupt everything and make you divide your whole happy life in half between me and your father. So, I stayed here.'

'But I needed a Mom,' Caitlyn insisted. 'All of my friends had their Moms around. I didn't know anyone else whose Mom had left them.'

'I didn't leave you on the side of the road with a bag of Doritos!' Janice exclaimed. 'I left you with your father who is an excellent parent and who has clearly done an incredible job. That doesn't mean it didn't sting. Caitlyn, you have no idea how much it stung. It still does.'

Caitlyn stayed silent and Janice couldn't make out the expression on her face, so she continued talking.

'I just want you to remember that it wasn't about who loved you more. It was about who could give you a better life.'

'I don't think I'll ever really understand it but I appreciate you saying that,' Caitlyn said slowly.

Janice hugged her and patted her on the back.

'It's still quite sad isn't it?' Caitlyn said with a slight smile as they broke from the hug.

Janice nodded not quite knowing what more to say. It was emotional talking to her daughter this way. She felt emotional all the time these days since those goddamn articles had come out but she needed to try to be strong when she was with Caitlyn. There was plenty of time to fall apart later at home in an empty house.

She took Caitlyn to an early lunch with her at the Russian market, a bustling local market so-named for the Russian expats that frequented it in the 1980s. Janice recalled that it had been one of the few places in Phnom Penh that Caitlyn liked when she was a teenager because they had bought reams of material covered in cutesy animal prints and Caitlyn had got several dresses tailored.

'Look at these owls. You love owls,' Janice pointed out, pulling out a slightly gauche pink and blue pattern to show her as they strolled around the market barely glancing at cheap souvenirs that had long since lost their exotic appeal for either of them.

'Owls haven't been my thing since high school, I'm afraid,' Caitlyn told her.

'Your favourite iced-coffee guy is still there,' Janice pointed out. The small, unassuming stall signposted *Best Iced Coffee* had been a favourite of locals and expats for more than twenty years.

'Oh, no way! I remember his iced-coffee being amazing!'

Caitlyn looked excited and rushed over to order one from the owner, a cheerful Cambodian as highly regarded by Phnom Penhers as his coffee.

'God, this is just as good as I remember,' Caitlyn enthused as she quickly mixed the condensed milk with a straw into deep fried coffee beans that had been blended into ice-water.

'Type 2 Diabetes in a cup!' Janice quipped.

'Oh, don't ruin it, Mom,' Caitlyn groaned.

Janice glowed a little at hearing her call her Mom. These days it was mostly Janice. They took their coffees to a noodle stall in the market and sat on wooden benches where they could smell raw meat emanating from the wet market facing them. Janice managed to eat a third of an enormous bowl of vegetables and noodles covered in soya sauce which was the most substantial meal she had been able to down in days.

'So, tell me all about the boy,' she prompted Caitlyn.

'Oh, god, I don't know if we are that kind of mother and daughter,' Caitlyn hesitated.

'Come on. Indulge me.'

'He's really good. I think he's pretty special,' Caitlyn grinned widely.

Janice could see that Caitlyn was smitten and wanted to share her joy but felt uneasy. Her daughter could have anyone on the planet. Why was she settling for Tom? He just seemed like any number of other uninspired UN clones that Janice had met over the years. He was so ... what was the word? Perfunctory. Yes, that was it. Perfunctory. She wasn't sure if a person could be described as perfunctory but it seemed like the right description for Tom. There was probably a sweatshop somewhere making guys like that.

'What's with the face, Janice?' Caitlyn challenged, noticing her frown. 'You are clearly not a fan of Tom.'

Oh no, I'm back to Janice again, she thought.

'Sorry, hon. I just want to make sure you know your worth and the many options out there before you settle,' Janice said, trying her best to be diplomatic.

'I know my worth, Janice,' Caitlyn snapped. 'Look if we are going to try and have a relationship without killing each other, you are going to need to park that obsessive need of yours to control everything. If dating Tom is a mistake, it's my mistake to make. Got it?'

'Okay, I respect that. I'll shut up,' Janice assured her. 'I suppose the curse of having a Dad as wonderful as yours means that it's going to be hard to find a man who lives up to what you grew up with.'

'We're agreed on that one. Dad sets the bar very high,' Caitlyn smiled a little.

They relaxed and sat silently while Caitlyn noisily slurped the end of her iced-coffee. Janice could have happily sat there all day watching the bustle of the market and making light conversation with her daughter but she had to get back to the shitstorm she was facing.

—

That afternoon, Janice had a call with the Cambodian Hands board. There were four board members. Kalyann; a Cambodian-Australian professor teaching South East Asian studies in the University of Melbourne, Gabriel; a retired French journalist now based in Marseilles who had reported on Cambodia for years, Vincent; a retired senior executive at a large professional services firm, and Vera; a senior HR person at UNICEF's South East Asian office in Bangkok.

It wasn't even required by law for Cambodian Hands to

have a board but Janice had been so keen to do everything so perfectly and ensure the organisation's survival if something ever happened to her that she had assembled them together years ago. Until now they had just acted as rubber stampers giving the go-ahead to her ideas without challenging them but since the two articles had come out in the *Phnom Penh Herald*, they had clearly gotten spooked and were being proactive. Vera's email tone about the need for an emergency board meeting had been far curter than Janice had ever seen from her and it was obvious that there had been some conversations between them without her.

She felt nervous as the call started. She didn't need to be worried really, she told herself. She was tough with her staff. Of course, she was. But she'd never bullied anyone in her life. Once they were all on the line, there was little small talk with Gabriel jumping right in.

'Janice, we'd like to hear your perspective on these allegations. Is there any truth in them whatsoever?'

She had always respected Gabriel. He had been utterly fearless in his questioning when she had known him in his reporting days, a skill she now felt a little worried about being on the other end of.

'Each of you know me and how I work very well,' Janice told them in what she hoped was a reassuring tone. 'We've had many staff come and go over the years. The majority of them have been wonderful but others haven't worked out as well and may have gripes. The same could be said for any long-running organisation.'

'Yes, but the specifics given in the *Phnom Penh Herald*. Are they true?' Gabriel asked.

'Come on. The people saying those things are not even

using their real names …' Janice started.

'Don't be evasive, Janice,' he interrupted her. 'You know we are asking if you really behaved as it is described?'

'Have I ever gotten worked up with my staff? Yes, occasionally.'

'Janice, this is really serious,' Vera chimed in. 'Have you called staff names and phoned them in the middle of the night?'

'Well, I've called staff outside of hours when emergencies have occurred.'

'And name calling?' Vera asked.

'Is this grilling of me really necessary? This is one newspaper article which can't even name its sources,' Janice grumbled.

'Janice, this is necessary,' Vera interjected.

'No, I've never called anyone a name. Not to anyone's face anyway,' she laughed a little nervously.

'We are doing our job as the board here and trying to protect Cambodian Hands. Please take this seriously.' There was an exasperation in Kalyann's usually calm tone.

'Okay, I'm sorry. I'm a little stressed out and perhaps I'm feeling defensive,' Janice admitted.

'How have you been managing your stress, Janice?' Vera asked.

Jesus, what was this? A fucking therapy session?

'Oh, I'm fine. You know me. This has just been time-consuming to manage and I'd really rather get things back to normal and to be able to put all of my focus on the actual work and particularly our plans around gender-based violence.'

'I doubt that'll be going ahead for some time.' Vera's tone was like a kindergarten teacher to a toddler. 'When was the last time you had a real holiday, Janice?'

'Vera, I'm fine,' Janice said tightly.

'Okay,' Kalyann interjected. 'I don't think this is very productive. Maybe the best way to do this is for us to talk to the staff directly and conduct an investigation?'

'Yes,' Vera agreed. 'That's the best way to come back and clarify with donors and others that there are no issues.'

'Fine by me,' Janice managed, feeling railroaded.

She got off the call feeling intensely angry. She wasn't sure if she wanted to cry or to punch something. She had to do something to take back control of her life. She left her office and searched around the building for her driver.

'Boran!' she shouted. Boran the driver was napping in the office kitchen and woke up with a jolt upon seeing her standing in front of him.

It wasn't a long journey and for once Phnom Penh's traffic worked in her favour. She wasn't really sure what she was going to do or say when she got there.

At the reception of the *Phnom Penh Herald*'s office, she told the girl behind the desk, 'I want to see Andre King.'

She sat on an ugly leather beige couch in the reception area and waited. When Andre came out, he was far younger than she had expected.

'Janice, at last we meet,' he greeted her with a thick, nasal Australian accent and a gloating smile. 'Come in for a coffee.'

'I won't be staying long enough. Thank you.'

'Okay, let's talk here then.' He sat down across from her and flipped open his notebook. 'I actually interviewed you a few years ago. Do you remember it?'

'No,' she said firmly. 'I can't be expected to remember every snot-nosed kid this rag sends my way.'

'Delightful!' Andre smirked at her, his voice spilling with sarcasm. He took out his dictaphone and switched it on. 'So, what did you want to talk about?'

'Get that thing out of my face. I refuse to talk on the record,' Janice snarled at him.

'Whatever you say is on the record to me, Janice,' he laughed. 'Your showing up like this is giving me a story for tomorrow, whether you talk or not.'

Janice felt the rage rise through her. This punk had some fucking nerve.

'You don't even have sources on record or any evidence and you call yourself a journalist? You think you are so fucking powerful, fucking with people's lives like this. If Cambodian Hands suffers, so do thousands of vulnerable people in this country. I insist that you write a retraction,' she demanded.

Andre rolled his eyes in contempt.

'Pathetic. Playing the "poor Cambodians" card is so predictable. You weren't exactly thinking about poor Cambodians when you were treating your Cambodian staff like crap.'

'You have no idea what you are talking about!'

'Well in that case, tell me your side of the story,' he goaded, gesturing at the dictaphone on the coffee table between them.

She felt frazzled and tired suddenly. What the fuck was she doing talking to him? She wasn't going to win this, Janice suddenly realised. It had been a stupid move to come here.

'You'll only twist my words. Your bias is clear. I'm leaving.'

She stood up and rushed out of the reception area into an open elevator without waiting for any response from him. She willed the elevator to go faster so that she could make it into the car before she broke into hot tears.

Kindly, Boran didn't mention her obvious sobbing as he silently dropped her home. She put her pyjamas on and began to boil water to make herself some tea. She managed to stop the sobs but was still feeling upset and anxious. Janice pulled at her own hair and a clump of bleached mass fell into her hands having broken as easily as dry spaghetti. It was so weak these days from neglect and cheap Cambodian shampoo. What a stupid and unsatisfying thing to do, she thought. She needed to talk to someone. What time was it in Sacramento?

'Janice, is everything okay? Is Caitlyn alright?' Liam answered her call.

'She's fine, Liam. We had lunch today, actually.'

'You sound terrible, Janice. I've been really worried about you.'

'Thanks … Thanks for worrying. I'm just so tired.'

'You have probably been exhausted for years. When was the last time you had a decent night's sleep?'

'Oh, I dunno. 1992 probably,' she uttered.

'Ah, a more innocent time. A good year for music. That wonderful mullet hairdo you had back then made for a soothing, natural pillow I'm sure,' he teased her. Hearing Liam's voice had a calming effect on her.

'That was a great mullet. I stand by it,' Janice responded with a weak laugh.

'But seriously, Janice. What's happening over there and how are you doing?' His voice turned to concern.

'It's hard at the moment. I'm worried that this isn't going to go away easily and to be honest, I'm unravelling a little, Liam,' she told him.

'Come home, Janice. Let me take care of you for a while,' Liam offered.

'That's lovely but you know I can't do that. I have to work through this.'

'You are so frickin' stubborn. Just think about taking some

time out. Please.'

'I will. I promise. Talking helps though. Hey, remind me why did I ever divorce you?' she said half-jokingly.

'Don't you remember?' Liam put on a mangled British accent in an impression of Princess Diana. 'There were three of us in the marriage. Me, you and Cambodia.'

'I think my second husband, Cambodia wants to divorce me.'

'Well, I'd call that karma,' Liam quipped.

'You asshole,' she laughed. It felt good to laugh.

They had first met in high school. They had been such different teenagers. She had been so highly strung and opinionated which made her quick to make enemies whereas he had been funny, easy-going and universally loved. The Leahys were such a big, loving and supportive family too which was the complete opposite of what she'd grown up with. She couldn't remember how exactly but at some point, they had become friends. Of course, she'd always known that he had a crush on her but it had taken them a while to become a couple. Janice had been reluctant to go there given how different they were.

'You are just more complicated than I am, but that's okay. I like that you are a firebrand. Life will never be boring with you around,' he had told her nonchalantly when she protested against his advances.

She had eventually given in to his pursuit after 3 a.m., at a house party during the summer before their last year in high school. Someone put on a Mamas and Papas record as the party was winding down and people were passing out asleep. Janice was getting her things and getting ready to go home when Liam got on his knees and serenaded her drunkenly to The Mamas and Papas's song 'Dedicated to the One I Love'.

He couldn't sing a note but his goofy, unselfconscious operatics to such a tender and emotional song made Janice and everyone else who witnessed this display howl with laughter. She had let him walk her home that night and they made out furiously on her doorstep. It was lovely thinking of them back then. It was as if they were characters in a book she had read.

She had loved Liam profoundly but she should never have married him. She hadn't been a good wife. Good wives were women like her mother who were fine being nothing else. She had spent their marriage scrapping for a life for herself outside of their relationship. For the first few years, it had been the ordeal of getting herself through dental school and paying her way through it by working all manner of gruelling side jobs from waitressing to packing sandwiches in a factory to cleaning houses. When she finally qualified, she quickly found that staring down rich people's mouths all day made her miserable even if it meant that she was able to make a comfortable living for the first time in her life. Her bliss at becoming a mother helped to shelve her nagging feelings of dissatisfaction temporarily but then one evening when Caitlyn was still only a few months old, she and Liam were channel flicking when they landed on a harrowing documentary about Cambodia by the Australian journalist, John Pilger. Janice had never thought of herself as a particularly political person but she was gripped. In-depth thoughts about Cambodia began to preoccupy her as she went about everyday tasks and looked after the baby. Images of the piles of skulls that the documentary had shown in the Killing Fields started to enter her dreams. When she started looking into ways to help and learned about the country's need for volunteer dentists, Liam was cautiously supportive even if he didn't really understand why it was so important to her.

When they had finally divorced, Janice told herself that in divorcing Liam, she was finally setting him free from all of her complications and bullshit. She knew that she hurt him deeply but he had never once gotten angry at her. He simply said with an unreadable face, 'If you need to be in Cambodia, you need to be in Cambodia.'

It was still only 9:30 p.m. but Janice got into bed with her tea and her iPod. She turned on The Mamas and Papas and closed her eyes, hoping that the music would somehow be able to drown out the rest of the noise in her head.

16

Tom woke up on Monday morning in a Valium-induced fog. The crash had rattled him. It shouldn't have been such a shock. It was so normal to hear about car crashes in Cambodia but of course he had never really thought about it happening to him. His mind had been jumping around after he got home from Sihanoukville and he needed to take two Valium to eventually pass out but now it was proving hard to shake the effects of the drug.

He pressed snooze on his phone alarm several times, sacrificing the slivers of time that he would usually have spent showering and ironing his shirt for work. After pushing himself to get to the office, he spent the day slumped at his desk in a wrinkled shirt downing coffee in the futile hope that it would motivate him.

Overnight, a sprawling bluish-purple bruise had sprung up around the cut on his eyebrow he got in the crash. He felt like a battered housewife lying to his colleagues, saying that he got it when he fell in the gym. But at least it seemed to make people keep their distance. His much-needed solitude was disturbed when Kerstin in Geneva called him just when he was counting down the last hour until it was an acceptable time to leave the office.

'Hi, Kerstin.'

'Hello, Tom. This is Kerstin speaking.'

Why did she always insist on saying 'Kerstin speaking' even though he clearly had her number programmed into his phone after more than a year of working together? Jesus. Had she not heard him say 'Hi, Kerstin'? He was only thankful that she hadn't video called so he didn't have to explain his banjaxed face.

Never one for small-talk, Kerstin jumped right in. 'Tom, what are you hearing about these bullying allegations against Janice Steiner?'

Fan-fucking-tastic. Good news travelled fast.

'There was a story last week in one of the local papers but nothing has been confirmed,' Tom explained.

'It's not just the local papers there. I read about it on a German website over the weekend where they were interviewing the journalist that broke the story. Imagine my surprise. Do we know if the claims are true?'

Fucking Andre. His whole career is made by this.

'Kerstin, I just know what was reported.' Tom could hear the defensiveness in his own voice.

'This is serious, Tom, and frankly it sounds like you should have been keeping a better eye on things,' Kerstin's sing-song German voice was up and down more than usual making it apparent that she was annoyed.

'Why didn't you inform us when the story came out?' she asked. 'This represents a risk to our programme. The last thing UNP needs is a scandal connected to our work.'

'I hear you, Kerstin. Sorry,' Tom responded through gritted teeth. What did they expect from him? Janice was a loon but they were only too delighted to work with her when she was a media star and donor darling.

Kerstin continued, 'The Cambodian Hands board are having an emergency meeting to discuss it. I've asked them to send us an update as soon as any decisions are taken.'

'Wait, the board are meeting? I didn't know that. What are

they deciding?' Tom felt undermined. Kerstin had clearly initiated conversations with the Cambodian Hands board without him. Surely that was his job?

'I don't know the specifics other than that it is very serious and that Janice's position could be on the line. Either way, if this story doesn't die down, we may have to consider pulling our support for the project.'

Fuck. Fuck. Fuck. He may as well just ask …

'Kerstin, what happens to my job if UNP stop supporting the hand-weaving programme?'

'Well if the project was gone, your role would be gone too so that would be something we'd have to work out.'

She sounded so ominous.

'For the moment. We need you to keep a closer eye on the situation and send us any updates as soon as you have them.'

'Okay, got it.'

Tom's stomach was twisted into a knot by the time the call ended. He was livid at the whole situation and especially livid at himself. Why hadn't he thought this through properly when he had first learned that Andre was writing about Janice? Like an idiot, he had just assumed that nothing would come of it.

If his job was finished, he'd have to go home to Galway. The shame of it. He hadn't even managed to save much money because he'd been enjoying the Phnom Penh lifestyle so much.

He had left Galway for Geneva four and a half years ago determined to make it so that he'd never have to live there again. Everyone had been so impressed with him leaving to go off and work for the United Nations.

Galway was to blame for his friend, Herpe's death, Tom felt. It was easier to blame Galway than to think about his own shoddy treatment of Herpe. Herpe's death had turned Tom's indifference about Galway into something close to hatred and fuelled his determination never to end up back there. It had happened in his final year of college, when the recession was at its most misery-inducing. While Rob was off fathering children and Tom was studying in Dublin, dousing himself in the tastes of his more sophisticated, political and ambitious college friends, Herpe stayed home in Galway working in a phone shop. The three of them were living very separate lives but Herpe insisted on trying to bring them together as often as he could. Tom would have happily let the relationships fade out if Herpe hadn't been so determined. He would text incessantly, pushing for him to come home for a night out until Tom would eventually give in to him whenever he felt sufficiently bad about the amount of time that had lapsed since they had last seen each other. Tom would need to pump himself with booze on those nights to tolerate the inane chatter with Rob who in Tom's eyes had become something of a housebroken bore focused on little more than producing babies and to endure Herpe's well-worn tales from the 'good old days' when they were at school together. The gulf between them felt self-evident but Herpe insisted that Rob and Tom were still his 'best mates' and Tom went along with it to spare his feelings.

Many people their age in Galway were emigrating to places like Australia and Canada at the time, as money and jobs were so hard to come by. Herpe talked about going to teach English in Dubai but it didn't seem like anything more than talk as he didn't have any kind of plan or be in any way focused on getting the money together.

The last time Tom had seen him, Herpe had turned up at Tom's student accommodation in Dublin uninvited, insisting on a night out. Brandishing two half-drank bottles of Buckfast, a fortified wine beloved of Galwegians as a cheap and easy way to get drunk, Herpe was jolly and persistent. He begged Tom to come out with him to Copper Faced Jacks, a notorious Dublin nightclub known for its cheesy music and the generally unhindered behaviour by drunken revellers there in everything from sex to fighting. Tom hadn't been at all happy to see him. He had been in the middle of a hefty college assignment and was exasperated at the unexpected invasion of his space and time which may have been easier to withstand if he hadn't felt so strongly that he had outgrown the friendship and was in need of a way out of it.

'Come on, man. Sure, I'm probably moving to Dubai soon and this could be our last night out together for ages,' Herpe had pleaded with Tom.

'I can't, Herpe. I have work to do. You can't just turn up on my doorstep and expect me to be ready for a drinking session,' Tom had responded, irritated, refusing the bottle of Buckfast he handed him.

'Poor form, man, poor form. More Buckie for me, I suppose,' Herpe said, as he took a swig from the bottle with a pasted-on cheery look upon his face. 'Will your housemates mind if I crash on the couch tonight?'

'I'm sorry, man. They are kind of dicks about stuff like that. You can't stay here,' Tom lied. The truth was that Tom was embarrassed. His housemates; one of whom was the son of a former Taoiseach and another who was the head of the university debating team wouldn't exactly have much in common with a Buckfast-downing guy named after a sexually transmitted disease who worked in a phone shop.

Tom had pushed Herpe to get the last bus back to Galway that evening. Five weeks later on a Saturday night while out drinking in Galway city, Herpe threw himself into the fast-flowing waters of the River Corrib. Rob had called while Tom was walking through the college campus and told him the news through unrestrained sobs down the phone. Maybe it shouldn't have been a shock, Tom would later reflect. Suicide in their community especially among young men was nothing new but he hadn't seen it coming. Apparently, none of Herpe's other friends or his family had either. Tom wanted to feel sad but the only emotion he could summon was pure volcanic anger.

'Clichéd little fucker throwing himself into that fucking river like so many other drunks on a night out. Why the fuck didn't he go to Dubai like he fucking said he would? That little fucking asshole!' Tom had screamed violently down the phone at Rob, not caring about the shocked looks that he was getting from students nearby having their lunch on the lawn in front of the science building.

The prospect of having to move home unemployed and live with his parents again at twenty-eight years old, in Galway of all places, was fucking humiliating to Tom. He had worked too hard and come too far for assholes like Janice and Andre to come along and fuck up his plans.

He needed to talk to someone. He needed comfort. Seeing Caitlyn would relax him and help him think through what to do. He texted her and they made a plan for him to call over to hers.

'How was your day?' She kissed him hello less than an hour later. The gash on her shoulder was covered up with a large plaster and her face was covered in more makeup than he had ever seen her wear in order to cover up marks from the accident. He felt a twinge of guilt. Thank god she hadn't been badly hurt.

'About as painful as getting a spinal reconstruction,' he groaned, scooping her into a hug. 'How was yours?'

'I'm so glad you texted,' she said putting a pot of water on the hob to make tea. 'I had kind of a crazy day. Not a bad day really but it's just given me a lot to process.'

When they sat down on her couch with cups of peppermint tea, Caitlyn launched into a lengthy retelling of the hours that she had spent with Janice and how a discussion of the bullying allegations had evolved into their first ever honest conversation about their relationship.

Tom felt a little frustrated as she talked. He had been hoping to unload on her about his job worries but obviously her family stuff was more intense, and he would have to give it precedence. He supposed that was what a relationship was; putting your own needs aside for the other person's. He nodded supportively as she outlined the specifics and analysed what she and Janice had said to one another.

'I still have lots of issues with her but it did help me understand a bit more where she is coming from. It feels really good but bizarre if you get me?' Caitlyn was saying. 'I'm still feeling quite worried about her with all this bullying stuff though.'

'Yes, how is she with all of that stuff?' Tom asked his first question in the conversation.

'She's kind of fine actually. She's so strong and is continuing as if it's business as usual.'

There was more than a hint of admiration in Caitlyn's voice. 'She says that the allegations are bullshit and that it will all blow over.'

'Ugh, I don't know about that,' Tom said. 'My HQ says that the board of Cambodian Hands are meeting to discuss it. Plus, I learned today that UNP are looking closely at whether or not to keep the hand-weaving programme. I'll be out of a job if they don't.'

'Oh, no. That's awful but I'm sure nothing will come of it. She says none of it is true and I believe her.' Caitlyn patted his arm.

Tom felt a surge of irritation. When did Caitlyn become so taken with Janice? Yesterday she didn't have a good word to say about her.

'I'm not so sure,' Tom muttered.

'Wait, what?' Caitlyn looked at him in disbelief and lifted her hand swiftly from his arm. 'You actually think she bullied those people?'

'It's possible, Caitlyn,' Tom said flatly.

'You barely even know her.' Caitlyn's big blue eyes were filled with hurt.

'That's true but even I've seen some pretty weird behaviour on her part.'

'Weird behaviour is one thing. She's intense and infuriating. I know that more than anyone.' Caitlyn's voice was rising. 'But she's not a bully. She cares so much about Cambodians.'

'Well, if that's the case then why would they lie about her?' Tom knew that he was probably being an asshole but he couldn't stop himself. She needed to see the truth.

'I don't know. She's been so critical of the UN and NGOs lately. A lot of people could have a motive to pay them off.'

'Seriously, Caitlyn?' Tom practically snorted. He wasn't holding back now. Maybe Caitlyn was a bit of a crazy bitch like Janice after all. 'You realise you sound like a conspiracy theorist?'

'You realise you are being an asshole?' Caitlyn retorted, her face was red and he could tell that she was holding back tears.

'If I'm being an asshole maybe it's because I'm probably going to lose my job because of this shit and there's not a lot I can do about it and the least you could do is be sympathetic,' he fumed.

'Look, if the worst happens and I really don't think it will, it will be an inconvenience,' Caitlyn countered. 'But you'll be fine. You are so employable. You can just get another job.'

'I don't want to go applying for jobs. The plan was to do well here and then get promoted somewhere else. This fucks up my whole career trajectory!' He was close to shouting at this stage.

'Your career trajectory? Jesus, Tom,' she gasped. 'If that's your attitude, you really need to get some perspective. You have so many opportunities. For Janice, what would she do? Her whole life is here.'

He needed to get the fuck away from her before he said some stuff he really regretted.

'Look,' he put his barely drunk tea down on her coffee table. 'I'm going to leave. Let's catch up later in the week, Okay?'

'Oh, don't do that,' she put her hand on his shoulder. 'We're just getting worked up. It's obviously an intense situation for both of us. Let's just watch a movie or something.'

'No, I'm sorry. I need some space.' He avoided looking at her directly. 'I'll call you.'

He quickly kissed her on the cheek and walked out of the place before she could stop him.

Tom was fuming and felt the energy pumping through him. He really needed a drink but he had no booze at home after being away all weekend. He didn't really want to go home anyway. He needed to be somewhere distracting. He took a motorbike taxi to a bar called Top Mango on Phnom Penh's

278 street, known as 'Golden Street' which was lined with touristy bars and restaurants. Top Mango was the kind of place that Phnom Penh's NGO and UN crowd typically avoided given that it was always full of backpackers. No one he knew would be there on a Monday night.

The rooftop was busy and he had to push his way through crowds of twenty-somethings wearing harem pants with no shoes on, dancing to an ear-piercing Katy Perry song to get to the bar. He parked himself on an empty stool which was placed practically on top of a Christmas tree. He'd nearly forgotten that it was Christmas in a few weeks. It was easy to do that in Phnom Penh. When it was still 30 degrees every day, it really didn't feel like the middle of November. Buddhists didn't celebrate it so very few places even had holiday decorations. He should probably figure out some Christmas plans at some stage.

The cliché of sitting on his own at a bar when he was feeling pissed off wasn't lost on him but the whiskey began to provide comfort as soon as he started to drink it. The cheerful Cambodian barman told him that today was 'double-up Monday' and handed him a second drink for free. He drank quickly and by his fourth whiskey he could feel that the 'buy one, get one free' system was helping him get well and truly sozzled.

It amazed him that these backpacker places were even cheaper than regular Phnom Penh bars. How was tourism ever going to truly help to elevate Cambodia's economy if it mostly consisted of backpackers spending no more than three days and a few hundred bucks in the country? He made a mental comparison to Galway where older American tourists came in their droves every year on nostalgia trips to the land of their ancestors spending thousands of euros in the process. As he imprecisely pondered Cambodia's tourism strategy, he felt a tap on his left shoulder. A sallow skinned brunette with a large, silver nose-ring stood in front of him, giggling.

'Hi there. My friend wants to know why you are in a back-packer bar dressed like a banker?'

God these backpackers were so fucking juvenile, he thought.

'I'm dressed like this because I work. Not everyone is on a gap year,' he snarked at her.

'Oh, my god. You actually live here? That's so cool. What do you do?' She had a faint accent that he would have placed as South African or maybe Dutch. He couldn't be certain.

'I work for the UN,' he told her. His voice softened slightly as he took the time to get a better look at her, belatedly realising that this girl was absolutely smoking hot.

She had caramel-coloured skin and looked like she was of Middle-Eastern heritage. She was wearing a tiny red mesh top that looked like a bikini top made out of a fisherman's net. Her boobs must have been fake as they were way too round and high and there was no way they could be that big naturally because she had a tiny, little flat stomach which was exposed entirely.

'You work for the UN? Wow. I'd love to do something cool like that when I finish college,' she slurred her words slightly.

'What are you studying in college?' Tom asked, keen to keep the conversation going.

'Oh, nothing yet. I'm on a year out after school.'

'Very cool,' Tom responded. 'So, which one of your friends wanted to know about me?'

'Ha. I have a confession to make,' she giggled looking sheepish. 'Actually, it was me who wanted to know.'

'Oh really, it was you, was it?' Tom teased. 'Take a seat'. He pulled another stool up next to his.

He was probably staring at her boobs but he couldn't help it. She was so exceptionally sexy. She was clearly hammered. But so was he or he was at least on his way there. He bought another whiskey for himself and a gin for her.

'Hey, what happened to your face?' She touched the cut and bruise above his eyebrow noticing it for the first time.

'Want to kiss it better?' He asked her. She giggled and leaned in to him and they began to kiss.

She ran her hand softly on his thigh and his dick instantly sprung to attention.

'So, do you live nearby?' She whispered in his ear as she began to suck his earlobe.

Fuck, that felt good.

'Mmmmm,' he moaned. 'Wait, how old are you?'

'I'm nearly nineteen,' she told him as he put his hands on her lower waist. He could feel the top string of her thong knickers underneath the thin material of her skirt. He had to get her naked. He had to see those boobs.

'You are not even old enough to become a pilot,' he nuzzled into her neck.

'Why would you want me to become a pilot?' she asked. 'Let's get out of here.'

'You're just a kid,' he said breaking from the kiss and looking at her.

She looked at him suggestively. 'I'm really not. Let me show you.'

She rubbed her hand lightly on his crotch again.

'Okay, then.'

Fuck it, he thought. Who was he to argue?

'Let's go to my place.'

17

The next few weeks involved several calls with Geneva about UNP's future involvement with Cambodian Hands and the weaving project. To Tom's irritation these calls were scheduled with very little notice and typically late at night Phnom Penh time. 'Conference call colonialism' was his private term for the European office's habit of scheduling calls without any consideration of the time difference. He was proud of how witty that was. It would have been a good one to tell Caitlyn actually, he thought as he sat at the desk of his home office waiting for Geneva to call him.

He had received several missed calls from her since that Monday evening in her place, all of which he had ignored, as well a text message which had come in late on the same night when he was pre-occupied with the backpacker from Top Mango.

I'm sorry that things were so awful tonight. It's a stressful time for both of us and the crash has probably made things worse. I didn't mean to be flippant about your worries about work. That was unfair of me. Would love to see you soon and get things back to normal. Xx

Without knowing how to respond, he had ended up ignoring it. He didn't really know how to deal with it and hadn't had a chance to think about it properly. Geneva had started taking over Tom's life with these incessant night calls about Cambodian Hands and he couldn't let himself get distracted by thinking about Caitlyn when he was so busy. They got Tom to write several inane papers. So far, there had been one on all of the media coverage of the Janice story, highlighting any mentions of her connections to the United Nations. Another paper they requested was a Strengths, Weaknesses, Opportunities, Threats analysis of the hand-weaving project. They fucking loved SWOTs. A third paper was a detailed timeline covering all the previous engagements Cambodian Hands had with the UN.

He had been given urgent deadlines for all these papers and they were sent to senior UN folk to supposedly help their decision-making on whether to keep their involvement with the hand-weaving project but there was still no sign of any kind of result. Tom was getting incredibly frustrated about their paralysis. He hated being in limbo about whether he had a job or not but knew his future prospects depended on his ability to deliver what they wanted so he had to jump to it and get working whenever new demands came.

That evening's call was with Kerstin and three of the more senior UNP folk. He doubted any of them had even set foot in Cambodia or could distinguish the country from any number of fucked up places in their vast portfolios. The video-call came in and through his connection, he could see the four dullards in suits in a white, non-descript meeting room. He was quietly amused at the irony of them sitting in front of a poster for one of UNP's zero-waste environmental projects while each of them sipped coffee through disposable cups and there were at least two plastic water bottles on the table.

'So, the big development is that the Cambodian Hands board have finally taken a decision and they have put Janice on a sabbatical of sorts,' Kerstin began.

'Wait, so is she suspended?' Asked one of the dullards, whose name Tom couldn't remember.

'Not suspended but the sabbatical isn't voluntary and it's quite open-ended,' Kerstin answered.

'Well, this is great news. So, we can continue working with them and avoid any potential scandals,' Tom jumped in.

'Well, not quite,' Kerstin put ice on his enthusiasm. 'If Janice is on a sabbatical, that doesn't necessarily mean that the system within the organisation that caused the problems has improved.'

'What kind of system would you want to see them adopt?' Tom deliberately over-emphasised the word system.

'We just need to be sure the risk is fully eliminated before we can continue working with them,' came her response.

These people don't have a clue what they want, Tom thought.

There was a slight silence before one of the dullards asked, 'Tom, will you write another paper weighing up the potential risks of staying involved even without Janice and start to outline what kind of safeguards we would want them to implement?'

'Yes, of course,' Tom practically grunted. This was never ending. He could write papers forever but they would need to take a definitive decision at some point.

'And could you send it to us before the weekend?'

When the video-call finished, Tom felt relieved that it was over but the thought of rushing together another paper made his already-tense neck muscles tighten. He was falling behind on his everyday work because of these calls and demands. He glanced at his phone and saw that he had a new missed call from Caitlyn and a text message.

Okay so I think it's shitty that you haven't responded to my text or been in touch. We both said nasty things including you making some very hurtful insinuations about my Mom. You said after the car crash that you are here for me. Where's that guy?

He couldn't deal with this drama right now. His office; converted from one of the spare bedrooms in his villa was far too big for a one-person office but the accumulation of take-away delivery boxes from all of these night calls was helping it seem less vast. Thankfully the maid was coming tomorrow, he thought. He sat at his laptop feeling unmotivated and contemplated ordering food.

His phone bleeped again. Seriously, Caitlyn?

He then looked down and saw that it was actually from Joey. He and Andre were heading for a Kobe beef steak at La Boulangerie to celebrate Andre being promoted to an Editor role at the *Phnom Penh Herald*. Tom winced at the idea of seeing Andre but felt a twinge of temptation at the prospect of Kobe beef in Phnom Penh's best restaurant. It had been a while since he had eaten something that wasn't from a takeaway box.

No, he told himself. Go for a swim and then get stuck into the paper. When he first moved into the villa, he had swum almost every day and appreciated the massive luxury of having a private pool but lately he'd practically forgotten it was there.

His swimming trunks felt tighter than when he had worn them last in Sihanoukville. He was starting to get a bit of a gut. He supposed it was inevitable that the booze and the Phnom Penh lifestyle were taking their toll. He shuddered at the thought of himself looking like a fat old sexpat on Street 51 and vowed to work out more.

Swimming lengths up and down the pool, he was careful to avoid the low-flying bats swooping down just above the water. The repetition of the movement forced his brain to enter into the thoughts he'd been avoiding.

What the fuck was he going to do about Caitlyn? If he was honest with himself, he missed her. But he wasn't sure what he wanted. He liked her but did he really want the hassle of the relationship? The whole thing was so messy. Caitlyn being Janice's daughter, Janice being the reason that his job was possibly on the line. Since when had he been the kind of guy who had a girlfriend anyway? Before Caitlyn he had an uncomplicated, happy life in Phnom Penh. This was his way out. He finished his swim feeling good about his decision. This was the right thing for both of them. He knew it.

He really didn't feel like starting another paper tonight after all. Maybe he could put it off until tomorrow and then blast through it. He did his best work under pressure anyway. He deserved a beer after all the bullshit Geneva were putting him through, didn't he? He told himself he would just go meet the boys for one drink after their dinner, but he only half believed himself.

Andre and Joey were on the city's riverside in one of the more touristy dive bars when Tom came out to meet them. A Khmer band were playing the jaunty guitar, psychedelic rock reimagining of 1960s Cambodian music that was becoming a hallmark style for emerging local bands. Joey and Andre were several beers in and quite drunk by the time he found them.

'It's the dark horse!' Andre greeted him loudly.

'Hey, man,' Tom put on a jovial demeanour.

'Let's get you a drink,' Joey slapped him on the back and then disappeared to the bar.

'Dark horse indeed. How are ya, mate?' Andre shouted over the music.

'Yeah, not bad.'

Tom knew he shouldn't take the bait but found himself

doing it anyway. 'So why am I such a dark horse?'

'Ha! I didn't know your little fire crotch was Janice Steiner's daughter. Did I? You kept that quiet.' Andre sounded amused. 'Joey just told me over dinner. Of course, now it all makes sense. This is why you wouldn't talk to me about Janice.'

'Oh, that's all ancient history now.' Tom was keen to change the subject. 'So, tell us about your promotion?'

Andre launched into a self-aggrandising retelling of how the *Phnom Penh Herald* editor was thrilled with his work on the Janice story and how many international media outlets had called Andre and the paper asking about the story, and how they had offered him a news editor role as they were worried he would leave. Tom zoned out as much as possible while nodding along to the details. He gratefully chucked back his beer when Joey finally arrived back with it after what seemed like weeks.

The two boys engaged in a lively chatter which seemed mindless to a far soberer Tom. Joey was recalling the details of a night out that they had a few weeks ago when Tom had been busy with Caitlyn. Andre had spontaneously stolen an unattended tuk tuk and they had drunkenly joyridden it around the Boeung Keng Kang 1 area for hours before dumping it in the Mekong river.

Tom had missed the 'best night ever' they both told him repeatedly. He smiled and fake laughed at the appropriate times but Tom felt bored and a little disgusted by them. They just seemed so juvenile. These guys were both in their 30s. Had neither of them thought about the Cambodian driver who needed that tuk tuk to make a living? Had they always been such idiots? Maybe he'd always been too drunk in their company to notice. He found Andre particularly obnoxious as he howled with laughter retelling how they had driven the tuk tuk past the dictatorial Prime Minister's house barefacedly violating the no tuk tuk rule for the surrounding boulevards.

Tom was regretting coming out. Pretending to go to the bathroom, he slipped out the bar's front door and jumped into one of the many tuk tuks waiting outside. He felt an intense relief at being out of there. They were so fucking hammered that they won't even notice, he thought. As the tuk tuk pulled past the white lighting framing the outline of Royal Palace, Tom reached into his pocket to check his phone and realised he didn't have it.

Fuck. He contemplated ignoring it and not going back for it until the morning but this was Phnom Penh and it would be sold off within hours if it had been pickpocketed. He reluctantly asked the driver to turn around and rushed back into the bar.

'Ah there he is. We thought you had done an Irish goodbye on us, buddy!' Joey exclaimed.

'Who me? No chance.' Tom quickly scanned around the place for his phone.

'Looking for this?' Andre grinned at him holding out his phone. 'Be careful, mate. You don't want this getting into the wrong hands.'

Tom grabbed it from him gratefully. He looked down to see another message from Caitlyn.

I have no idea if this is how you normally treat people when you are in relationship but if so, you will end up a very lonely, unhappy person. If you were hoping to hurt me then you have succeeded. I have pride and you won't be hearing from me again.

Oh fuck. The message gave him a jolt. Was he ready for that kind of finality? He wasn't sure. He scrolled through his phone to her contact details and almost pressed the call button before stopping himself. This wasn't the right time or place and anyway he had made up his mind and he just had to stick with it.

'I think it's your round, mate.' Andre gestured to his near-empty glass.

Tom dutifully ambled his way up to the bar feeling pained.

18

Caitlyn had assumed that it was just a shitty fight that would blow over. She and Tom had a real connection. They were passionate people and things had just gotten a bit intense, that was all. He was probably just getting his space. He would get in touch.

She told herself to be patient and that he would call but it was hard not to obsess about him. She was fixated on her phone. Every time it beeped, she willed it to be him. When it inevitably wasn't, she felt a plunge of disappointment and then irritation at Ella, her Dad or Lucy or whomever else had the nerve to text her. She had never felt less sexual in her life, but she masturbated furiously because she found that the functional orgasms were the only way that she could her knock herself to sleep.

She was starting to look like shit from lack of sleep. She stopped putting on eye-liner even though without any definition on her eyes she probably looked like she was decomposing. She would love to be one of those women for whom heartbreak made them lose their appetite and lose weight. By contrast, she felt like it had given her a tapeworm and she was constantly ravenous. She felt unmotivated to cook or go out so instead, she spent several evenings at home eating full tubes of Pringles until they gave her a headache.

After a few days of no contact from him, she caved and called him again. She let the phone continue ringing until the very last ring but he didn't pick up. Disappointed, she hastily text him an angry message criticising his lack of contact. It felt marginally more dignified to be angry than to be hurt.

Again, he didn't respond. Later that night, she sent him her third text message saying that he wouldn't be hearing from her again. It was pathetic but she knew it was a last ditched attempt for him to suddenly say *No. Don't cut off contact. I love you.* When she still didn't hear back, it became apparent to her on an intellectual level that it was over but her emotions would be slower to catch up.

She gave herself a mental pep talk and decided to submerge herself in work. Caitlyn anticipated that her colleagues would ask her about Janice but so far no one had mentioned it. Even Vic hadn't said a thing. Caitlyn theorised that perhaps Pheary had told them not to and was quietly relieved.

Caitlyn was making an effort to check in more with Janice since the Cambodian Hands board had put her on sabbatical leave while they investigated the bullying claims. Janice was very up and down about it all, flipping from casual and confident one minute to angry and remorseful the next. She was still strongly denying that she had ever treated her staff as badly as the newspapers claimed. Caitlyn believed her. As flawed as Janice was, she didn't believe that her mother could be abusive.

At the staff meeting that Friday morning, Pheary told the team that she was going into Prey Sar prison to visit the land activist, Savat Nou who was still languishing there without a court date after several months. Caitlyn spontaneously volunteered herself to join her, feeling the need to get out of the office and distract herself from thinking about Tom. She could see Vic's punchable face looking on disapprovingly as Pheary agreed to her coming but for once he stayed silent.

After a short drive to the outskirts of Phnom Penh, she and

Pheary arrived at Prey Sar. Her prison reference points from television shows and some reading about Prey Sar's appalling conditions in Save Cambodia's reports left Caitlyn unprepared for how vile the place really was.

They came in to a reception area flanked by several surly-looking guards with AK47s who couldn't have been much more than teenagers. Pheary handed the guard behind the counter an envelope filled with notes as a 'facilitation fee' in order to get proper access to Savat. Three or four guards crowded around the envelope and counted it several times. Once they were satisfied, they guided Pheary and Caitlyn towards a meeting room on the other side of the prison complex.

Walking down the cell-lined corridors, Caitlyn had to try her hardest not to retch at the overpowering smell of sour urine and other things she didn't want to try to identify. It was so pungent that she could taste it in the air and began to cough. Pheary, in her usual dignified fashion didn't react to the smell so Caitlyn tried hastily to make her own reaction as discreet as possible and covered her mouth.

The guards led them to a small meeting room with chipped magnolia coloured paint and a loud, weak ceiling fan which acted as a useless substitute for air-conditioning. Savat was there waiting for them, sitting behind a plastic screen. When he saw Pheary, he broke into a wide smile and stood up expectantly. They greeted each other warmly in Khmer.

She usually found that Cambodians looked younger than their years but Caitlyn was shocked that Savat was only forty-two when he looked so much older. He was far thinner and more worn-looking than in the photos she had seen in the media reports too. Caitlyn was surprised to see that he was wearing a navy-blue cotton t-shirt and matching pants with white writing in Khmer. She felt a slight embarrassment at having been expecting an orange jumpsuit.

'Hello, I'm Caitlyn,' Caitlyn introduced herself in Khmer talking loudly into the microphone that was set up so they could hear one another through the screen.

'Hello Caitlyn. I studied in the US. We can talk in English if you like,' Savat responded kindly in English.

'Oh, no, you both can talk in Khmer if it's easier. Pheary can brief me later. I don't mind,' Caitlyn told him shyly.

'English is good for me. I don't get to use my brain too much these days so it will be nice,' he smiled at her.

'Savat, tell us about your conditions here,' Pheary jumped right in, taking out her notebook and pen.

'For me the main problem is sleeping,' Savat began. 'Sleeping is very difficult because there is no space so we have to sleep on top of each other or with our arms over each other or breathing on each other.'

Caitlyn took notes quickly while Pheary nodded sympathetically.

Savat continued, 'But really, I'm one of the lucky ones. I am very fortunate to have many people come to see me and help with money. The guards here need money for everything from water to soap and because I have some help it's easier for me than lots of the other men.'

Pheary continued to nod as if it were all normal. 'How is your health, Savat?'

'I have a rash on my leg.'

He lifted his leg on top of the table and pulled up his pants to show what looked like severely raw skin with angry-looking scabies on his lower calf. Caitlyn winced at how painful it looked. Pheary indicated to her to photograph it and Caitlyn did her best to get a clear image pushing her phone up against the plastic screen.

'My heart condition is okay though as I am taking my medicine every day,' he continued.

'What about beatings?' asked Pheary. As she spoke, Caitlyn noticed for the first time that there was a faint bruise on Savat's cheek.

'Nothing very bad,' Savat said quietly. Caitlyn noted the guard in the corner in the room who was clearly trying to monitor the conversation even though she doubted that he spoke English.

'Okay. We're very glad to see that you are doing well,' Pheary told him. 'What's your lawyer saying about the court date?'

'They still haven't given my lawyers a time. They said before the end of the year is unlikely at this stage,' Savat sounded properly dispirited for the first time.

'Okay.' Pheary looked exasperated. 'We'll keep working on it. Is there anything else you want to share with us?'

Savat looked emotional. 'When my family come to visit me, we can only read each other's lips because of the huge glass barrier in the visitation room. My daughter is only eight years old. I want to be able to hear her voice. It's awful. I really want to keep up with the news and about what's happening with our land but they won't let me listen to the radio.'

'I'm sorry, Savat. That's unacceptable. We will raise this with the head of the prison,' Pheary said kindly.

'Thank you,' he said.

Their short visit was closed abruptly by the guard in the room who began to brusquely usher Caitlyn and Pheary out. They hastily said goodbye to Savat, and Pheary told him she'd be in touch soon.

'I am so grateful for your help,' he told them, his voice beginning to crack.

Pheary spent the journey back to the office talking on the phone in Khmer to Savat's lawyers and leaving voice messages for the head of the prison who the guards said was unavailable in person.

Caitlyn sat in the backseat and as the jeep stalled in heavy traffic, she reflected on Savat's harrowing situation. She felt like crying thinking of him in that foul place missing his family and having no basic comforts. He was probably suffering all kinds of beatings and deprivations that their brief conversation hadn't captured. She scolded herself for having let herself get so worked up about trivial things like Tom fucking Fenton when there were people facing real issues.

Vic approached her and Pheary as soon as they arrived back at the Save Cambodia office.

'How was it?' He asked Pheary while ignoring Caitlyn.

'Not good,' Pheary sighed. 'He looks awful but he's doing okay under the circumstances. There's still no sign of a court date and I'm worried about how long it's taking.'

'You know,' Caitlyn interjected. 'Maybe we should do another press release? It's been months since our last one and the international media coverage of Savat's case seems to have disappeared.'

'I don't think that's a good idea at all,' Vic said flatly. 'We have made some good strides with the government since World Press Freedom Day. A press release could set all of that progress backwards.'

'I agree with Vic,' Pheary said. 'Let's not take risks. Let's see if we can raise these issues behind the scenes a little more. I'll call the US embassy.'

Caitlyn felt frustrated and couldn't stop herself. 'What is the embassy going to do? It's awful in there and he looks really sick. Isn't there something more immediate we can do?'

'Your passion is appreciated, Caitlyn but this is the way we are moving forward,' Pheary's tone was sharper than usual and Caitlyn stopped herself from pressing further.

Vic practically gloated at her and she felt a visceral rush of hatred for him. What a fucking dick he was.

She went back to her desk and tried to focus on the report she was editing which was a deeply academic critique of China's various investments in Cambodia that conflated with human rights. Interesting stuff but right now it felt far less important than helping Savat.

She couldn't concentrate on it at all and of course Tom still hadn't text her. She started reading again about Savat's case. He had been peacefully protesting against bulldozers from a Chinese corporation. He didn't have any kind of weapon on him and yet they were accusing him of 'intentional violence'. It made her so angry that a government like Cambodia's could treat its own people so terribly.

She opened up a blank word document and typed a few paragraphs capturing her thoughts. *Today I had the difficult experience of visiting the land rights activist, Savat Nou in Prey Sar prison ...* she typed. She screenshotted the paragraphs which talked about Savat's appalling conditions and called for his release and posted them to her Facebook and Twitter accounts. She only had about 300 followers on Twitter and her 557 Facebook friends were mostly people from college but it felt productive to at least inform a few more people of what Savat was going through.

Not long after she had posted, she was enjoying seeing

several likes and retweets emerge when her phone rang. It was a number she didn't recognise. She answered it without thinking.

'Hello, is that Caitlyn Leahy? It's Andre King here calling from the *Phnom Penh Herald*. I wanted to ask you some questions about your Mom.'

Oh, god.

'Have you any comments on your mother being put on sabbatical? What are her plans post-Cambodian Hands?'

'How did you get my number?' Caitlyn stammered.

'Actually, I believe we've met. We have a mutual friend. You've been dating Tom Fenton from UNP, right?'

'Don't call me again!'

She hung up quickly.

Caitlyn was shaking and could feel the adrenaline running through her. She hadn't been expecting that the media would call her. Fucking despicable. The worst part was the part about Tom. Would Tom actually have stooped so low as to give that asshole her number? Why would he do that? What could he possibly have to gain?

'Caitlyn!' Vic appeared in front of her as if out of nowhere and gestured at her to come in to his office. She jumped up and trailed after his quick pacing.

'Sit!' he told her, gesturing to the chair in front of his desk. She had never been inside of his office before and it struck her as eerie how minimalist it was. He had a large desk with nothing on it other than his laptop, not even a stray notebook. His walls were completely empty. Pheary's office was the same size and by contrast it was full of personality with NGO posters, Khmer art and clutter.

'What the hell is this?' He turned his laptop around to face her. On the screen was her post about Savat Nou.

Oh, fuck.

'It's my personal social media. I wanted to make more people aware of Savat's case,' she explained unsteadily.

'Pheary and I told you this morning that we are working behind the scenes on this one. It's very delicate stuff. Do you have some kind of problem understanding that?' His voice was raised and his eyes bore into her.

'I get it. But I thought it might help,' she managed, feeling her face heat up.

'What good would it do having a few kids in California or wherever knowing about Savat's case? Do you really think it would change anything?' His eyes flashed.

'But it's on my personal account,' she protested.

This seemed to particularly rile him.

'Why you feel such a need to share online is beyond me. Your generation have no discretion,' he fumed.

'While you are interning here, you represent Save Cambodia and posting about this online goes against our strategy of being quieter on this case. What if a government person sees this post and identifies that it's come from someone who is working here? Think, Caitlyn.'

'Okay, I get it. I'm sorry.' She knew she was beaten.

'I want you to remove this post right away,' he demanded.

'Okay, I will.'

She stood up to leave but he gestured at her to wait.

'Consider this a formal warning and know that if it were up to me, you'd be gone. We're already compromised because you are here and because of who you are. Don't make things worse for yourself.' The venom in his voice was startling to her.

'Okay, got it.'

She raced out of his room feeling a lump rise in her throat

and willing herself not to cry. Maybe he was right, but did he have to be such a dick about it?

19

Caitlyn loathed feeling like she was in trouble. Her Dad had rarely scolded her as a child and whenever teachers or other adults had reprimanded her, she instantly went on the defence. That same wounded, armoured feeling, like a puppy caught chewing a shoe, was how she felt now having been rebuked by Vic. She reluctantly removed the online post. In just a few short hours it had accumulated 32 retweets on Twitter and 176 likes on Facebook. In hindsight, it had probably been a bit of an impulsive move to post about Savat. However, she still felt adamant that her intentions had been good. With her confidence somewhat slashed, she passed the next week at work quietly, editing reports and writing meeting notes dispassionately. She was careful to avoid asking questions in the staff meetings or drawing much attention to herself.

Maybe Tom was the real issue and it was clouding her judgement on everything else. She still hadn't heard from him. She was so angry with him for the lack of contact and even angrier about him giving that creep, Andre her number but mostly she just missed him terribly. She read over their entire stream of text messages since the day they had met obsessively until she knew them off by heart. David Bowie's 'Space Oddity' kept automatically popping up on her YouTube account convincing her that the song was following her around to torture her like the Stevie Wonder song 'My Cherie Amour' does to Bradley Cooper's character in the movie *Silver Linings Playbook*.

It was a tired cliché but everything really was a reminder

of him. Her bed had been the location of hours of sex, coffee, wine and packets of peanut M&Ms. Her kitchen was where she had made him spaghetti Bolognese, but stupidly put in far too much chili powder making it inedible but he had choked it down anyway without saying anything. Her couch was where they had watched nearly all of Tim Burton's movies and he had talked about how much he loved Oscar Wilde. It was relentless.

On Saturday morning, she woke up to her Dad calling, reminding her that they had a regularly scheduled call on his Friday night, which was her Saturday morning.

'So, I talked to your Mom and I'm worried about her, Cait,' Liam launched in.

'I know. Me too,' said Caitlyn. 'It's not clear if this sabbatical is actually a firing.'

'I agree. Either way I think she needs a break and she needs to get out of that country,' her Dad's hatred for Cambodia was evident in his refusal to name it.

'Yes, probably.'

'So, the news is that she's going to come and stay with me in Sacramento for a while. I think you should come home too.'

'What? Wow.' Caitlyn was taken aback. 'I mean isn't that a little dysfunctional her coming to stay with you?'

'Your Mom and I have always been good friends, Caitlyn. You know that.' Liam said. 'She needs some support and Sacramento is a good place for her. It will help to take her mind off it all.'

'It's admirable of you and I agree she needs support. I suppose it's just a little weird that's all.' Caitlyn didn't really know how to feel about her parents spending time together. It was hardly normal for divorced people to act as one another's support system. Maybe the oddness of it might have been more acute if the circumstances were less intense.

'It will be fine, sweetheart. What about you coming home?'

'I dunno, Dad. I still have two more months to go in this internship.' Caitlyn didn't know what the hell she was doing at work but coming home early felt like failing.

'I suppose you have your young Irish stud muffin there too?' his tone became more playful.

'Ugh, that's over. Don't ask,' Caitlyn groaned.

'Ah, Caitlyn. I'm sorry to hear that. If he hurt you, I'll happily kick forty shades of green out of his shamrock ass,' he ventured.

Caitlyn laughed in spite of herself. 'So offensive! Don't worry, Dad. I'm fine.'

'Well, if you change your mind, my offer still stands. You know, I think we have some distant cousins who are in the IRA. I could set them on him,' Liam offered mockingly.

'You are ridiculous. I love you.'

She felt a lump in her throat as she realised how much she missed her darling Dad and how great a hug from him would be right now.

'I love you too, sweetheart. Think about coming home with Janice, hon. Please.'

—

In her desperation to talk to someone about Tom, Caitlyn had been texting Ella who had been in Bangkok for work for the past number of weeks. Her unique brand of supportive messages consisted of sending Caitlyn smutty memes and daily unsolicited pearls of motivational wisdom such as: *In the words of my late grandma who never experienced an orgasm in her life, 'Every day is a great day when you can get up and put your panties on.'*

As soon as she arrived back in Phnom Penh, Ella arrived at Caitlyn's apartment with a bottle of wine. She was looking pretty and newly tanned with red chunky statement earrings off-setting her blonde hair. Caitlyn felt a sting of jealousy at how nice her friend looked which wasn't typical of her.

'So, what exactly happened? Walk me through it all,' she prompted after hugging Caitlyn tightly.

'I don't know really. We had a fight about the shit that's happening with my Mom. We were both stressed but he was an asshole and basically implied that Janice was a bully so I got riled up too. I think we were reeling from the car accident too. I thought it would be fine and we'd just get over it but he's ignoring my messages and I think it's over. So, you heard that my Mom has been put on sabbatical right? She's basically been suspended. He would definitely know about that through his work. But he hasn't been in touch. I can't help but wonder how he hasn't managed to be in touch. Did he ever even give a shit?' Caitlyn rambled. Her words tumbled out in relief at finally getting to talk to someone.

'Okay, how long has it been?' Ella asked sipping her wine from Caitlyn's cleanest mug.

'I haven't heard from him since I saw him on Monday two weeks ago so it's nearly three weeks,' Caitlyn answered.

'I'm so sorry, Caitlyn. That's torture. What an asshole for just ditching you. So, fucking spineless,' Ella's voice held unconcealed anger.

'I know. How did I fall for such a dick? I thought he was a decent guy but clearly I was blinded.' Caitlyn tried not to cry.

'Don't be so hard on yourself. The girls and I all thought that he was this charming, eligible guy, Cait. It's understandable how you fell for him.'

Ella got animated: 'Look, you are having a shitty time all round at the moment. You need some fun and it's Friday night. Let's go out!'

Caitlyn welcomed the distraction. She showered and put on a loose black sundress that was quite shapeless but she felt too hideous to wear anything that showed her body. After weeks of intermittent crying and lack of sleep, her face was stripped of its colour. Her freckles, which she hated, seemed more prominent than usual, so she piled on extra foundation to help make herself look somewhat normal. Ella had brought her a beautiful silk turquoise scarf from Bangkok. She put it in her hair to bring some kind of colour to her washed-out face. Ella handed her a large mug of white wine, which she gulped down gratefully.

They went to Jade, a small wooden shack-like bar beloved of expats for its cheap cocktails and the fact that anyone was allowed to jump behind the bar at any moment and connect their iPod or phone to the bar's sound system to put on their own music.

The night was beginning to get started as they arrived. Ella ordered them double vodkas and red bull which Caitlyn hadn't drank since college but the familiar syrupy taste and its subsequent kick of energy elevated her mood significantly. Someone put on a playlist of 80s rock and the dancefloor filled up with people jerking about to INXS's 'Need You Tonight'. Caitlyn and Ella joined them with Caitlyn dancing mindlessly as if she was being puppeteered by the music.

The rest of the night beyond INXS became almost entirely wiped from her memory. She vaguely recalled talking to a guy at the bar. He was handsome and had very blonde hair and she remembered thinking he could easily get work playing a Nazi in a World War II movie but that saying it to him would probably be a little offensive.

Her next memory was of kissing him in a single bed and being in her underwear. But then she realised she was somehow kissing a guy who had dark hair. What the fuck?

'You know I'm not the same guy you came up here with,' he laughed as he pulled at her clitoris roughly through her thin panties.

The unexpected pain jolted her into sobriety. Oh, shit. What was happening? She felt her stomach heave as if she was going to puke. Her head was all messed up. Was she dreaming or awake? She needed to sleep. She turned away from him and crossed her arms over the naked breasts she had no memory of exposing. He grunted and she felt him spoon into her. She recoiled as she felt him place his naked and unmistakeably hard erection at the crevasse of her ass and breathed heavily. She felt a jolt of fear and moved towards the edge of the bed. She hoped that he was sleeping. She closed her eyes tightly willing her dizziness to stop. She soon passed out. She woke up later after what must have been a few hours with a dry mouth and a pounding headache that made it difficult to fully open her eyes without squinting.

She glanced around the room to see two single beds and several backpacks strewn around. A guy with dark hair was asleep next to her in the bed and another guy with almost white blonde hair who she guessed may have been the 'Nazi' was passed out in the bed across from them. A third guy was asleep in a loose foetal position on the floor. She quickly pulled on her dress which was on top of a man's pair of jeans on the floor and grabbed her bag from the nightstand. She didn't know where her bra was but it didn't matter. She just had to get the fuck out of there. Braless and with her sandals in her hand, she opened the door cautiously hoping desperately that it wouldn't wake any of them.

It was a hostel she had never been to before. Where the fuck was she? She practically ran down the stairs and sped past the reception desk without making eye contact with the girl sitting behind it until she was out the front door. Outside on the street, she was in some kind of industrial park in a part of Phnom Penh she didn't recognise. She realised her vagina felt sore as she bent down to put on her sandals. She had clearly had sex but couldn't remember it at all. Fuck.

She started to walk on the motorway avoiding speeding cars and motorbikes, unsure which direction to go in. After a few minutes, a lone motorbike taxi driver slowed as he saw her and she gratefully hopped onto the back of his bike. They drove for what seemed like hours before arriving near the Russian market which Caitlyn was relieved to recognise.

She felt rancid with the bumping of the motorbike testing her fragile stomach. She had to stop herself dry heaving. What the fuck had she done last night? Had she had sex with two guys? The thought of it disgusted her. She had never done anything like that in her life. The whole thing was honestly so patchy. She had been so out of it. Oh fuck, had they worn condoms? She had no idea.

She had a lone message from Ella on her phone. *Be safe and have fun xx*.

She called Ella as soon as she got home.

'Heyyy! You're up early,' came the jovial response.

'Ella, I'm trying to fill in the blanks from last night,' Caitlyn began, desperate for information.

'So, we were both quite drunk but you told me you were fine. You insisted on going home with that blonde backpacker.

You were all over each other. What was his name? Stefan?' Ella recounted enthusiastically.

'Oh, god. I don't remember much at all. I ended up in a random hostel out past the Russian market'.

'Oh my god. Go you! Way to get over Tom! That guy was so hot. Whoop!' Ella cheered down the phone at her.

'The whole thing is a blur,' Caitlyn responded weakly.

'Don't worry about it. You needed some fun. He seemed really nice,' Ella sounded so proud of her. She couldn't bring herself to tell her the full story. She didn't want to think about it herself.

'Yes, I suppose. I feel a bit guilty though,' Caitlyn managed.

'This drives me crazy,' Ella started getting impassioned. 'It's perfectly okay for women to have casual sex but society tells us we can't which is a complete double standard. You did nothing wrong. It's all part of the break up process. You're allowed to be a little crazy.'

Maybe Ella was right. This was normal stuff and she shouldn't feel ashamed.

'I feel so hungover,' she moaned.

'Ah, that's probably the vodka red bulls,' Ella laughed. 'We'll take it easier next time.'

'I don't think I can do a next time. I'm putting my vagina in storage for a while,' Caitlyn joked.

Ella gave a high-pitched snort of laughter. 'Ha! Even if you are walking like John Wayne, he totally was worth it. So damn hot!'

Caitlyn retreated to her bed for the day. The feelings of disgust still rippled through her. Bury it, she told herself.

She left the house after a few hours to pick up a morning after pill, which thanks to a French NGO, was only two dollars in the local pharmacy. She swallowed it down in between bites of a cheese pizza hoping that she wouldn't vomit it up.

She busied herself by watching the movie *Sister Act* which she had picked up in one of Phnom Penh's ubiquitous pirated DVD shops a few weeks prior. As a child she had an obsession with Whoopi Goldberg's musical comedy about a sassy nightclub singer who posed as a nun after witnessing her married gangster boyfriend kill someone. A preposterous storyline in her adult eyes but the 1990s nostalgia and Motown soundtrack was exactly the comforting distraction she needed. She drifted into a nap early into the movie as Whoopi Goldberg's character begins leading the nuns' choir.

—

Later that week, Caitlyn went to Janice's place to have dinner with her. Janice had made plans quickly and was due to leave Phnom Penh for Sacramento the next day. Her deputy, Sophorn had been made the temporary head of Cambodian Hands and Janice had reluctantly put an open-ended out of office message on her email account. Andre had written a piece in the *Phnom Penh Herald* about her 'indefinite sabbatical' in unbridled gleeful tones as if it were a firing, adding to the list of insults that were accumulating against her.

'It's fucking humiliating,' Janice fumed while chopping chunks of ginger to add to the noodle soup she was preparing while Caitlyn sipped a glass of wine at the large teak kitchen table.

'All the board care about is avoiding scandal. They don't actually care that there's still no proof I did anything wrong.'

'I'm so sorry. I thought the board would support you.'

'I did too. None of them are even based here anymore. They're a pack of washed up retirees who are more worried about their own legacies than doing the right thing for Cambodian Hands,' Janice vented.

She seemed so angry.

'So, what happens now?' Caitlyn asked.

'They told me it's a sabbatical while they investigate and interview staff so I suppose all I can do is wait it out. The truth will come out. It has to.' Janice sounded determined.

'Do you really think it will all die down and you'll get to come back?' Caitlyn asked.

'I do. I mean I have to, right? All I have is my reputation. What else will I do with myself?' Janice looked at her with sadness in her big blue eyes. She ladled some soup into a ceramic bowl and handed it to Caitlyn.

Caitlyn didn't really know what to say so she changed the subject.

'So, you're going to be staying with Dad? That's weird.'

'It's unconventional, of course it is. But you know your Dad and I have never given a shit about convention. It will just be a short trip and I can take stock and plan my next move. I hope this madness dies down so I can get back here as soon as possible. But it's not a bad idea to get out of here for a while'. As if to illustrate her point, Janice pressed decline on an incoming call on her phone which Caitlyn assumed was another reporter.

She sat down across from Caitlyn with her soup and looked less serious all of a sudden.

'I haven't seen your father in ages. How do I look?'

'You've looked better,' Caitlyn said truthfully. Janice's hair was looking greasy, her lips were flaky and dry and the dark circles around her eyes looked carved in stone.

'Thanks. You have definitely inherited my lack of diplomacy,' Janice laughed. 'Will you come home for Christmas?'

'I don't honestly know what I'm doing.' Caitlyn couldn't face decision-making.

'Plans with Tom?' Janice prodded.

'Nope, that's definitely over.'

'Your Dad told me. I know you don't want my advice but I really think you dodged a bullet there. He wasn't right for you. A yes-man if ever there was one.'

'Maybe.' Caitlyn smiled a little.

'Oh, and I heard a rumour about you getting into trouble at work? Fuck them. I have to say, I'm pretty proud of your rebellious streak.'

'Well, I didn't get it from Dad, did I?' Caitlyn laughed.

'Probably not, no,' Janice grinned broadly. 'You know what I always say; well behaved women rarely make history.'

'I'm pretty sure one of the feminist writers said that long before you ever did,' Caitlyn quipped.

'Yes, but unlike them, I actually live it,' Janice said mockingly.

'No arguing with that.' Caitlyn clinked her wineglass against her mother's.

20

Sacramento, California, December 2013

'How are you feeling today, Janice?' Ruth asked as Janice sat down in the armchair across from her and poured herself a glass of water from the omnipresent floral-patterned jug on the side table. Everything in Ruth's office was a little bit floral including the lavender blouse she was wearing that day which looked as if springtime had vomited on it.

Ruth was a heavy-set woman with reams of dark, curly hair and a generous bosom which made her look like she'd give wonderful hugs. Janice wasn't sure how much she was really getting out of these therapy sessions with her, if anything. She hadn't been to therapy before. It was something that she advocated for other people but had been more reluctant to do herself. The Cambodian Hands board had pushed her to go while she was back in Sacramento and she wanted to do everything she could to get herself back to Phnom Penh, and to work. The first few sessions had basically consisted of Janice filling her in on the history of who she was and the whole sabbatical issue. It was like answering a journalist's questions and then paying them extortionately for it.

'I'm okay. I'm feeling a little powerless and upset, I guess,' Janice started, taking a sip of water.

She waited awkwardly as she anticipated the next question. Ruth's strategy seemed to be to just nod wordlessly and wait for Janice to fill the silence rather than to ask any follow up questions. It was proving to be quite an effective way of getting

Janice to spill her guts.

Janice continued, 'Whenever I call Sophorn; my deputy in Phnom Penh who's now in charge, he tells me what's happening with our work but it feels frustrating that I'm not there to direct it. I'm worried about keeping the organisation going while this sabbatical drags on.'

Liam had joked about her dependency on news from Cambodia being like that of an addict, calling her phone calls to Sophorn, her 'relapses'. She had been very up and down since she arrived in Sacramento. It was hard to feel a sense of purpose without Cambodia and Cambodian Hands. The calls from the media had died down and the board seemed happy that she was cooperating, so things were kind of going in the right direction but it was incredibly hard for her to switch off and just wait around. The board were due to meet again after the Christmas holidays and take a decision on the next steps and whether she could go back to work.

'Powerless is an interesting choice of word,' Ruth observed. 'What made you use it?'

'Well, it's not just with the work stuff. I also feel powerless because I'm not able to defend my reputation and I feel powerless because I'm not helping the people I am meant to be helping, like Pagna. We should really be moving on the gender-based violence work that I was planning but instead I'm stuck here in limbo.'

'I'm hearing a strong sense of urgency from you.'

'Yes, I definitely have that,' Janice agreed. 'But only because I want to get shit done and all of this feels like an unnecessary delay.'

'It sounds like you are very burdened by responsibility.'

Jesus, this woman knew how to state the obvious.

'Yes, but well, who isn't?' Janice responded.

Ruth nodded while scribbling something into her daisy covered notebook.

'If you could wave a magic wand, what positive changes would you make happen in your life?' she asked.

'I think I'd prefer a time machine to a magic wand,' Janice laughed weakly.

'Interesting,' Ruth sat forward. 'What would you do with a time machine?'

'Oh, many things. Well, for a start, I'd go back in time and change my behaviour with my staff. I mean the claims in the media are exaggerated and make me out to be far more extreme than I have been but I think I could have been kinder at times and maybe less intense with them,' Janice mused. 'But the reality is that I don't have a time machine, so I'm left dealing with the present.'

Ruth put down her notebook and looked at her intently.

'You don't have a time machine but you do have the ability to consider the past in your future actions. You can also start to forgive yourself for actions that have already occurred. Acknowledging that there are some changes that you would make if you could is a very positive step and shows real growth.'

'Hmmm. Maybe.'

'You seem sceptical,' Ruth said.

'Yes, well … I think I've gotten very accustomed to carrying guilt. It wouldn't be easy to leave it behind.'

'What do you feel guilty about?'

'Many things,' Janice said.

'Like what?' Ruth prodded.

'My daughter mostly,' Janice admitted.

'I'm glad you brought her up. We haven't talked much about

her yet. Tell me about your relationship with her.'

'She's a wonderful young woman,' Janice smiled thinking of Caitlyn while she talked. 'I'm so proud to be her Mom but it's hard too because she was raised by her father.'

'Why is it hard?'

'I suppose I feel guilty about not being there enough for her but it made sense at the time.'

'What's the source of this guilt?'

'I dunno. Maybe society? I know I didn't fit a particular standard as a mother. I sometimes wonder did I violate some kind of natural order by letting Liam raise her. I think if the genders were reversed it might be different but I know that people judge me for not being more of a traditional mother and I judge myself for it too. We still view traditional motherhood as mandatory and traditional fatherhood as voluntary.'

'I think there's a lot in what you've just outlined that we should unpack over the next few sessions,' Ruth said.

Janice groaned internally. She thought she was here to talk about work. How had she ended up unloading all of her personal stuff?

'Tell me about your own parents. How did they influence you as a parent?' Ruth began.

'There's not a lot to say. They have both been dead for decades.'

Ruth paused again and Janice rushed to fill in the silence without even realising that she was doing it.

'My Mom had a tough life. She worked very hard for hardly any money and was treated badly by her shitty husband. It seemed like she was constantly pregnant when I was a child but she had lots of miscarriages.' Janice didn't like to think of her Mom and the tough life she had led. It made her desperately sad.

'Why was her husband shitty? I assume that's your father?'

'Yes. He was a man of the time. He was controlling and beat the shit out of her. Typical, stereotypical stuff.'

'Why do you say it was stereotypical?'

'Well, it just was, right? It's a common tale for people of my age,' Janice said matter-of-factly.

'How was your relationship with him?'

'Difficult. He fucking despised me and I despised him.'

Why was she paying $90 an hour to have this woman insist on picking at long scabbed-over wounds?

'Why do you say he despised you?'

'Well he beat me at any opportunity he could. He hated that I was opinionated and hated that I insisted on getting an education instead of focusing on bringing home money. He wanted me to be meek and obedient like my Mom and my older sister were but I wasn't going to let him rule my life.' Janice could feel herself getting upset.

'What connection could there be between your father and what happened in Cambodia?'

Janice sighed. It was so typical that the therapist wanted to connect everything and find a fucking pattern.

'There is none,' she didn't disguise the irritation in her voice. 'The two things are decades and light years apart. It was the 70s and 80s. Most people had a shitty Dad. I haven't thought about him in years.'

'Why do you want to dismiss his terrible treatment of you? It sounds like it was a tough childhood.'

'Maybe, but it's just how it was,' Janice said tightly.

Ruth cocked her head and smiled gently at Janice. 'You seem to dismiss the hard things as if they don't matter, Janice.

But everyone needs to self-care and acknowledge the difficult parts of life no matter how strong they may be as individuals. How do you self-care?'

'I don't know. I suppose I don't really self-care. I don't have the time. I have too much to do.'

'I think you are very burnt-out Janice. I think it's good that you are taking this time out even if this sabbatical isn't exactly voluntary. You have this opportunity to rest and look after your health.'

Janice nodded wordlessly, feeling emotionally drained.

'Our time is up for today but excellent work. I think we did a lot and I know it wasn't easy. I want you to continue meditating over the Christmas break. You should try to spend some time socialising and I hope you can keep the contact with Cambodia to an absolute minimum.'

Janice stood up to leave feeling relieved that it was over. Ruth walked her to the door and pulled her into a quick lavender scented hug with a pat on the back, confirming Janice's earlier suspicions about her being an excellent hugger.

'Merry Christmas and remember, you never know what's around the corner,' Ruth told her smilingly.

Janice noted the triteness of the statement but felt too tired for it to bother her. She was grateful for a two-week Christmas break from these intense sessions.

She walked from Ruth's office to a Cambodian-run donut shop a few blocks away. Although donuts weren't part of Cambodian cuisine, donut shops set up by refugee families who had fled the Khmer Rouge were very common in California. It was a little out of her way but she had noticed it on the way in and she wanted to feel some kind of connection with Cambodia.

'*Soksabi*!' Janice cheerfully greeted the Cambodian teenager with a mohawk behind the counter who was glued to his phone. He looked up at her quizzically and responded in an accent so Californian it was practically surferian.

'Sorry, my Khmer is terrible. Hella embarrassing for my parents.'

'Oh, don't worry,' she smiled. 'Mine is too and I actually live in Phnom Penh.'

'Oh, cool,' he looked down at his phone again, clearly uninterested in making conversation.

Janice was a little deflated but nonetheless bought a box of glazed donut rings which she knew Liam loved. The man still had the palate of a twelve-year-old.

She had to take the light rail train back to Liam's house as her drivers' license was expired and she hadn't yet had time to renew it. Sitting in a filthy, graffiti-covered train carriage, Janice contemplated how public transport in Sacramento really showed the city's racial and social divide. Hers was the only white face on a full train with several people seeming really down on their luck or looking unmistakably homeless. Had it always been like this? It had been so long since Janice had lived in the US that she had forgotten the depth of her own country's challenges. Was this blatantly unequal society the kind of so-called 'development' she and others were fighting so hard to achieve in Cambodia? The thought disgusted her.

She turned her attention to happier considerations. Caitlyn was arriving home tomorrow and Janice was excited to be spending Christmas with her daughter for the first time in a long time. For years she had just worked on Christmas Day. It wasn't even an official holiday in Cambodia, so she was never even alone in the office. Of course, Liam was Christmas-obsessed, and his excitement was infectious. He had completely overstocked the house with wine and food and had been playing 'A Holly Jolly Christmas' on repeat for days. He had fixed up Caitlyn's old room and bought a Britney Spears bedspread on eBay and put it on her bed to surprise her. When Janice had questioned whether Caitlyn was a Britney fan, he had laughed and told her that Caitlyn had an ironic love for Britney and considered her an unlikely feminist hero 'given everything she had come through'. Janice didn't understand the reference and felt a slight sting remembering that they shared so much that she couldn't be part of.

But in spite of the occasional strange moments, being around Liam was the only truly comfortable part of being back in Sacramento. With him, she could at least be herself. She'd long given up thinking of Sacramento as home but it seemed that the city had moved on in her absence too. The global re-cession had hit hard and gutted the place of much of its soul. Everything looked grimier than she remembered and many of the stores and restaurants that she had grown up with had gone derelict or been turned into Starbucks or Dollar Trees. So many of her old friends had moved elsewhere leaving her at a loss for people. Even her sister, Anita had moved to New Mexico with her vile republican husband, who Janice hadn't spoken to since 2004 when he referred to a Middle Eastern waiter serving them in a diner as a 'sand N-word'. She and Anita had never been particularly close but Janice had always tried to see her on trips back no matter how strained it felt and was now feeling her absence in Sacramento.

Last week, she had met up with an old friend from dentistry school, Amy, and realised how little they now had in common. The conversation had been polite small talk about their families and the old days until somehow out of nowhere it had taken a swerve onto the subject of feminism.

Chomping on a biscotti, Amy had nonchalantly stated, 'You know, I don't really see the need for feminism anymore. I mean, we've basically achieved equality.'

Janice practically spat out her green tea in revulsion.

'Oh, you think we've achieved equality, do you?' she barked across the table at Amy.

'Then why do we have more than sixty million girls denied an education all over the world? How come four out of five victims of human trafficking are women? How come one third of all women have or will experience some kind of gender-based violence? And that's not even getting me started on the gender pay gap and the lack of women in positions of power,' Janice ranted at her.

'Whoa! No need to get so worked up.' Amy raised her hands in mock defensiveness. 'I suppose given where you've been, you've seen a lot of bad stuff but what I meant was that here in *America* things are pretty much equal.'

Janice felt irrational levels of rage towards Amy and her yellow Lacoste sweater. What kind of person pays $50 more for a plain sweater just because of an infantile crocodile logo anyway? She shook her head in disbelief and with uncharacteristic restraint held back from saying anything further. Amy was clearly a lost cause. They sat in awkward silence as Amy gulped down the remainder of her chai latte as quickly as she used to down vodka when they were students. She hastily told Janice she had to hurry to her ceramics class and bolted away mumbling something about meeting for drinks soon.

Liam had howled with laughter when she recounted details of the reunion to him.

'Oh, to be a fly on that wall. Poor Amy!'

'Poor Amy?' Janice scoffed. 'You mean poor Janice!'

He laughed again.

'I'm sure you and your militant feminazi ways have given her an anecdote that she can dine out on at ceramics classes, Pilates classes and boring dinner parties for years. Generous of you really.'

Janice arrived home that evening to a spirited Liam who insisted on cooking her dinner to celebrate her last therapy session of the year.

'How did it go, hombre?' he asked her while tossing around chicken and bell peppers on what seemed like an absurdly high heat while she sat across from him at the kitchen countertop.

'Pretty good. I'm officially a manic-depressive activist,' she told him with mock cheerfulness.

'I could have told you that for free,' he quipped. 'But well done! Let's get you a margarita. We're going Mexican tonight.'

'Oh, I don't know if I could handle one of your margaritas. They're basically straight tequila,' Janice protested.

'Come on, it's Christmas. Feliz Navidad and all that.'

'Have you always been this exhaustingly jolly?' she asked.

'Yes. In fact, I think it's gotten worse with age,' he said. 'I'm very excited to see our girl tomorrow.'

'I know. Me too,' Janice smiled as she popped a salsa covered chip into her mouth. 'Incidentally, I've never told you what an amazing job you've done with Caitlyn.'

'Thank you,' Liam beamed as he poured the strawberry margarita mix into a jug. Never good-looking in the conventional sense, Liam had always been the kind of man who had 'something about him'. He had fully lost the shoulder-length, rusty-blonde hair that he had had when he and Janice were younger but he wore his baldness with confidence and when he smiled like he was now, his whole face broke into creases of joy.

Janice started: 'I wish ... '

'There's no need to say it, Janice,' Liam interrupted her. 'I am loving seeing Caitlyn become as formidable a woman as her mother is.'

Janice felt incredibly touched. He really was an exceptional man.

'You've been so good having me here too. Truly. I don't know how I would get through this without you,' she told him.

'Oh, don't mention it. Well ... actually seeing as you are mentioning it, you know I may have an ulterior motive or two,' he wiggled his eyebrows while handing her a margarita.

'You are ridiculous,' she burst into a laugh. He really was exactly the same person he had been when they were teenagers.

She sipped his industrial strength margarita and picked aimlessly at the depleting bag of chips while he continued to cremate the chicken. She had always expected that he would marry again. She knew there had been occasional girlfriends but the announcement he was engaged that she was expecting for years had somehow never come.

There hadn't really been anyone else since him. No one of actual significance anyway. She had shelved that part of herself for so long that she almost forgot it existed. Work had become her main focus to the detriment of everything else.

By the time they finally got to eat, Janice was more than a little tipsy for the first time in a long time. They laughed at how inedible his chicken had become.

'This is why you shouldn't cook while drunk on margaritas!' she exclaimed, animatedly waving around a forkful of the blackened meat.

Liam placed a hand over her hand. 'You know, I was serious

earlier, Janice. I've never been able to get over you, my darling. Can I get back under you?'

Janice howled laughing. 'Where on earth did you hear that terrible pick up line? That's a Liam Leahy hall of famer right there!

'Wait, are you serious?' her body rippled with nerves as she asked while looking at him expectantly.

'Janice, I'm very serious but only if it's something you want,' he squeezed her hand.

Fuck it, she thought as she leaned in to kiss him. Ruth and her platitudes had been right after all.

21

Tom was surprised at his sense of urgency to get home to Ireland for Christmas. He hadn't bothered to leave Asia for the holidays the previous year because it had seemed like a waste of money to fly all the way back when he had the option of enjoying a luxury few days in a five-star hotel in Bangkok with Joey and some other expat 'orphans' uninterested in flying home to be with their families.

But this year was different. He needed to get the fuck out of Cambodia for a bit. If he was honest with himself, he needed some normality. He was sick of boozing, irked with the heat, bored with girls. He wanted to wear a jumper, have a decent pint of Guinness and catch up with Ireland.

Christmas was the time when everyone came back to his hometown of Glenmora, just outside of Galway city. He was looking forward to running into people that he went to school with and getting to tell them about his life in Cambodia. He knew that it was shallow to want to show off but he had worked hard so why shouldn't he be proud of his achievements?

He was even a little excited to see his family. Phnom Penh wasn't always an easy place to buy gifts but he had done well in the Russian Market picking up imitation designer handbags and scarves for his mother and sisters-in-law, knock-off converse trainers for his older brothers, books for his Dad, and toys and 'I heart Cambodia' t-shirts for his young twin nephews.

He landed in Dublin airport groggy from the three flights but exhilarated with Chris Rea's song 'Driving Home for

Christmas' stuck in his head. The airport's arrivals were full of the Irish diaspora coming home for Christmas and he was warmed at the cheesy but touching scenes of incoming travellers having emotional reunions with their loved ones to a backdrop of festive music.

He spotted his older brother Conan in the crowd. He was looking tired, more bloated and greying since Tom had last seen him, as if he'd been surviving on a diet of nothing more than cider and chips which knowing Conan was probably accurate. They gave one another an awkward back slap resembling a hug.

'Where's Mam?' Tom asked, excited to see his mother. Josephine Fenton worshipped her youngest son and Tom, in turn adored her.

'She was wrecked with getting everything ready in the house for you, so I told her not to bother coming on such a long drive. She's getting older you know,' Conan told him pointedly.

'Oh, okay.' Tom felt a squirm of disappointment.

Conan had always been something of a dickhead and perceived Tom to be spoiled because he was the youngest. His eldest brother John was a much warmer guy and Tom had a better relationship with him. It was going to be a long two-hour drive to Glenmora with just the two of them.

As they walked outside to the airport carpark, the blast of Dublin's bitterly cold December air gave Tom a chill.

'Jesus, it's fucking freezing,' he shuddered.

'Oh, I remember coming home from Oz and trying to adjust to the Irish weather. It's a shock to the system alright,' Conan chuckled.

Tom inwardly groaned. Conan had spent a couple of years in Australia before coming home and getting married. He still made frequent references to the good old days in Bondi Beach in 2002 as if it were yesterday which Tom felt was more than a little pathetic.

'So, how's life in Phnom Penh?' Conan asked as they drove their way out of the airport on to the motorway. He incorrectly pronounced it *Nom Pen* in the assumption that the first P was silent which made Tom recoil a little.

'Pretty decent,' Tom told him. 'Still loving the lifestyle and getting to do some very interesting work with local communities.'

'And you don't pay tax at all out there, do you?'

Tom had almost forgotten how money-obsessed his brother was.

'Nope. UN staff are exempt from tax,' Tom explained matter-of-factly.

'Jaysus, it's well for you,' Conan exclaimed with a tinge of bitterness. 'I'm getting absolutely fucked for tax here. It's an absolute joke.'

Conan was some kind of engineer at a big American pharmaceutical company. Tom found it hard to believe he was doing too badly. Keen to move to a gentler topic, he asked about Conan's wife, Saoirse and their young twin boys.

'Ah grand, grand. The little feckers are now in their terrible twos and we don't get a moment's peace,' Conan grumbled.

'You guys should come visit me in Asia. The boys would love the pool in my villa,' Tom offered without really meaning it.

'Villa is it? Aren't we posh? Once you have kids and a mortgage, Tommy, it's not that easy to feck off to the other side of the world. We don't all have the freedom you do,' Conan said pointedly.

Tom was irritated. You'd swear Conan hadn't been the one making any of the decisions which had led to his dismal life. He lied and told Conan he needed to get some shut-eye as he hadn't gotten any sleep during the flights in spite of the fact that he had slept quite well after taking some of Cambodia's finest unregulated Valium. They spent the rest of the journey in silence with Tom closing his eyes and feigning sleep.

They arrived in Glenmora after what seemed like an aeon. The family home was a detached large bungalow that his parents had built in the early 1980s sitting on an acre of farmland. His eldest brother John and his wife Ciara, Conan's wife Saoirse and their children, as well his parents were all there waiting for him. His mother threw her arms around him as he walked through the door. She seemed smaller to him than she had when he had left for Cambodia. He was touched to see that she had decorated the house far beyond the level that would be considered normal in order to welcome him home. There were three separate Christmas trees; one in the dining room, one in the conservatory and one in the living room. Each room had large red ribbons draped on them like they were wrapped up Christmas presents. His mother had prepared an enormous spread of his favourite childhood meal; roast ham, cabbage and roast potatoes.

They crowded around the dinner table. The roast ham he had loved so much as a child now seemed so bland and taste-less compared to the more sophisticated meals he had become accustomed to in Geneva and Phnom Penh, but he forced it all down knowing his mother had spent hours lovingly preparing it.

His father, Terry, a kind but detached man with whom Tom had a respectful if slightly awkward relationship prompted, 'Son, tell us all about Cambodia and the great work you are doing there.'

'It's been really fascinating,' Tom launched in. 'I'm working on a project which helps rural, mostly indigenous women produce their traditional products, like baskets, and sell them to external markets. It's a great way of helping them earn money so they can stay in their communities and don't have to leave them to get work. It also means that traditional methods of production aren't being forgotten and can be passed down to future generations.'

There was a short silence as everyone waited for someone else to ask Tom a follow up question.

'Oh, right, it sounds great, son,' Terry eventually responded. 'I suppose it's a bit like roof-thatching here. It's an old traditional method and there aren't half as many people that can thatch a roof as there was forty years ago.'

'Well, not really ...' Tom started.

'That reminds me!' Tom's mother interrupted him excitedly. 'I meant to tell you, that thatched cottage near the Bray Road is on the market for three hundred thousand euro.'

'Three hundred grand for that old place? That's extortionate!' Tom's brother John said in disbelief.

The conversation then turned into a lively discussion of rising property prices and who they each knew who had bought a house, where they had bought it and for what price. Perhaps it shouldn't have surprised him but it stung Tom a bit that his family obviously had so little interest in his life in Cambodia. His mother must have identified the slight disappointment on his face. She turned to him.

'And you are safe out there, hon, aren't you? I know they have all sorts of problems.'

'I'm fine Mam, honestly. It's very safe,' he smiled warmly at her.

'I went to Thailand on holidays with the girls a few years before I met Conan. Mad place but the people were so lovely,' interjected Saoirse. Conan's wife was a sweet woman but she wasn't known for her intellectual prowess.

'People think that they are quite similar but Thailand and Cambodia have a very complex relationship actually. The two countries have had lots of rivalry over culture and land that goes back centuries,' Tom chimed in.

He could see the faces of his brothers and their wives weren't exactly riveted by his contributions and that he would probably need to pare it down to their level.

'Anyway, enough about that. What have I missed here?' He asked jovially.

'Ah, same oul shite,' Conan uttered.

Jesus, he's gotten so dour, Tom thought.

'Actually, we have some good news and we wanted to wait for Tom to be here to share it,' John began excitedly.

'Oooooh, is it what I think it is?' His mother exclaimed. 'You better not be messing with us, John Joseph Fenton!'

'It's what you think it is, Mam! Ciara's pregnant!' John exclaimed. He kissed his wife who was beaming shyly beside him. Everyone stood up from the table excitedly and hugged them both.

'I have a bottle of champagne in the shed saved for this,' Terry shouted excitedly as he rushed out of the dining room to fetch it.

This was very welcome news in the family. John and Ciara were in their late thirties and had been trying for several years to have a child. Tom wasn't sure of the full details but he imagined that IVF had been involved.

John was nine years older than Tom. In his younger years, he had been a star rugby player who played for their provincial team, Connaught. Back then, he could have had any girl he wanted, and did. Tom couldn't care less about rugby but his teenage-self had been delighted to have a local celebrity as a brother. He had enjoyed using his brother's name to get into nightclubs and he had even managed to kiss a few girls who were into rugby by mentioning who his brother was.

After a few injuries, John's hopes of playing for Ireland were never realised. Without rugby, John's ambitions seemed to gradually dissolve. He'd gotten fat and married Ciara and seemed happy enough just selling insurance and going on the occasional bland holiday to resorts in Portugal or Spain. Now that he was having a kid, his eldest brother's transition to an ordinary, boring life in Galway was complete in Tom's eyes.

Thinking about John and what he had become after being such a legend saddened Tom. It was amazing to him how people in Ireland insisted on following the same unimaginative formula in life; find a job, date someone for a while, marry them, buy a house, breed some kids. It was all just so uninteresting.

His Dad's shed champagne wasn't enough to make his family's inane baby chatter more stimulating to Tom. After about an hour, he left them, blaming jetlag which once again proved to be an unexpectedly valuable excuse. He went to bed in his childhood bedroom. It still had his much-prized poster of Kurt Cobain performing on MTV Unplugged above the bed and tickets of all the gigs that he had gone to as a teenager blue-tacked onto the walls. His mother had sprinkled lavender water on the clean sheets and the fresh familiar smell provided him with some comfort but his mind was still restless.

His thoughts turned to Caitlyn. He imagined telling her about his somewhat disappointing homecoming. What would she make of Conan's bitterness and John becoming a Dad? He realised that he was craving a conversation with her. He wondered where she was for Christmas. She was probably back in Sacramento. He took out his phone and checked her Facebook. She had changed her profile picture from the one of Talia Shire in *The Godfather* to a new photo of herself that he didn't recognise. She was smiling her slightly pouty smile and wearing a turquoise headscarf which made her gorgeous blue eyes stand out like they were in high definition. He felt a stab of longing and took another Cambodian Valium which helped him to pass out asleep.

22

The holidays at home continued in an anticlimactic fashion for Tom. Christmas Eve had once been an indulgent night out in Galway city. A big group of the people he went to school with would meet for a pub-crawl down at the bar-lined streets near the Spanish Arch by the city's waterfront. These nights would be so debauched that he had become accustomed to spending Christmas Day with a raging hangover.

However, when he had sent out a group message asking who was around and what the plan was, everyone began to list their excuses. People had a series of pre-determined dull commitments such as having to be at home to prepare Santa Claus's presents for their kids or visiting their in-laws. And so, Tom's Christmas Eve was spent watching Fawlty Towers with his parents.

Rob Kelly messaged to welcome him home. He had just become a father for the fourth time so couldn't make it out but he invited Tom to his newest baby's Christening party on the day after St Stephen's Day.

A fourth kid? Jesus Rob. It might be time for the snip. Tom had responded.

I'm creating my own football team, mate. Had been Rob's cheerful response.

Christmas Day was spent receiving uninspired gifts such as men's bath sets from his family and listening to Conan complain about topics as wide-ranging as the cost of petrol and the cost of childcare. He paid minimal attention to his family while he deliberated over whether or not to text Caitlyn and wish her a Merry Christmas. He eventually decided not to. She wouldn't want to hear from him. He was sure of that. Kind of.

By the time the day after Stephen's Day came around, Tom was itching to get out of the house and have some fun. So much so that Rob's child's Christening may as well have been a party on a yacht with Leonardo Di Caprio and a slew of super-models. In 2013 lapsed-Catholic Ireland, Christenings were less about the child entering the Catholic Church and more about the parents having an excuse to drink during the day and get free baby gifts. The Christening reception was in a non-descript local pub with battered leather couches and sludge-coloured carpets. Tom had last been there before he was old enough to legally drink as it was the kind of place that didn't bother asking kids for ID.

'Fenton! Welcome home, man!' Rob greeted him warmly giving him a big, hearty hug.

He looks like shit, thought Tom as he handed over his gift which was some baby clothes his mother had picked out. It was hard to believe that Rob had ever been Glenmora's answer to Johnny Depp. His cheap, striped shirt was stretched across his gut with the buttons fit to bust, and his forehead was lined like the inside of a copybook.

'Come and meet the baby!' Rob steered him through the crowd to where his wife was sitting with the baby girl, whom they had named Ava. Tom wracked his brain to remember Rob's wife's name. Something Irish. Niamh, Maeve or maybe Sinéad. Fuck, which was it? She was looking well for some-one who had had four kids aside from the fact that she was practically radioactive-looking from liberally-applied fake-tan. Why did so many Irish women insist on painting themselves the same colour as an orangutan? The new baby looked the same as any other did to Tom. She was draped in a white gown as was traditional for Christenings. It had always struck Tom as creepy that the Catholic Church insisted on essentially the same white virginal outfit for women at their Christenings, their communions and their weddings.

'Congratulations, guys. She's a beauty,' he told Rob and Niamh or Maeve or Sinéad.

'You remember Tom? He's living over in Vietnam,' Rob said to his wife.

'Cambodia,' Tom corrected.

'Sorry, mate. You remember I was always shite at geography in school,' Rob laughed.

'You don't have much of a tan for someone living over there.' Niamh or Maeve or Sinéad looked at him quizzically, her black, heavily pencilled eyebrows standing out from her tangerine skin.

Caitlyn would get such a kick out of this, he thought, suppressing the urge to laugh. Tom began to put on his best baby-interested performance, using his tried and tested baby-related questions. *Who in the family does she look like? Is she sleeping all through the night yet? Where does her name come from?* Rob needed little prompting and launched into an enthusiastic diatribe about all things Baby Ava.

'Dylan! Get down off that couch!' Niamh or Maeve or Sinéad screeched suddenly. Handing the baby over to Rob, she rushed to grab a little blonde boy who must have been their second or third child who was jumping vigorously on a sofa.

He and Rob sipped pints and picked from a basket of over-cooked chicken goujons while the baby slept in Rob's arms. Tom felt a little awkward realising that he was running out of things to say to Rob. Herpe's absence always felt particularly pointed whenever he and Rob were alone together.

'Mad how things work out. Me, a father of four and you off saving the world?' Rob mused, as if both paths were on equal footing.

'Yes, indeed.' Tom nodded marvelling at how genuinely happy he seemed to be all domesticated.

'Are you seeing anyone, yourself?' Rob asked him.

'Ah, I was. An American girl. Not anymore though. Lots of drama.'

'I hear you. Here, Niamh has a lovely mate. I'll introduce you,' Rob said enthusiastically.

Niamh, that was his wife's name!

'Ah, no, man. I'm not really up for it.' Tom had no interest in being set up.

'Come on. Just say hello and see what happens,' Rob winked.

'Ah, Rob,' Tom started to protest but it was too late. Rob was calling: 'Fiona, come over here.'

A pale blonde in a yellow dress made her way over to them.

'Hi, Ava,' Fiona started gushing over the baby who was facing outward in Rob's arms.

'Fiona, this is my mate Tom, the one who lives in Cambodia. He's home for Christmas. I'll let you two talk. Baby Ava needs to see more of her fans.' He grinned at them as he scuttled away.

They shook hands awkwardly. Her dress seemed too big for her but she was quite pretty in an understated sort of way.

'I hear you have some big job. You work for NATO, is it?' Fiona started.

'Very different thing. I work for the United Nations,' he corrected her.

'Oh, right, sorry.' She seemed genuinely embarrassed. It was a little endearing. 'Fair play to you over there doing that. It must be a mad place.'

'It's not a bad life actually,' He told her. 'What about yourself? What do you do?'

'I'm a science teacher. I just transferred to a new school actually. It's a very rough school, very different from the posher schools I was in before, but I love it.'

'Ah, very good. How Michelle Pfeiffer in *Dangerous Minds* of you!' He quipped.

'What? Sorry who's that?' Fiona laughed loudly in spite of not getting the reference.

'Just referencing the 90s movie. Remember the one where Michelle Pfeiffer teaches in a rough school? Coolio's 'Gangster Paradise' was on the soundtrack?' He waited for it to click with her.

Fiona was apologetic. 'Sorry, I'm useless at remembering films. I don't really watch much television.'

'Sorry, we can't be friends.' Tom joked. 'I spend my life watching television and movies. What do you do for fun?'

'I don't know really. Different things. I'm always so busy. At the moment, I'm taking sign language and I just finished a candle-making course.'

'Wow. Okay, I have to ask. Can you make a candle of a hand signing something?'

She laughed a big hearty laugh. 'Do you know? I haven't tried yet, but I definitely should.'

'Fancy a shot?' Tom asked. Fiona really wasn't his usual type but she was nice, and he was craving some fun.

One sambuca shot led to three and Tom let a warm tipsy feeling come over him. It felt good to let off some steam. The kids and the older members of Rob's family soon cleared off and those who remained began to get more sloshed. The dry chicken goujons had clearly failed to soak up the copious amounts of alcohol that had been consumed all afternoon. The loudspeaker began to play Queen's 'Don't Stop Me Now' and people filed their way on to the grimy dancefloor.

'Come and dance!' Fiona demanded. Clearly made boisterous by the booze, she pulled him onto the dancefloor.

She bopped along enthusiastically to the music even doing a little air guitar motion when the song's instrumental came on. He enjoyed watching her as he pumped his fist in the air. She was utterly lacking in self-consciousness. AC/DC's 'Thunderstruck' started and they were joined by Rob and some others.

'You're clearly in there, mate,' Rob slapped him on the back gesturing to Fiona.

Tom was enjoying himself as the soundtrack continued to pump out crowd-pleasing hits.

'I love this song!' Fiona shouted to him as David Bowie's 'Let's Dance' began to play.

It wasn't 'Space Oddity' but it was impossible to hear any Bowie and not think of Caitlyn. He felt a twisted feeling in his stomach. He still wasn't sure whether it was guilt or regret that he was feeling. Probably both. He left the dancefloor and got a pint at the now-deserted bar. He pulled out his phone and started to type out a message.

Hi Caitlyn, just wanted to check in and say hello. I'm in Ireland for Christmas. Where are you at the moment? I hope wherever in the world you are, that you are happy and having fun. I heard Bowie just now and it made me miss you. I'm so sorry if I hurt you. Sometimes I'm just an immature dick and I'm not able to see the brightness in front of me. Never change, you brilliant bitch. All my love, Tom.

He was debating with himself about whether or not to press send when Fiona appeared beside him suddenly.

'I was worried you'd left,' Her cheeks were red from dancing. 'I owe you a shot. You bought the last one.'

'Oh, okay, go on then.' Tom saved the message to drafts and put his phone away.

'Are you okay?' She put a hand on his shoulder and looked at him with kind, grey eyes.

'Yes, I'm fine. It's just been a bit of a weird Christmas,' he told her.

'It's a tough time of year for a lot of people,' she said sympathetically.

'I think I just hate this idea of having to be exceptionally happy because of a specific time of year like birthdays and Christmas. People build them up so much and of course they end up let down because reality can't possibly live up to our demented expectations. True happiness is spontaneous and can't just be summoned on particular calendar dates.' Tom knew he was venting a little but she was nodding encouragingly as he talked.

'The things you come out with. You're really funny,' she giggled as the barman placed the sambucas in front of them.

'Shots time!' She cheered.

They clinked shots against each other and knocked back the sticky, acidic liquor in unison. Tom gasped at its strength and supped his pint to rid his mouth of the harsh liquorice taste. She laughed at his wincing face as he leaned in to kiss her.

—

Tom woke up in Fiona's apartment realising that he was alone in her bed. Her bed had strings of fairy lights overhead and there were big silver words *Live Laugh Love* hand-painted on the wall facing him. This was the kind of thing Caitlyn would definitely mock.

It had been pleasant. Pleasant seemed like a strange word to use for sex but it was the right one. He wasn't quite sure if he was madly attracted to her but there was something just so lovely about her.

'Good morning! Fancy a cup of tea?' A cheerful Fiona poked her head around the door as if she had sensed him waking up.

'No, I'm fine. Thanks, though.' His mouth was as dry as a sandbox from the hangover.

'Are you sure? My housemate's just made a pot.'

Jesus, housemates. It was like being in college again.

'No honestly, I really need to make a move. I have to put some family time in before I fly back in a few days,' he told her pulling on his jeans.

She looked disappointed and he felt bad.

'I'm sorry. It's just hectic being home. But I had a really fun time with you. Keep educating those young minds and kicking ass.'

'I will,' she smiled broadly.

'I really hope we see each other again' she said as they kissed goodbye.

He taxied back to his parents' place feeling proactive. It was time to make some changes in his life and take back some control of his career trajectory. He grunted a hello to his Dad who was watching television in the sitting room and went straight to his room. He pulled out his laptop and under the watchful gaze of Kurt Cobain, he started to search for UN jobs in Europe.

23

The prospect of the holidays alone in Phnom Penh seemed bleak once Caitlyn had learned that Ella and everyone else that she knew were going home to be with their families. At the last minute, she had caved and booked a flight home to Sacramento for Christmas.

It had been a surreal week at home with her parents. Even thinking of them as one entity in the same place, her parents, was still bizarre but somehow it had been quite enjoyable. Janice was more relaxed in Sacramento. Her usual intensity was softened by Liam's natural joviality and Caitlyn could see that she seemed to have more of a sense of humour around him. Janice had downloaded a meditation app and she and Liam had taken to meditating together every morning at the kitchen table before eating breakfast. Caitlyn had initially mocked them but it seemed to be working for her as Janice mentioned Cambodian Hands far less than Caitlyn would have anticipated over the Christmas week.

On Christmas Day, none of them felt like cooking the traditional turkey dinner so they ordered Chinese food. Janice hadn't had American Chinese food in years and noisily exclaimed her appreciation for every greasy bite of orange chicken and egg fried rice much to Liam and Caitlyn's amusement. Afterwards, they had watched *It's a Wonderful Life* while squashed beside each other on the old grey coffee-stained couch in the living room. Caitlyn and Janice were both in full blown tears at the end when the townspeople all gathered in George Bailey's house to help him, singing 'Auld Lang Syne'. Laughing at each other's tears, Caitlyn felt a momentary stab of sadness wondering what life would have been like if her Mom had been around for more Christmases when she was growing up.

She and Janice took to playing nightly games of competitive scrabble in the kitchen. Caitlyn had always loved scrabble but had struggled to find someone to properly contend with. Her Dad had never proved much of a challenger, unable to beat her at it since she was a teenager. Nick hadn't been much better, easily beatable given his refusal to take the game as seriously as she did.

But Janice was ruthless, brilliant and impossible to defeat. She put down lengthy, high-scoring, obscure words like quercine, xanthan and paroxysm while Caitlyn cried foul insisting that she was making the words up and then gasped in dismay when the dictionary proved Janice right. Liam opted out of playing with them claiming it was 'too competitive' for him but he took occasional smiling glances at them from over his Kindle, clearly revelling in seeing them together.

She speed-dated her way through the rest of the week at home catching up with various friends and family and buying all of the things she couldn't get in Cambodia like decent chocolate, underwear and books that weren't photocopies.

Over Mexican food, she caught up with Lucy who had just gotten engaged to one of Travis's New York management consulting friends, Damon after a rapid-fire romance. Caitlyn had yet to meet him in person but he sounded flawlessly adoring and based on his Facebook photos, he looked like the perfect encapsulation of teeth-prominence and wholesomeness that Lucy went for.

'When you know, you know,' Lucy gushed, recalling the

details of how he'd gotten down on one knee as they walked through Central Park on their three-month anniversary.

Caitlyn was happy for her friend but she had to laugh a little at the cliché. Even when they were kids, it had been obvious to Caitlyn that her own life would be far less straightforward than Lucy's would be. Lucy moved through the world with impeccable ease and didn't possess an ounce of self-doubt.

Caitlyn's mind wandered as she chomped down on her quesadilla while Lucy got animated while describing her wedding Pinterest board in detail.

'Oh, I'm sorry. Am I totally boring you?' Lucy asked, catching Caitlyn's disinterest. 'You have to stop me whenever I become a wedding asshole. We've barely talked about you. How are you doing? Have you heard from Tom?'

'Nope. Still no word,' Caitlyn sighed. 'I have accepted that it's over though or at least I'm trying to.'

'God, he's a dickass,' she fumed, reminding Caitlyn of Lucy's ferociously held loyalty. 'I'm sorry but can I just say that I absolutely hate him? Seriously. Fuck that guy. I can't understand his lack of integrity in not even sending a text message to let you know it's over.'

'I know. It's shit. I've obsessed about it so much though. I'm really trying not to give it more airtime in my life,' Caitlyn said.

'Just come home and marry my brother, please! He still asks about you all the time. Imagine, we could totally do a double wedding!' Lucy looked excitable and Caitlyn knew that she was only partially joking.

'Oh god, can you imagine?' Caitlyn laughed.

'Okay, we won't plan a double wedding just yet. But at least consider calling over to my parents' house to see Travis before you go back to Cambodia and he goes back to New York.'

'I dunno, Lucy.' Caitlyn protested. Any mention of Travis just resurfaced the images in her mind of her blue medusa paint on Travis's mouth and Nick's cold look of disgust as she told him about it.

'Just a tiny cup of coffee to say hello … ' Lucy prodded.

'Oh my god. Stop pimping out your brother!'

'Okay, I'll shut up. Sorry. You know I just think it would be amazing to see my two favourite people on earth, both of whom are incredibly kind, smart and funny getting together and making each other happy.'

'Stop trying to manipulate me!' Caitlyn was getting exasperated.

'Just think about it,' Lucy smiled at her with mock-maniacal eyes diffusing Caitlyn's irritation.

Caitlyn had to laugh.

'Fine. I'll think about it but only to shut you up.'

—

She spent New Year's Eve in her Aunt Mary's playing video games with her young cousins. They wore paper hats and blew into cheap paper horns while counting down to midnight and the beginning of 2014. After putting the kids to bed, Mary opened a bottle of red wine and asked her how things were going with Janice.

'I don't know if our family will ever be the Waltons but I feel much warmer towards her. I kind of like her as a person and understand her a bit more. It's nice not feeling infuriated with her all the time,' Caitlyn said. 'And she seems calmer here too which can only be a good thing.'

'That's so great. And she and your Dad seem to be getting on well too,' Mary said knowingly, topping up their large glasses.

'Wait. Do you think that something is happening between

them?' Caitlyn asked taking the bait.

'I honestly don't know for sure and I could be wrong, but I have a suspicion. Your Dad seems so happy to have her here …' Mary trailed off. 'I only mention it so that you are prepared.'

Caitlyn hadn't really thought about it but recapping her parents' warm interactions with one another over the past few days she thought that Mary may have a point.

'I mean it would definitely be weird but maybe it would be okay?' she mused. 'It's nice for Dad to have company. He's never really prioritised that side of his life.'

'You are amazing, Cait. Truly.' Mary said suddenly with a look of admiration on her face.

'Ha! Mary, I didn't do anything!' Caitlyn laughed.

'No, you didn't but not everyone would be able to be as strong as you are. I always knew you'd be brilliant but I'm just so proud of the woman you have become,' Mary sounded emotional.

'Mary, you're drunk!' Caitlyn laughed, feeling touched. 'But thank you.'

—

When it was time for Caitlyn to go back to Phnom Penh in early January, Liam and Janice drove her the two-hour drive to San Francisco airport. She could tell her Dad was nervous about her going back. He was quieter than usual and gave her an inordinately tight hug which winded her slightly as they said goodbye. Janice hugged her too and told her that she would see her soon without mentioning whether she'd see her in Cambodia or not. It was strange turning back and seeing her parents standing there together as she walked through the departures gate.

The short break at home had been good for Caitlyn. She

had ignored Lucy's relentless text messages about calling over and seeing Travis. She wanted to be the strong woman that Mary had said she was. Entertaining something with Travis because she was still reeling from Tom felt like the kind of juvenile move.

She was excited to be back in Phnom Penh and do as much work as possible before her internship came to an end in a few weeks' time. She had managed to keep her promise and had not messaged Tom again in spite of having to fight against an intense yearning to text him on Christmas Day and wish him happy holidays.

However, once she was back in the city where he lived, it was harder to keep Tom out of her mind. She wondered whether she would run into him in a bar when she went on a night out with Ella or when she was in any of the city's multiple coffee shops. She rehearsed the details of a potential run-in several times in her head, preparing herself to confidently tell him exactly what a mediocre idiot she thought he was. As part of her preparation, she was careful not to be outside without makeup or with greasy hair so she wouldn't be caught looking like shit when it inevitably happened.

He had been tagged in a photo on Facebook with a blonde girl called Fiona Sheehan in a bar in Ireland. It wasn't a particularly intimate-looking photo but Caitlyn instantly sensed that they must have been together. She delved into Fiona's profile and saw that Tom had liked one of her previous profile pictures which confirmed her suspicions. Fiona's profile was protected but Caitlyn could see that she was a teacher in Ireland and a fan of sharing competitions from Irish hotels in the hope that she might win a free weekend away.

Caitlyn found herself thinking snarkily that she was

probably better looking than this fairly bland-looking girl. This was confirmed emphatically by Ella who told her that Fiona looked like a 'basic bitch'. She asked herself if it would have been easier if his new girl was more beautiful and seemed cooler than she was. Not really. It had nothing to do with the girl really. Tom had pursued her and she had been utterly herself and then seemingly out of nowhere, he had abandoned her. She already had some fairly sizable abandonment issues to contend with and Tom fucking Fenton hadn't helped.

She was jetlagged for that first week back but Caitlyn pushed herself to get back into work, grateful that Pheary wanted her to prepare the first draft of a proposal that Save Cambodia were sending to the European Union to try and get funding.

A few days after Caitlyn got back, the staff were coming back from a lengthy Khmer barbecue lunch for someone's birthday when Pheary urgently requested for everyone to come into the conference room. The twenty or so of them assembled themselves in the room and readied their pens and notebooks looking expectantly at Pheary. She looked ashen-faced and her voice sounded uncharacteristically fragile as if it could crack into a sob at any moment.

'I wanted to inform you all that I have just received a phone call informing me that Savat Nou was found dead in his cell in Prey Sar prison a few hours ago,' she told them.

There was a collective gasp from much of the room.

'What happened?' someone asked.

'We don't really know the full story other than that it was heart failure,' Pheary continued, seeming numb.

'His family are saying that he was asking to go to hospital because he was struggling to breathe and that the prison authorities ignored him. If this is true, this is a very serious situation and they will need to be held accountable for this tragedy.'

'What do we do now? Is there any way we can help?' Caitlyn heard herself asking.

'Not for now, Caitlyn. We are just trying to get more information. Vic is working on a press release which we'll send out within the hour. We will also need to check on his family. I don't think they had any money saved for a funeral so we might want to start a fundraiser.'

'That's all for now. If anyone who has been working on this feels upset and wants to leave the office and go home and take some time for yourselves, please do so.'

The staff collected their things and shuffled out of the conference room looking visibly devastated. It was clear that none of them intended to do anything other than get right back to work. Caitlyn turned to follow them out then stopped herself when it was just herself and Pheary left in the room.

'Pheary, can I ask you a question and I'm sorry in advance if it sounds naïve?'

Pheary nodded.

'How do you cope with situations like this and not let the anger just overwhelm you?' Caitlyn asked.

She smiled sadly at Caitlyn.

'At the pagoda, the monks tell us to cultivate a heart of love that knows no anger. Anger will not help this country's problems, Caitlyn. Only love can.'

Caitlyn smiled back out of politeness as she didn't really know how else to respond. She knew that Pheary genuinely believed in what she was saying but her answer didn't feel helpful to Caitlyn. She did feel angry about Savat. She felt absolutely enraged.

She left Pheary and sat back down at her desk, scarcely bothering to make it look like she was working. It was devastating, just devastating. Maybe devastating was too weak a word but she didn't have a better one. She could feel the anger bubbling up in her at the prison authorities who had let this happen, at the shitty, despicable government who had put this good man in prison in the first place for defending people's homes and at the NGOs and UN who should have done more to help him.

She sat with a clenched jaw as her brain wandered into dark territory. She thought about what it must have been like for him not being able to breathe, the excruciating pains in his chest knowing he was dying as he languished in a disgusting pit with no personal space. He was only forty fucking two. Far younger than either of her parents. And he had an eight year old daughter. How would she ever be able to get over something like this?

In the midst of her anger Caitlyn wondered if it was wrong of her to feel so pained. She hadn't known this man intimately. What right did she have to feel so upset? She could leave this country whenever she wanted. Maybe she didn't have a right to monopolise Cambodian grief.

Savat's name was already trending on Twitter with NGOs and activists expressing their shock at his death. Reuters and BBC had posted the story, quoting an anonymous source claiming that deaths were common in the prison due in part to a reluctance by prison authorities to transfer sick prisoners to hospital in time for treatment.

Caitlyn came home quickly as soon as it turned 5 p.m. Feeling comfortable at last in the sanctitude of her grimy apartment she called Janice and cried down the phone to her so hard that her sobs choked her attempts to speak. Janice sounded calm and let Caitlyn talk for a long time.

'I know I don't have a right to be this upset but it's so awful,' she wept.

'I know it is, hon. Believe me. It's maddening that people so often die in needless circumstances in Cambodia. I've seen a lot of that over the years.'

'It just makes me so angry. I feel so useless not being able to do anything,' Caitlyn sobbed.

'I understand that feeling very well but I think you should try and distance yourself as much as possible,' Janice cautioned.

'What do you mean "distance myself"?' Caitlyn asked.

'I mean that it's okay to care and to do good work but that you don't want to take the problems of Cambodia onto your shoulders,' Janice explained.

'Wow. Isn't that what you've spent more than twenty years doing?' Caitlyn snapped at her.

'Yes and look at where that's gotten me. It's not a path that I would like for you to follow. Believe me. Look, I was going to wait until your birthday in a few weeks, but I have a gift for you. It's some money to help you plan your next move when the internship ends.'

'I don't need money. I'm fine.' Caitlyn went into her default defensive mode.

'This is a gift to help you plan your next move and give you some downtime after your internship if you'd like it. I think you should think very carefully about where you are going and why,' she offered.

'Okay.' Caitlyn didn't really have energy to argue.

'I'm transferring it to your account now. You are about to be unemployed which is hard enough without having any money.'

'Okay. Thank you, Mom.'

Caitlyn got off the phone feeling slightly better. She texted Pheary. It was after hours but she doubted that she would mind.

I would like to make a donation to Savat's family. Can we find time to talk about the details tomorrow? Thank you.

24

Janice had given her $3,000. The amount had come as a complete shock to Caitlyn. This was far more than she had ever had in her bank account at any one time. She gave about a third of it to the fund that Save Cambodia was putting together for Savat's family. It would help to go towards his funeral and his daughter's schooling. She worried a little about it being a white saviour kind of a move but decided not to overthink it. Fuck it, she thought, this is a practical way that I can help.

She made the arrangements with Pheary directly telling her that she didn't want the rest of the staff to know. She didn't want to make a thing of it and could only imagine that Vic would find a way to be a dickhead about it.

She had to write a final report of her experience interning at Save Cambodia and submit it to Pheary. One of the key questions in the report format was 'List your key achievements in this internship'. This gave Caitlyn pause. She had written proposals and press releases, helped with social media and editing reports but what had she actually achieved? For want of a better answer, she wrote that she had learned a lot about the country and its challenges that would help to guide her future career. It felt feeble but at least it was honest.

The last few weeks in Phnom Penh were bittersweet for Caitlyn. On one hand it had been a skid mark of a year and she was ready for something new but on the other hand, she wondered whether it was too convenient to just leave the country instead of staying on and somehow trying to truly make an impact. Janice's advice had resonated with her though. She had no idea what to do next but whatever she did, she needed to think carefully about why she was doing it and where it would bring her.

On Caitlyn's last night in Phnom Penh, she and Ella went for a rooftop dinner in the Foreign Correspondent's Club.

'I have some pretty big news,' Ella shared after they had ordered.

'You better not be pregnant,' Caitlyn joked.

'Jesus, can you imagine?' Ella shuddered. 'No fucking way.'

'So, when I was in Bangkok for work two weeks ago, I met a guy. Like really met him, not just had sex with him,' Ella was grinning broadly.

'Oh, amazing. Tell me everything!' Caitlyn said excitedly.

'So, I had some time to kill before my flight back and wanted to do something touristy, so I went to the royal palace which I hadn't been to before,' Ella recounted sipping her red wine.

'I took my camera and was taking photos of a beautiful fountain in the gardens and when I looked through the lens, I saw in my shot that someone else had the same camera and they were taking pictures of the fountain from the other side. You know mine is like this really rare vintage Nikon? What are the odds? Right? So, we both look up from our cameras at the same time and kind of give each other this like, knowing look. But the thing is, he's gorgeous. Not like, mildly attractive. Like insane, mop up my underpants, fine as fuck.'

'Excellent,' Caitlyn enthused.

'So, of course, we got to talking and he's really great. He's Indian but just moved to Bangkok for a job at the Indian embassy there. So, I ended up missing my flight and staying on a few extra days to spend time with him.'

'This is insane. It's like something in a movie,' Caitlyn gushed.

'I know. If I heard someone else tell this story I would want to punch them. It's so cheesy but I'm pretty, goddamn happy right now,' Ella laughed.

Wow. Non-committal Ella was all mushy and in love. Caitlyn had to laugh at the ridiculousness of the story but she was happy for her friend. Hearing about someone else's love life success was still a bit raw for her given her own failings in that department but she was working on it.

After dinner, Ella left to get to bed for an early work meeting the following morning. It felt quite final saying goodbye to her. Caitlyn wasn't sure how sustaining an expat friendship would work in practice. She wondered if expat friendships were destined to be intense but fleeting. She and Ella had shared a particular slice of time together and would certainly keep in touch but it was probably unlikely that they would ever find themselves living in the same city again.

She was in a reflective mood and stayed in the restaurant after Ella had gone and sipped a cosmopolitan as she looked out over the rooftop views of the Mekong river and soaked up her last few hours in the city. She was ready to leave, she told herself excitedly. Bring on the next adventure.

As she made her way downstairs to get a tuk tuk home, she passed through the second floor of the restaurant, she suddenly saw the back of a familiar head sitting at a table in the distance. Fuck. Even her insides felt like they were trembling.

His back was to her and the restaurant was crowded but it was definitely Tom. She recognised his friend Joey at the table with him which confirmed her suspicions. Who else was there? Was it? Yup, it definitely was. It was that sleazy reporter, Andre.

Her first instinct was to go over and talk to Tom. Of course, she had been dying to see him and his presence was pulling her towards him like a magnet. She wanted to walk right over and for him to see her and kiss her, and for everything between them to be as it was. She could see the side outline of his face as he talked spiritedly. She willed for him to turn around and see her standing beside the stairs.

Logic slowly crept in. He doesn't want you, she reminded herself. He made that clear by ignoring you.

She hurried down the rest of the restaurant's stairs and hopped onto the first motorbike she saw waiting outside before she could change her mind. As the bike weaved through traffic, she felt tears coming as the trembling began to ease.

—

Caitlyn decided to stop off in Rome for a few days on her way back home to Sacramento to face unemployment. It wasn't really on her route home but she had never been to Europe before or gone on a solo holiday and basing her decision purely on movies, Rome seemed like exactly the kind of place where an adventurous, solo, female traveller would go to find herself.

Janice's money meant that she could treat herself. She booked into a sleek, modern hotel at the top of a winding, cobblestoned street dotted with cute little trattorias. It was expensive but she justified it by deciding that it was her 25th birthday present to herself. She arrived late in the evening full of jetlag and after checking in, she took herself to dinner at one of the side street restaurants. She had an indulgent plate of cheese and pepper spaghetti which her taxi driver had recommended as the best Roman dish, alongside a small carafe of white wine. She felt a burst of joy at her own feeling of independence. Here she was alone in Rome eating the best pasta she had ever tasted. She was like a woman in a romantic comedy but obviously with much shittier outfits. The horrible aftertaste of seeing Tom began to lift.

After allowing herself to have a lie-in on her first full day in the city, she Google-mapped her way to the Vatican. It wasn't even peak tourist season but the queues were intense. She joined a guided tour group and marvelled at the vast ornate beauty of the various rooms throughout the enormous complex. It was impressive of course but her thoughts couldn't separate the beauty that she was witnessing from her revulsion at how the Catholic Church had managed to profit so significantly from exploiting people's fears, blatant misogyny and other despicable behaviour that she didn't want to think about.

Nick used to mock Caitlyn's inability to look at things without making them political. He joked that she had a superhero power for finding sexism, racism or cause for offence almost anywhere. The Vatican was so gratuitous in its display of wealth that it wasn't exactly difficult for her. She found after a while that oohing and aahing at gorgeous tapestries and sculptures knowing why they were there was making her feel disgusted. She could not just look at them objectively and appreciate them as art.

As the tour concluded in the crowded Sistine chapel, she spent a few moments gazing at Michelangelo's intricate ceiling artwork before making her escape. She found an English language bookshop on the way back to the hotel and bought a book about clerical sex abuse. She read fervently while eating a magnificent margarita pizza at a trattoria so close to the edge of a busy road that the tables shook whenever a car sped past. She was enraged and compelled by what she was reading but her brain was so happily occupied she realised that for the first day in weeks she hadn't thought about Tom once.

After a day of sightseeing, Caitlyn's feet were sore and her thighs were chafing with ire. She went back to the hotel and took a nap. It was a Saturday night, she realised once she was rested. In the movies about these independent women, they never showed what they did by themselves on a Saturday night. She looked at the leaflets the hotel had given her in search of something to do and saw that there was a Michelin starred restaurant a few blocks away which had been lauded for having the world's best spaghetti carbonara.

This is exactly what a woman in a romantic comedy would do, she told herself. She arrived at the restaurant and realised that in her faded jeans and black sweater, she was massively underdressed compared to the other patrons there. The maître d' who greeted her at the door was a booming, bald man in an expensive-looking suit. When she told him that she had no booking and that she wanted a table for one, he looked at her a little strangely and said they had been booked out for weeks but that she could sit at the bar.

Caitlyn propped up at the bar and took out her book for social armour. She was the only solo diner in a sea of glamorous-looking couples. The handsome sommelier behind the bar introduced himself as Matteo and offered her some wine samples. He was a little older than her. She would have guessed mid-thirties. He was damn cute, she couldn't help but acknowledge, kind of like a more Mediterranean version of Jake Gyllenhaal with big, brooding eyes. The maître d' brought out a trio of seafood appetizers which she hadn't ordered. There were crostini with seabass mousse, mussels and octopus carpaccio. Caitlyn couldn't really tell which dish was which but each was incredible.

Matteo asked her where she was from as she sipped from the small flutes of wine he kept putting in front of her for tasting. When she described Sacramento as being near San Francisco, he got enthusiastic.

'Wow. Jefferson Airplane! Janice Joplin! Jack Kerouac!'

'We can totally claim Jefferson Airplane and Janice but I'm not sure that Kerouac was even from California,' she said.

'Oh, I know that,' he laughed. 'I just thought it sounded good for alliteration purposes. I personally think that Kerouac was a bit of an overrated tool.'

'Yes. 100%!' Caitlyn enthused, laughing a little at his charming, accented pronunciation of 'overrated tool'. 'I absolutely hated *On the Road*.'

'Me too. I couldn't finish it actually. No plot at all and so sexist with every female character being so submissive and one dimensional. It's so unrealistic and we're supposed to declare it a masterpiece?' he said getting animated and placing another flute of wine in front of her.

'Here. Try the Vermentino di Gallura. It's from the island of Sardegna. Very crisp.'

'Oh, wow. I like you!' Caitlyn exclaimed taking a sip. She knew nothing about wine and would never remember how to pronounce these names but it tasted delicious to her. 'I would so love to get you in a room with some of the guys I was in college with who insisted that Kerouac was a genius.'

'I'd say most of them were just following one another's taste and jumping on what was perceived to be cool, as men of that age tend to do,' he said thoughtfully.

'Yes, you are probably right and young women are definitely guilty of doing that too,' Caitlyn said, enjoying their conversation. 'During my teenage and college years, it seemed as if any kind of art that was typically masculine, like Kerouac, was automatically considered to be so much more high-minded than typically female books, movies and music which were often dismissed as trivial or not serious enough.'

'If you are talking about the early to mid-2000s. I think it was a poor time for art all round,' he smiled at her. 'But if you are going to try to get into the Beat generation work, I recommend you try Allen Ginsberg. He has so much more to say about the world and that particular time and place and his writing is just of a higher literary value by any standards. It'll be more your thing, I promise.'

'I've never read Ginsberg so maybe I'll do that. Thank you,' Caitlyn was impressed and feeling a little flirty from the wine. 'So how are you so well-read?'

'I studied literature. I'm an aspiring writer by day and a free-handed sommelier by night. Ernest Hemingway, eat your heart out.' Matteo winked at her as he turned to take a drinks order from one of the waiters and Caitlyn blushed a little.

When the carbonara arrived, it was as magnificent as all the reviews had described. Caitlyn did something that she had never done before and had mocked others for doing and took a photograph of it with her phone. Matteo caught her in the act and smiled at her in amusement.

'I never do this. I swear,' she told him laughingly. 'But this may well be the best thing I've ever eaten.'

When she had lapped up every last bite of the carbonara and was relaxing happily with another of Matteo's wine samples, the maître d' brought out a trio of desserts and placed them in front of her.

'Oh goodness, I'm so full,' she protested.

'The chef insists,' he told her.

Jesus, this was like nothing else that she'd ever experienced. She managed to devour the desserts of white chocolate mousse, tiramisu and raspberry panna cotta.

She was a little worried about being charged a fortune. But when the cheque arrived, to her surprise, they had only charged her for what she actually ordered which was one glass of wine and the carbonara. Caitlyn left a 20% tip and thanked the maître d' profusely. She was going to have to leave this place an incredible TripAdvisor review.

'What are your plans for the rest of the night?' Matteo asked as she said goodnight.

'Oh, nothing really. I think I'll just go back to my hotel,' Caitlyn told him.

'Would you like to join me for a drink when I finish here?' He asked.

Shit. She hadn't been expecting that. Caitlyn was taken aback by his offer. It was certainly tempting. There was no denying that the guy was interesting, not to mention insanely attractive. But she didn't need to, she told herself. The night had been wonderful enough already.

'I really enjoyed chatting to you but not this time, thank you so much,' she responded.

When she later told Ella about the evening, she would chastise Caitlyn for not 'lapping up Italian Jake Gyllenhaal like he was made from that damn carbonara that you keep banging on about.'

But Caitlyn left the restaurant feeling more joyful than she had in months. Good things were ahead, she told herself, she could feel it.

25

Phnom Penh, February 2015 (12 Months Later)

Sitting in a tuk tuk as it bumped its way down Street 51 on the way to the Cambodian Hands office, Janice felt ripples of excitement. The excessive honking from cars on the street, the death-defying driving of helmetless motorcyclists whizzing past and the strong smells emanating from fried rice stalls and overflowing bins were all magnificent to her today. Even the despicable sexpats still out from the night before sitting at street side bars with women young enough to be their granddaughters weren't able to dampen her mood. She was finally back in her beloved Phnom Penh.

It had taken far longer than she could ever have imagined. The board had insisted that she take a full year off and really take the time out to rest. Gabriel had come back to Phnom Penh to lead an intensive investigation where he interviewed dozens of former and current staff. They had found that while Janice had been an autocratic and difficult manager, some of the reported claims by her former staff like the allegation that she punished staff by making them clean toilets were disproven. The woman who made the claim had admitted to Gabriel that she had been goaded by Andre King into making things sound worse than they actually were. Gabriel concluded that Janice had been unreasonable with staff over everyday mistakes and had displayed erratic behaviour at times. However, in Vera's words, Janice had 'narrowly avoided being outrightly abusive'.

Even with the slight saving of her reputation, Janice still

had to face up to the fact that she had behaved so poorly. More than a year's worth of intensive therapy with Ruth had helped her to work through the self-shame and to understand that it was the by-product of more than twenty years of insomnia and burnout. But Janice knew that she was by no means 'fixed' and that she was going to have to take better care of herself and those around her.

She had been so frustrated initially at having her life put on pause but she had quickly fallen into a content little existence in Sacramento with Liam. Janice had even managed to get a small role as a guest lecturer on a course about South East Asia in Sacramento State University. She had found that she had a decent aptitude for getting young people passionate about Cambodia and its challenges. Caitlyn had been there briefly before she had got her new job and moved to Myanmar and it had been an enjoyable, if a little surreal, time with the three of them living together as a family.

As the new year started, the board told her that they felt happy with her progress and were allowing her to go back to work. Janice had been overjoyed and had hastily made plans to get back to her old life. The only downside was how clumsily she had left things with Liam. He was very upset about how abruptly she booked her flight and readied herself to leave. Perhaps they had both been in denial about the fact that their renewed relationship could only work temporarily. It had probably been irresponsible to start it up again.

He stopped speaking to her during the few days before she left Sacramento and didn't even offer to bring her to the airport which was very unlike him. As the plane took off, she felt nauseous at how horribly familiar it all felt. But she didn't want to think about that today.

Seeing the familiar blue and green Cambodian Hands logo as the tuk tuk turned around the corner towards the office gave Janice a rush of happiness. Sophorn greeted her warmly. He had assembled the organisation's fifty staff members including those who were typically based in rural areas. They were all waiting for her in the large staff room. Janice was very touched to see that they had got a celebratory cake and a Welcome Back banner was hanging from the ceiling.

They all cheered as she entered the room. Sophorn made a short speech.

'This is a wonderful day for all of those working at Cambodian Hands. We're thrilled to welcome back our inspirational and hardworking founder and director,' he said while everyone clapped enthusiastically.

Janice could see how intently the staff listened to everything he was saying. Sophorn had really proved himself to be an excellent leader while she was away. He had managed to keep the organisation's important relationships with donors and the UN going smoothly which was a great relief to her.

He continued, 'I am also pleased to announce a bonus piece of good news. We just got word that the European Union has agreed to grant us $150,000 to set up a new gender-based violence programme. We'll be hiring an expert colleague who will begin to roll it out very soon. Of course, this was all Janice's brainchild too.'

Everyone cheered enthusiastically while Sophorn smiled. He seemed so much more of a commanding presence than she recalled.

'So, let's have some cake and celebrate and then let's get back to work as we have many important things to do to continue to help the lives of Cambodian women,' he concluded.

Janice approached him as the clapping died down and the crowd dispersed with slices of cake on paper plates.

'Sophorn, how did you manage to get that EU funding? That's amazing!' She enthused.

'Oh, we just applied with a proposal through their regular process. It was very tough and bureaucratic but the EU really agreed with us that the programme was needed,' he told her.

'Well done. I'm so impressed,' Janice marvelled. 'This means that we can really help women like Pagna!'

'Actually, I meant to tell you about Pagna.' Sophorn quickly swallowed a mouthful of cake in his enthusiasm to speak. 'She's left her husband. Properly this time.'

'Wow. What happened?'

'She came to me a few months ago and said she wanted to get a job in Phnom Penh, so we helped her with her CV and provided her with a reference. She's now working at a cleaning job in a hotel. She and the kids are living in a nice new apartment out near the airport. They are still getting used to their new lives but she keeps in touch. Things seem to be going quite well for her.'

Janice was amazed. It felt wonderful to hear of all these great things that were happening for and around Cambodian Hands. However, later that night when she was at home and back to her old habit of not being able to sleep, Janice felt a feeling clawing at her that she couldn't swat away. What if Sophorn was better at leading the organisation than she was?

—

Her first few weeks back passed by slowly. It was taking Janice longer than she had anticipated to get resettled into life in Phnom Penh. Weekdays were fine as she could focus on work but weekends were a real challenge for her. She was trying not to work during weekends in order to avoid getting herself into the same state of exhaustion and burnout that she'd gotten into before. But what did people do when they weren't working?

If she were in Sacramento, she and Liam would be watching documentaries or going for walks but in Phnom Penh her weekends were so empty. She took to spending her Saturday mornings at the overpriced gym that she had joined out of boredom. She found spinning class to be an enjoyable new hobby. She had tried yoga at Caitlyn's recommendation but concluded that it was far too mellow. Getting verbally abused by a muscular Brazilian instructor while sweating her face off on an exercise bike was as therapeutic for her as a session with Ruth was.

After the gym, she'd stroll down Street 240, a leafy few blocks of coffee shops and clothing boutiques selling formal wear and artisanal trinkets for tourists. She never bought anything; the silk gowns and high heels they sold didn't exactly suit her lifestyle but it was a nice routine nonetheless. After Street 240, she'd wind up back home at around midday and realise that she had completed all her weekend activities already. It would still be a few hours before she could order a pizza and open a bottle of wine. She hadn't been lonely before, at least she didn't think so, but she felt a little lonely now.

She was determined she wouldn't call him. Calling him after having left him again would be a selfish, assholeish thing to do, she told herself. She managed to avoid it for the first few weeks but after a particularly easy-to-drink bottle of pinot grigio one Friday night, she reached for her phone.

'Hi, it's me,' she said gingerly, relieved that he had actually answered.

'I know. Your name comes up on my phone,' Liam answered

standoffishly.

It was awful to hear him be so uncharacteristically cold.

'Yes, well … How's all with you?' she asked awkwardly.

'Fine, yes. Is there a reason you called?'

'Yes … It feels weird being here. I miss you terribly,' she said.

'I thought you wanted to be there. I mean you practically ran there as soon as they gave you the go ahead.' He was angrier than she had ever heard him.

'I know I did. I thought I was needed here.'

'Have you never in your life felt like you might be needed in Sacramento?' He snapped. 'Why did you call me, Janice?'

'I don't know if I'm needed here anymore and I want to come home to you … if you'll have me?' She blurted out. She hadn't realised it was what she wanted until the words left her mouth.

'I don't think so, Janice,' he told her. 'This time it was really painful. We're not kids anymore. I think it's high time we both moved on.'

'Okay,' Janice managed, feeling her chest and throat begin to swell up.

—

Janice couldn't recall if she had ever properly experienced heartbreak before. Maybe it was so long ago that she couldn't really remember but the first break-up with Liam had never seemed this painful. She called Ruth for an emergency session which calmed her down slightly. She upped her meditation to twice daily but still found herself unsettled and upset, and her insomnia returned at full throttle.

Outwardly, she slowly settled into her role again. She took back her old tasks from Sophorn and began to take external meetings. After a few awkward 'how was your break?'s, it began to seem as if it were business as usual at Cambodian Hands and Janice had never taken her little intermission from Phnom Penh.

They had even replaced good old UN robot, Tom with a younger Dutch guy. Apparently, Tom had moved on somewhere to a more senior role which didn't surprise her in the least. As she had told Caitlyn who had asked about him with feigned nonchalance, 'Room-temperature yogurt, yes-men always do well in the UN.'

Meanwhile, nagging feelings of insecurity about Sophorn continued to occupy her thoughts. During a staff meeting where he gave an engaging presentation about the new gender-based violence programme, she couldn't help but notice again how the rest of the staff were hanging on his every word. How had she underestimated him for so long? Had she been so blinded by her own need not to relinquish control over the organisation? She asked him to have a coffee with her in her office.

'Sophorn, can you tell me honestly, did you like being acting director? How do you feel it went?' she asked.

'Pretty okay,' Sophorn responded slowly. 'I mean it's stressful and it has long hours and initially it was a little daunting but then when I got used to it, I really did like it. I think I managed to put some good ideas in place and do some things differently.'

'Okay,' Janice sipped her tea. 'Let me ask you honestly. What are the things that you found most difficult about the role?'

Sophorn didn't have to think for more than a few seconds.

'Honestly, some of the more political stuff like dealing with foreign donors. I found that a little challenging,' he said. 'For that stuff, it really helps that you are ... well, you.'

'Okay,' Janice contemplated. 'Thank you for your honesty, Sophorn and thank you for taking such good care of the organisation for me. I'm very grateful.'

She stood up in an indication that the conversation was over but Sophorn continued sitting and leaned towards her with a contemplative look on his face.

'Janice,' he said earnestly. 'I really want to change my country and make it better. I have learned lots from you but I also have my own ideas about many things that we could be doing.'

'I'm happy to hear that, Sophorn.' Janice said, meaning it. 'I think if Cambodia really is to change, people like me need to step back and let people like you lead the way.'

Janice continued to think through her conversation with Sophorn later that night while she paced around her home office with an overflowing mug of tea in her hand which kept dripping onto the floor. The questions were jumbled up in her mind and she needed to write them down into a list format.

Was she still needed to lead the organisation? Was there a different role that she could take on? What would that even look like? Some kind of figurehead role dealing with the foreign donors while Sophorn managed the day to day? What was right for the organisation?

She was lost in her thoughts when her phone rang. It was an unlisted number but she thought it might be Caitlyn calling. These days they were speaking more frequently. It was nice being just a thirty-minute time difference apart with her living in Myanmar.

When she answered, Janice heard a song playing in the background which was instantly recognisable to her. It was The Mamas and the Papas song, 'Dedicated to the One I Love'.

'Hello, hello,' she called into the phone but there was no

one on the other end speaking while the song played.

'Is this some kind of prank?' She asked down the phone.

'It's me, you idiot!' Liam's familiar laugh came suddenly. Janice felt a hit of joy in recognising it.

'Oh, thank goodness. I was getting freaked out.'

'So, this is my cheesy way of asking … Is your offer still on the table?' He asked hopefully.

'Yes, of course!' Janice exclaimed in surprise.

'Well then, I suggest you get on a plane and come home to me as soon as possible, you absolute firebrand,' he laughed.

26

Geneva, March 2015

'Can we do some touristy stuff this weekend?' Fiona asked Tom eagerly as they broke away from the Friday evening crowds at Genève-Cornavin train station. 'I know that you've seen everything before and I don't want it to be boring for you but I feel like every time I visit you here all we do is hang around with your UN friends.'

'Of course,' Tom told her. This was Fiona's fourth or fifth time visiting him and it was true that he had been a bit lazy about showing her around Geneva. He stopped outside of the station and wrapped his arms around her waist, taking her pink hard rolling suitcase into his hands behind her back.

'Why don't we go out for a traditional fondue dinner tonight?' He ventured. 'I know a place that is literally and metaphorically completely cheesy. Yodelling, an alpine horn, massive pots of fondue. You'll love it.'

'Yay!' Fiona clapped her hands together in enthusiasm like a seal, a frequent habit of hers when she was pleased. 'That sounds perfect.'

It was a lovely attribute of hers that she was so easily made happy, he thought to himself.

Ending up back in Geneva meant that things had come full circle for Tom. He had initially been hoping for a job in Paris or Vienna but he had managed to land the first UN job he applied for back in the UN's Palais des Nations in a promising UNP role. It had no doubt worked in his favour that his old boss

Caroline had been on the recruiting panel.

His new job was quite prestigious. He was enjoying getting to fly around to conferences in European capital cities giving keynote speeches about the work that UNP was doing in developing countries. Acknowledging the importance of visibility and creating a profile for himself, he had become more active on social media. He was learning that the more he tweeted about UNP's work or made posts on LinkedIn, the more his profile raised and the more he was invited to speak at conferences.

Fiona and Tom squeezed into the tiny lift of his building and made their way into Tom's apartment.

'I forgot how gorgeous this place is,' Fiona exclaimed, walking over to peer out onto his French balcony. 'You've been here ages and you still haven't bought anything to give it any personality though. It looks like a soulless hotel.'

'Soulless but swanky. It's my bachelor pad,' Tom said teasingly. He still had his paintings from Cambodia sitting in storage. It didn't seem right to him to recreate his old apartment from Phnom Penh and all of its memories here.

'It definitely needs a woman's touch.' She punched him affectionately as he pulled her in for a kiss.

He had ended up in a thing with Fiona around the same time he moved from Phnom Penh to Geneva. He wasn't exactly sure when it officially became a relationship but somehow it had. He was just at ease around her. They were long-distance while she was still in Galway but her being a teacher meant she had lots of holidays so she could come visit him in Geneva or meet him if he was at a conference somewhere in Europe. They would have a lovely time and then she would leave which Tom considered the perfect arrangement. He knew that she wasn't seeing anyone else and she didn't ask questions about whether or not he saw other people but he kept his flings with the occasional hot intern to a minimum all the same.

Geneva was healthier for him than Phnom Penh had been and he felt more polished and together. He was drinking far less and had got into CrossFit, looking better and leaner for it. He quickly acquired a pleasant if somewhat reserved group of expat friends who mostly worked at the UN. They were more serious and outdoorsy than the friends he had in Phnom Penh. He wouldn't have imagined it a year ago but he was enjoying spending his weekends hiking, skiing or at fairly tame dinner parties where no one drank more than three glasses of wine.

—

A short while later, Fiona and Tom left his apartment near Lake Geneva to go to a Swiss-themed restaurant a few blocks away. Fiona was looking pretty in a very Irish girl abroad sort of way. She was wearing a floral summer dress and cream high heels which showed the tops of her toes. He hadn't wanted to tell her that no one in Geneva dressed up for a night out and her outfit made her look like an obvious tourist.

'I love how posh everything looks in Geneva,' she was saying as they walked along the picturesque streets lined with 18th century buildings kept in pristine condition. 'Everyone is so good-looking too. It's insane. How can they eat all that cheese and chocolate and look so well?'

'I think having shit tons of money probably helps a lot,' he laughed. 'This is what the world looks like when you have everyone else's money but you keep out of all of their wars.'

'I know they are rich but what do you mean keep out of the wars?' Fiona asked.

Fiona had told Tom that she avoided politics because it was too depressing but sometimes it irritated him that she knew so little about what he considered basic world affairs.

'You know Switzerland is very famously a neutral country?' he told her.

'Oh right, yeah. Silly me. I think I must have known that,' she said giggling.

They arrived at the restaurant just as a live folk band was starting to play the cowbell. They ordered a pot of cheese fondue and Tom began to explain the history of fondue to Fiona while they waited for it to arrive.

'Nowadays, it's perceived as a high-end food but it has quite humble origins. In the 15th and 16th century, it was originally eaten by mountain-dwellers living very poor, nomadic lives. They were essentially bandits who used to attack French explorers passing through the alps. The only ingredients in fondue are hot cheese, alcohol, some herbs and of course the basic bread. Fondue gave them just enough to survive in the snow and ...'

'Sorry, Tom,' Fiona interrupted him excitedly. 'I love when you tell me all about history and stuff but I have something important that I need to tell you and I just can't hold it in anymore.'

Her big grey eyes looked intently at him as the band began to break into a loud and lively accordion song.

Oh fuck. He felt a wave of nausea coming over him. He knew what was coming before she said it.

'I'm pregnant,' she announced slowly.

Fuck, fuck, fucking fuck he screamed internally.

'Oh, wow,' was all he could manage to say.

The waiter arrived, interrupting them and placing a steaming pot of fondue and a basket of bread between them. Tom had lost his appetite and the strong-smelling cheese was enough to make him want to heave.

'But you're on the pill! How did this happen?' He asked her, trying unsuccessfully to make his voice sound relaxed.

'I don't know. I suppose it's not 100% and it just happens sometimes,' she said nonchalantly placing a segment of bread onto her fondue skewer. 'But it's great news isn't it? I mean, we are together a while and we are both thirty so it's not like we're too young or anything.'

How the fuck was she so fucking casual about this?

'Yes, yes, okay,' he managed, taking a large sip of his beer.

'I mean I know it's not ideal timing with us still living in different countries but I'm sure you can get a job in Galway,' she mused, biting into a cheese-covered lump of bread.

He wanted to scream. What the fuck? What decent fucking job could he get in fucking Galway?

The band broke into a yodelling song and several customers began clapping in time with the music. This fucking restaurant was like his personal Guantanamo Bay.

'This place is so noisy. I can't fucking hear myself think,' he grumbled.

'I think it's fun,' she giggled. 'This fondue is unreal. Try it.'

He skewered some bread and ate it mindlessly forgetting to dip it into the cheese.

'Tom, I know it's a shock. It was for me too. But you are happy, aren't you?' She looked at him hopefully.

He exhaled deeply.

'I'm sorry, Fi,' he took her hands across the table into his. 'It's lovely news. Really. It's just a bit of a surprise.'

She beamed at him.

'I love you so much, Tom.'

'I love you too, Fi.'

—

On Saturday afternoon, they did a tour of the UN Palais des Nations. He had always thought that it would be utterly tacky to be a tourist when he worked there but it seemed like a good distraction from talking about a baby that he was still in denial about.

Fiona was tired afterwards so they just stayed in his apartment for the evening and watched a movie. It was her turn to choose what they watched so she chose Armageddon as she had a thing for Ben Affleck. They had watched Pearl Harbor on her last visit to Geneva. He had a lot of bland Affleck movies in his future, he realised tragicomically.

Fiona snuggled into him on the couch and seemed utterly relaxed while Tom remained too numb to bother paying attention to the film's plot. By the time Bruce Willis died, Fiona was fast asleep on his shoulder and Tom put her to bed.

It was still only 10 p.m. and he felt restless. He threw on a hoodie and left the apartment. He wished Geneva had some decent pubs. It was hard to find a place to have a drink without someone eating dinner beside you. He walked up Rue Rousseau and saw a small divey-looking bar that he had never been to before. He sat down at the bar and ordered a carafe of white wine. He had developed a real taste for Swiss wine since moving back to Geneva and considered it far superior to French wine. He thought that the Swiss were crazy not to export it but of course they didn't really need the money.

'Avez vous une cigarette?' A craggy-looking middle-aged guy asked him.

'Non, je ne fume pas,' Tom responded in his bad French. He hadn't gotten around to taking lessons again and was still a little embarrassed at his secondary school level French.

'You are Engleesh?' He asked him while tipsily swigging back the last of his red wine.

'No, I'm Irish.' Tom responded curtly. He wasn't really in the mood for stranger chat.

'Ireeesh, ah, I love the Ireesh. You are good craic, no?'

'We have that reputation, yes,' Tom responded flatly.

'Are you from Dublin?'

'No, the west coast,' Tom's monosyllabic responses didn't seem to be giving this guy the hint.

'You work for the Red Cross?'

'No, UN.'

'Ah, very good. I am a dog walker,' the man said.

'Oh, that's fairly random.'

'Specifically, a dog walker for the ladies who work in the red-light district.'

'You mean, you walk the prostitutes' dogs?' The man had caught Tom's attention all of a sudden.

'Yes, of course. They sleep during the day so can't walk the dogs.'

'An intriguing career choice. Is the money any good?'

'I charge twenty swiss francs per hour, per dog.'

'Fuck me, that's not a bad living!' Tom exclaimed. The Swiss scale of wealth never failed to surprise him. Imagine an economy where the prostitutes' dog walkers earned more than double the hourly minimum wage in Ireland.

'I give you my card. If you ever need a dog walker or anything else, you call me,' the man gave Tom a bloodshot-eyed smile as he stood up unsteadily to leave the bar.

'Thanks, man, but I doubt I can afford you,' Tom laughed, slotting his card into his wallet.

When the dog walker left, Tom was finally alone and able to

begin to spiral through the specifics of his situation. He didn't want this kid. He had nothing against kids but he had never been interested in having one. Would he have to marry Fiona? His parents would think so. Fuck that. It wasn't the 1950s. What did other men do in his situation? A lot of them fucked off. Well he wasn't going to be that kind of douchenugget. He would do the right thing. He would have to spend the next 18 years performing. You can probably do that, he told himself gulping his wine. You are good at that.

But it still felt like his whole future had been stolen from him. He was exactly where he wanted to be. It would be career suicide to have to move back to Galway but he didn't really have much of a choice. He had suggested Fiona moving to Geneva but she said she didn't want to be away from her family.

'It's nice to visit Geneva but it's not home,' she had said.

She was a total home bird and had never even lived out-side of Galway. Maybe he could start consulting from Galway and that would tide him over for a while until the baby got a little older and they could leave Ireland. He would figure something out, he tried to reassure himself, ordering another carafe of wine.

—

Tom brought Fiona back to the train station for her to leave for the airport early on Sunday morning. What he wouldn't do to go back to two days ago when he'd been in the same station waiting to collect her and his whole life had seemed perfect.

She was taking the early Aer Lingus flight back to Dublin. From Dublin airport, it would still be a two-hour bus back to Galway for her and she needed to get ready for school on Monday morning. She hugged him for a long time before say-ing goodbye.

'I know this whole baby thing is scary, Tom, but the three of us are going to have a really great life together,' she said earnestly.

'I know we will,' he told her, trying in vain to look enthusiastic.

Fiona was still only about nine weeks gone and they promised one another that they wouldn't tell anyone until she reached twelve weeks. He speculated that she had probably already told her mother and she had more than likely told Rob's wife Niamh too as they were close friends. God knows Niamh knew enough about kids given that she had already had four of them. Fuck, if Niamh knew then Rob must know too, he realised. They were probably already planning fucking playdates.

Back in his apartment, he felt relieved at getting to be alone in his misery. He was flying to a conference in Bonn, Germany the next day and was glad for the diversion of getting to go and spout UN spiel rather than having to deal with his problems. Tom decided to take an eight-hour train to Bonn rather than flying. Choosing the more environmental option gave him brownie points at work but mostly he just loved travelling on overland European trains and looking out of the window. The Swiss landscape always looked so manicured and perfectly distributed. It was such a contrast to the wild, uncontrolled landscape he had grown up with in the west of Ireland.

He packed for the conference and began to prepare his speaker notes. He was careful to never use the same remarks too many times as everything said these days was recorded and tweeted so creative rephrasing was needed. At the last conference he had said that 'poverty is about more than people's income, it's about all of their deprivations'. He wrote a slightly revised version in his notes. 'People experience poverty by lacking the many essential things they need to live good lives' which he felt worked pretty well.

The Bonn conference had one of those basic websites set up with the programme details. He was scanning the agenda to see what time his session was on at when he saw it …

Well, holy fuckballs …

At 3 p.m. on the schedule, on a panel entitled 'Myanmar's Move towards Democracy', one of the panellists was listed as Caitlyn Leahy from an organisation called The Myanmar Coalition for Human Rights.

Wow. Shit. His heart pounded. He had thought that that was a cliché from books and songs but he actually felt a drumming in his chest followed by a flush of nervous excitement. Her session was on just a few hours after his. He didn't have to see her. He could easily just go to another session and avoid her. But knowing she was nearby and not seeing her? Could he really do that?

He had known that she was in Myanmar because he was still in the habit of checking her Facebook a couple of times a week. She didn't post very much but he'd seen that she had been tagged in some photos at a big golden temple in Yangon, Myanmar's main city and that she was looking as pretty as ever. He had been left craving more information about what she was doing and what her life was like but annoyingly she wasn't on LinkedIn or Twitter or any other social media.

He had to admit to himself that the prospect of seeing her gave him a thrill. She probably hated him. Things had ended badly and he'd been a dick, he knew that. But God, she'd been so damn sexy, he remembered wistfully. He had never met anyone who could get him as hard as she could.

He went into the bathroom and began to shave. He knew it

was a long shot that anything would happen between them but
he could at least make sure that he was looking his best.

27

'The only exciting thing about Bonn is that it's where Haribo sweets were invented so they are everywhere you go,' Tiago told her and Caitlyn soon found that he was absolutely right. She had never been to Germany before and had been quite excited to attend a fancy UN conference. But after getting in a few days early, she very quickly grew bored of walking around the grey, non-descript city where everything shut down at 5 p.m. Out of boredom, she indulged herself in the cheap and ubiquitous Haribo candy but after an initial high they made her feel nauseous and remorseful.

She hadn't been to many big conferences and the thought of speaking at one was still a little intimidating but none of her more senior colleagues were available so her boss had encouraged her. She had jumped at the chance because it came with a free flight to Europe meaning that she could stay on a few extra days afterwards and visit Tiago in Amsterdam.

Like almost every new couple she knew, they had met on Tinder. In Myanmar, apps were the only outlet for meeting someone in an otherwise dismal dating scene for expats. Her newly acquired circle of accomplished female friends in Yangon were all on it and had guided her about how it worked. They helped her in choosing the right photos for her profile which according to them had to be ones where she looked both fun and attractive and had to show both her face and her body (but not too much of it). They had also told her that she had to look as if she had some interesting hobbies leaving her with little to work with other than a picture of herself bowling with Lucy in 2010. They also helped her through a lengthy drafting process for her profile, wording which needed to make her sound smart, but witty and fun. It was a more complicated process than she could have imagined and Caitlyn had disliked feeling she had to sell herself like a product, but conceded when her friends assured her that it was the new normal.

The more experienced among them warned her not to date any of the many travellers coming to discover the country which was newly opened up after fifty years of military dictatorship. She had quickly flouted this rule upon swiping on Tiago who had been passing through on a trip around South East Asia with his friends. She had found herself lusting after the images on her phone of him with a red t-shirt hanging broadly on his tattooed arms and big smiling teddy bear brown eyes standing beside a canal in Amsterdam.

They met in a bar after days of messaging and build up which had essentially acted like foreplay. He was incredibly confident and greeted her with a massive, suggestive grin which gave her an instant feeling of motion in her underwear. They had got drunk quickly and barely taken the time for a substantial conversation before going home together. When he left her apartment for the airport the next day, she assumed she'd never hear from him again.

But when he got home to Amsterdam where he worked as a graphic designer, he texted her and continued to text her. At first it was inane questions about her day and what she was up to but then it got deeper. He told her stories about growing up as one of the only black kids in an overwhelm-ingly white community in Lisbon and talked lovingly of his parents who had migrated to Portugal from Cape Verde with hardly any possessions in the 1980s. His mother had never even seen a hairdryer before arriving in Lisbon. Caitlyn had known embarrassingly little about Portugal and lapped up his insights on the country's culture and history. He had led a hard life in many ways but at his core he was an innately happy person and she began to feel a deep admiration beyond her physical attraction to him.

One Sunday evening when he was back in Amsterdam and she was at home hungover in Yangon, they had been texting so much that he had asked if he could just call her to save time. They gradually fell into a routine of video calling each other every day during his lunchtime, which with the time difference was at the end of Caitlyn's workday when she was sitting in the back of taxis in Yangon's excruciating traffic. On the weekends they did longer calls where he gave her in-depth and often hilarious reviews of whatever movies and television shows he was watching. During one such conversation, Tiago outrightly asked her to be his girlfriend.

'Life's short,' he told her. 'I like you a lot and I think you like me. We could keep dating other people who we don't like as much or we could give this a real try and see what happens.'

Caitlyn was initially floored at his frankness. The practical side of her told her that it was a ridiculous idea.

'But I live in Myanmar and you live in the Netherlands,' she had protested.

The prospect of taking the risk was frightening to her. She and Tom had only been together a few months but it had taken her so much time and energy to recover and then before that she had had months of fallout from her relationship with Nick. Did she really want to put herself through all of that again?

Tiago's optimism eventually swayed her.

'What if I'm the man of your dreams and you look back on this when you are eighty years old and regret it?' he had teased. 'It'll be fun, I promise.'

That was about seven months ago and Caitlyn was still taking her time and feeling protective of her independence but she could feel herself getting more comfortable in the relationship.

Tiago had flown out to Sacramento for a week over New Year's when she'd been home for the Christmas holidays. Even Janice had been charmed by him saying that he had 'real substance' which was as high a compliment as anyone could ever hope to receive from her. Janice was calmer and slightly easier to please these days. It was becoming less strange for Caitlyn that her parents were together. She particularly loved seeing how happy Janice made her Dad and was enjoying sharing in his excitement now that Janice was moving back to Sacramento permanently.

Her new relationship had come just as she was getting settled into life in Myanmar which Tiago became part of despite him not being physically there. Yangon was leafier and less built up than Phnom Penh but also far less liveable and developed. She spent most of her time sitting in traffic in taxis which lacked air conditioning while trying to trundle through the expansive city to meetings. It didn't have the same collection of fantastic bars and restaurants that Phnom Penh had either so her downtime was less hedonistic, but Caitlyn felt invigorated to be there.

She had got a job with a small British NGO working on the forthcoming general election. They were monitoring the political situation and helping to train candidates to run for election. It was gruelling work but immensely exciting.

To Caitlyn and many of the other expat NGO workers there, Myanmar seemed to be a place of promise. The election was eight months away and she and others were feeling enthusiastic about how it was going to turn out. She had seen the opposition leader and Nobel Peace Prize winner Aung San Suu Kyi speak about ending corruption and bringing peace to the country on the campaign trail. She had been struck by how elegant and committed the Oxford-educated Suu Kyi seemed. Unlike the powerlessness that Caitlyn had felt about making impact happen in Cambodia, Myanmar was showing all signs of actually wanting to change and it seemed to be driven by local people themselves rather than being imposed by outsiders.

The Bonn conference was a week-long event hosted by the UN which they termed a 'festival' rather than a conference. To Caitlyn's mind there was nothing particularly festive about it. Having a smattering of colourful stalls where NGOs showcased their work and handed out leaflets hardly made it Woodstock. There were panels and workshops on all kinds of major world issues from climate change to conflict, to gender economics featuring various eminent speakers from NGOs, academia and the UN. Caitlyn was glad that her panel discussion about Myanmar was on the first day so that she could spend the rest of her time as a participant learning about all of these important topics.

She found it stressful figuring out what to wear in these formal settings. She had tried on a few pantsuits, but they had either made her look older and more conservative as if she was trying to look like Hilary Clinton, or they had been too well-fitted and made her look like she was trying to look sexy. She settled for a black blazer over a formal-looking grey woollen dress which made her look older but would do. Looking older at least meant that she was less likely to get mistaken for an intern. She was resentful thinking of how much easier it was for men who just had to throw on a suit.

The festival was taking place in the old German parliament building in Bonn with tiered theatre seating around them while she and the other two panellists sat on a stage in the middle. Caitlyn had received the questions that were going to be put to them in advance and had prepared the answers with the help of her colleagues but she still felt nervous. The other panellists, a Burmese-British academic and a Director of a major American NGO who worked a lot in Myanmar were a good deal more senior than she was.

When they introduced her, she tried to ignore her feelings of imposter syndrome and responded in a relaxed sounding voice, 'Good afternoon and thank you for having me.'

She had taken out her pen and notebook and was jotting down points to remind herself of her prepared answers when she saw him coming into the room and sitting down close to the back.

It couldn't be. Could it? It fucking was. She could feel the blood pump through her. He had shorter hair and was looking more muscular than when she had last seen him but it was un-mistakably Tom. It hadn't even occurred to her that he could be there. She tried to compose herself and focus on what the other panellists were saying. Shit, which question were they on?

'Caitlyn, can you tell us about how the opposition party are being received by ordinary people in Myanmar? And will Aung San Suu Kyi actually be able to become President if they win the election?' The host was asking.

Okay that's a fairly easy one, she thought. She glanced at her notes where she had written down 67%, unclear constitution, good momentum as her bullet point prompts. Caitlyn's mouth felt dry and she sipped some water. She stole another glance at Tom in the audience and saw that he was positioned with his hands in front of him as if he were waiting intently for her response.

'The constitution deems that Suu Kyi can't lead the government because she has foreign sons and because her late husband was foreign but this clause was very likely implemented to target her directly and there is a possibility that they will remove or somehow work around it,' she explained. 'The opposition party will need to win 67% of the parliament's seats to gain a majority because 25% of seats are still reserved for the army so it's a highly significant number of votes needed. But momentum is really good and if the polls are correct, they will reach and exceed this.'

She was probably speaking too quickly and it was possible that she sounded overly-rehearsed but fuck it, she knew her topic. She wasn't going to let him distract her. Without even looking in his direction she was cognisant of Tom's presence and could feel his eyes on her. Each time the moderator asked her a question she just spouted off her rehearsed remarks and hoped that she sounded logical.

When it was over, she felt the relief wash over her. She shook hands and exchanged business cards with the other panellists as the audience cleared the room. In the back of her eye, she could see Tom standing on the steps and checking his phone. With her stomach wrapped in a knot, she slowly walked over to him.

'Hello, stranger. What brings you here?' She greeted him.

He air-kissed her cheek a little awkwardly and she got a whiff of his aftershave, the familiar smell instantly reminding her of being in his bed in Phnom Penh.

'Hi!' the overly enthusiastic tone in his voice matched hers. 'I saw your name on the speakers' list and couldn't resist popping in. I was on a UNP panel earlier about economic empowerment.'

'Oh, wow. That's great. Good for you.' Caitlyn could hear herself sounding almost giddy in her effort to be breezy. 'How are you?'

'Good. Very good,' he nodded as he talked. 'How are you?'

'I'm great, thanks,' she said.

Jesus, one of them was going to have to ask a real question.

'So, you are in Myanmar now?' He asked at the same time as she asked: 'So, you are still with UNP?'

They laughed awkwardly.

'You first,' she told him. He was definitely balding since she had last seen him and up close, she could see the faint smatterings of pleated skin around his eyes like mini accordions. There was also an outline of a bicep bulge in the tight shirt he was wearing which was bigger than she remembered. He looked well.

'Yes, I am. It's a hard place to leave,' he laughed at his own attempt at a joke. 'I'm based in Geneva these days.'

'That's great.'

'You got a haircut. It's really nice,' he pointed out. Caitlyn's formerly waist length hair was now cut into a long bob. She found it was much more manageable that way given Myanmar's climate intensities between extreme heat and monsoon rain.

'Oh, I've probably had several haircuts since we last saw each other,' she answered mockingly.

There was a pause again and Caitlyn rushed to fill it.

'It's great to see you Tom but I should leave. There's still a panel that I want to catch,' she told him.

'Oh, yes, me too. So many good panels. I'm stuck on choosing between the one on the rise of right-wing parties in Europe and the one on water resources vulnerability but there's also one on digital activism that sounds good. Who knows where I'll end up?' He laughed nervously as he spoke.

He is really babbling, she thought with a hint of satisfaction.

'Take care,' she smiled at him.

'You too, Caitlyn. The panel was great by the way. Sorry, I should have said that earlier,' he told her.

She started to walk away before he called her back.

'Wait, Caitlyn! This is crazy. We should grab a drink tonight to catch up properly. It's been so long,' Tom suggested.

She could tell him she wasn't free. She could easily blame a meeting or a deadline but the answer tumbled out of her mouth before she had a chance.

'Yes, that would be great.'

They parted with plans to meet at her hotel that evening. She was giddy with nerves and couldn't remember which workshop she had originally planned to go to next so she just walked into the adjacent room and slipped into an empty seat down the back. There was a bearded man presenting a PowerPoint with a slide entitled Quantitative Indicators.

Fuck. There was no way that she could bring herself to pay attention to quantitative indicators right now. Seeing Tom had really thrown her. Caitlyn was thankful that the indicators session was the last one of the day.

As soon as it ended, she walked back to her hotel, practically sprinting in her eagerness to get ready. She ordered room service while she rummaged through her suitcase for something to wear but could barely do more than pick at her chicken pasta. She needed to look good but not like she was trying to look good. She took out a red and white vintage polka dot dress that she had been saving for a night out with Tiago in Amsterdam. No, fuck it. Tom wasn't worth this level of effort, she told herself. She put on black skinny jeans and a grey sweater. Tiago texted her just as she was applying a cherry-coloured lipstick.

Hey baby, dying to hear about how your panel went today! I bet you kicked some UN ass. Give me a call when you are done saving the world. Can't believe it's just two more days until I get to see you. X

She couldn't talk to him now. She felt a stab of guilt. Wait, what did she have to feel guilty about? It was just a catch-up drink with an old friend.

Tom was waiting for her as soon as she stepped out of the hotel elevator into the lobby. He had changed into a denim button down shirt and when he kissed her cheek, she could smell that he had liberally topped up his aftershave. He took her to a charming cocktail bar a few streets over from her hotel.

'This place is great,' she exclaimed upon walking in and seeing it was a cosy, little place with vintage photos on the wall, full book shelves and light, background jazz music.

'I've been here for days and have only seen the cheesy beer gardens.'

'Ah, you just needed the right guide,' he winked at her.

They sat in a corner table and Tom slid in next to Caitlyn on the couch rather than taking the small stool in front of her. Caitlyn tingled at the heat of his body next to hers.

'So, tell me all about life in Myanmar. I want to hear everything,' he prompted after buying them both expensive espresso martinis.

'It's really good,' Caitlyn proceeded enthusiastically. 'Working on the upcoming election is fascinating. I'm completely exhausted but it just feels like there are real changes underway and I'm witnessing history.'

'That's so great, Caitlyn. I'm so glad to hear it. I know how passionate you are,' Tom said with his eyes locked on hers.

She took a deep sip of her cocktail. She was enjoying herself. She couldn't help it. It felt so good feeling him look at her like he wanted her.

'Anyway, what's new with you?' she asked him.

'Same old, same old really,' he told her. 'My life in Geneva is fairly quiet. My work these days is just so much more global. I think it has way more impact than the Cambodia work which was so limiting. It's mostly representational work, talking at conferences like at the festival today and making sure we keep connecting with all of the stakeholders and policymakers who are observing UNP's work.'

Jesus, she thought. He sounded so ridiculously robotic and unnatural. Had he always been like that? She was sure that she remembered him being more genuinely passionate.

'So, what exactly are you working towards? What's the UN work really all about for you?' she asked him wanting to hear some shred of authenticity.

'Well, UNP's strategy for 2015 through 2018 calls for increasing the advocacy for country-level work on a global level so, my role involves ensuring that the work is well-represented and featured at all of the right high-level fora and that means it can translate to greater support on the ground.'

Caitlyn felt a little bored. It felt like she was listening to a government minister give a dull speech.

'Wow. You really are properly one of them now, aren't you?' Caitlyn said mockingly. 'You've gone full UN on me. The jug of Kool-Aid is long drunk.'

'Oh yes, you've got me figured out. The shadowy UN illuminati that control the world have brainwashed me. I'm hard at work establishing a new world order for my lizard over-lords,' Tom's voice was full of smiling sarcasm.

Caitlyn giggled loudly. Damnit, the asshole still knew how to make her laugh.

'Since I'm clearly boring the shite out of you and you don't even have the decency to pretend otherwise, that's probably enough talk about work,' Tom chuckled. She felt his hand hover lightly before resting his fingers over hers.

'You look incredible by the way. I shouldn't tell you that but you should know that you do. Tell me more about you. Are you seeing anyone?'

'Ah! It's none of your business but as a matter of fact, I am,' Caitlyn smiled, reluctantly pulling her hand from under his.

'I bet he's some rich Silicon Valley douchebag, isn't he?' Tom sighed.

'Nope, not even close.'

'And you are clearly not telling me any more about him even though I'm obviously dying to know?' He prodded.

'I'm not saying a word,' Caitlyn laughed.

'Okay, fine. But I sincerely hope whoever he is, he knows what a lucky fucking bastard he is!'

'Oh, don't worry, I'm pretty sure he does!' Caitlyn said with mock self-confidence. 'What about your love life? Have you found yourself a gorgeous but dull Scandinavian wife yet?'

'Nope. I've dated a little but I honestly haven't met anyone special,' he paused. 'You know how it is … It's my bad luck that no one out there is quite like Caitlyn Leahy.'

He stole a cautious look at her to gauge her reaction. Caitlyn's stomach jumped. Was he serious?

'Oh god, you are really on it today, aren't you? These martinis work fast,' she laughed a little nervously but couldn't stop herself smiling.

'You know what, fuck it. I have to ask,' she stated suddenly. 'What happened in Phnom Penh, Tom? I mean one minute we were together and it was going really well and then the next you just disappeared and completely ignored my calls and messages.'

'I'm so sorry, Cait. I was a bit of a mess. I've grown up a lot since then. Really,' he looked over at her and gave her the lopsided grin that used to make her melt.

'It was shitty what you did to me,' she told him.

'I know it was. Truly,' he pulled her hands into his and stared at her intently. 'I can't apologise enough. I was just so convinced I was going to lose my job when all that stuff happened with your Mum. It was stupid and I freaked out. You were always incredible and seeing you kick ass on that panel today really reminded me of how special you are.'

His touch made her flush. She wanted to believe him.

'I really think you are wonderful,' he said quietly.

She took her hands back from his and silently swigged back the end of her espresso martini.

'I owe you a drink,' she stood up and went to the bar and contemplated her situation. She definitely still felt a strong attraction to him. Fuck.

The barman prepared the espresso martinis with precision as Caitlyn found herself willing him to hurry up so that she could get back to Tom.

'So, where were we?' Caitlyn asked placing their fresh drinks on the table.

'We were talking about how amazing you are and how

much of a tool I am,' Tom moved in closer beside her as she sat down.

'That sounds about right. Please continue,' she joked.

'Whenever I hear David Bowie, I think of you. It's awful. You've ruined one of my favourite musicians for me,' he laughed wearily.

'That can't be true,' Caitlyn said slowly.

'It is and you know it is. Look, I'm not at my best right now.' Tom suddenly stood up and drank back his full cocktail in one gulp. 'I'm feeling a little silly for pouring all of this out. I should probably leave before I say some more embarrassing stuff and make a bigger fool of myself.'

Caitlyn began to panic slightly. She didn't want him to leave.

'Tom, wait! Sit down. You're being ridiculous.' she instructed him.

'Am I?' he asked, looking at her expectantly.

She couldn't help herself. She stood up and grabbed his shirt from the neck and pulled him towards her into a kiss. She felt joy race through her as he kissed her back passionately cupping her face in his hands while she ran her hands through his hair. Oh god, it felt so good being back there. It was like a high. He sat down and pulled her onto his lap and began edging his hands up her thigh. She was crazy wet already. In truth, she had probably been wet for the entire time they had been in the bar together. She was already thinking about how good it would feel to grind against the firm bulge in his pants that she could feel underneath her but stopped short given that they were in public.

'Oh god, these poor Germans are going to think we're disgraceful,' Caitlyn murmured.

'Oh, come on. All that sausage? They're all complete

perverts,' Tom joked as he began kissing her neck.

She could feel his hands moving towards the top of her waist and she desperately wanted them to reach into her jeans. She didn't even need foreplay. She wanted him now.

As he sucked her earlobe he whispered, 'I want you so much, Cait. You have no idea.'

His phone started to vibrate and jerk about on the table in front of them, interrupting them. He grabbed it quickly and rejected the call but not before Caitlyn had seen that the name Fiona had come up as the caller.

'Sorry, that's just work. Where were we?' Tom launched back into kissing her.

Caitlyn felt like she had been punched in the stomach. She instantly recalled that that was the name of blonde Irish girl she'd seen pictures of him with on Facebook.

'Oh, my god. I'm a fucking idiot. You are so full of shit.' She quickly pulled away from him and moved off his lap. 'That's clearly your girlfriend.'

'It's not. I swear, it's work,' he leaned back in to kiss her. She pushed him away again.

What a dick he was. Why had she ever thought that he was so goddamn special?

'You are pathetic. I saw the name Fiona come up and I know from Facebook that you were seeing a girl with that name. I'm not stupid, Tom.'

'You're right,' he conceded, looking upset. 'I'm sorry. I completely messed up. But you and me. This is really something. It's not like that with her.'

'You have a girlfriend, which you lied about. But I have a boyfriend too so this can't happen. We're fucking idiots,' Caitlyn fumed, sinking her head into her hands.

'It's not the same with other people. You know it's not!' he protested.

'You're such a liar. It's impossible to tell what's genuine with you and what isn't.' She quickly swigged back the end of her espresso martini and stood up before he could change her mind. 'But this is my fault too. I should leave.'

He looked pained.

'But I think I---,' He stopped himself.

'You what?' she challenged him, pulling on her leather jacket. 'Don't say something that you don't mean. We're not two halves of a whole or any of that bullshit.'

'I---, I---, I don't know, Cait,' he shook his head unable to look up at her. 'Maybe, I'm a bit of a mess right now and seeing you confuses things.'

'It's the same for me,' she agreed.

'Come have another drink,' he pleaded with her, looking dismayed. 'I'd like us to be friends at least.'

'I don't think we can be anything, Tom,' she told him, feeling sad all of a sudden as she realised the truth in what she was saying.

'Goodbye Tom.' She grabbed her sweater from the couch and started walking towards the bar's exit.

'Hey Caitlyn!' Tom called after her. 'I've been wanting to say something to you.'

'What is it, Tom?' She sighed, turning around to face him.

He had regained his composure and looked like his cock-sure self again. He was giving her the broadest possible version of his signature lopsided grin.

'Never change, you brilliant bitch!' he shouted, laughing a little.

Caitlyn let out a loud laugh and smiled back at him. 'Thank

you ... I think.'

'Take care of yourself, Major Tom.'

She turned around again, walking out of the bar without looking back at him with a half-smile still fixed on her face.

As she came around the corner to her hotel, Caitlyn took out her phone.

'Hi Mom, wait until I tell you about the crazy day I've just had. Lots to fill you in on ... ' she started when Janice answered the call.

Acknowledgements

Thanks to Cambodia and her people; one of the greatest loves of my life and the most frustrating, fascinating and wonderful setting on the planet. Cambodia friends, thank you for the conversations and support that fed into this story, I hope that it pays tribute to our real-life experiences. In particular, Jenny Hickey; thank you for all of the loving hours you put into this and for keeping me going when I was full of self-doubt.

I am, for better and worse, the product of a lot of colourful friendships, all of whom I value massively, many of whom directly and indirectly inspired elements of this book. To namecheck a few key people who support me; Aisha, Orla, Anna-Claire, Keith, Emma, Jane, Naureen, Nikki, Ashley, Kinsy, Orla, Sammon, Sal and Ali. To my college friends for always providing heart, my Bray friends for reminding me to take myself less seriously and my Speranzans who accommodate my double and sometimes triple life while we're trying to change the world. Sinéad Hayes, thank you for your fire and soul. Jill Tucker, thank you for being the best mentor and champion anyone could ask for.

To the wonderful folk at Merdog Books, thank you so much for taking a chance on this and making it come to life and to Fiona at the Editing Hub for helping to get it into shape.

Thank you to my hilarious and never-dull family who I adore. Billy, thank you for being a wonderful source of joy and wisdom in my life. I'm so lucky to have you. My darling Mum, thank you for a million things but mostly for your strength, your wit and your ridiculous level of belief in my abilities. Being half the woman you are isn't half bad at all.

Finally, to my person. Marcelo, thank you for rereading and critiquing, for keeping me laughing, for keeping me sane and for literally and metaphorically holding my feet throughout this. Te amo muito, meu bem.

About the publisher

Merdog Books is an independent publisher based in Donegal, on the northwest coast of Ireland. The mythical merdog is a symbol of what excites us about literature. The raw power, beauty and danger of the sea are combined with the boundless curiosity of a dog unleashed along the shore.

Merdog Books publishes fiction and nonfiction titles that reflect our love for powerful and affecting storytelling, and probing, persistent investigation of important issues.

merdogbooks.com